I0673052

THE
ECHO STONES

Wallace F. Brown

Solebury Press

SoleburyPress@comcast.net

The Echo Stones

The Echo Stones

The journeys most fraught

with danger

are the journeys

of the heart

Prologue

In the last still hour before dawn, she awoke from a frightening dream and sat up in her bed. The room was lit by the dying embers of the night fire and by the cool, dim light of a waning moon. Everywhere, things seemed to move silently in the shadows. She fought against the sudden fear and the suffocating feeling of dread that had become all too familiar to her through the long nights of a gray and lingering winter. Out beyond the castle walls, a wolf howled in the forest and her hands began to tremble. She pulled the heavy quilt up around her neck and struggled to calm herself. The dream always came when she was troubled and the world around her felt cold and threatening.

In the dream, she was a little girl again, sitting on the floor in the hallway outside her mother's chambers. What she remembered most clearly where the faces. There were bad things happening all around her. She knew they were bad things because people were screaming and crying and there was a horrible noise that wouldn't stop. Still, she couldn't look away. She sat in the middle of the dark hallway, on the cold stone floor and she looked at the faces as the flames climbed up the tapestry and sent black smoke crawling across the ceiling like an angry storm cloud. People were running by, but no one seemed to see her sitting there. One by one the faces on the tapestry began to glow with a strange golden light and then they came alive. They smiled at her for a moment and then they closed their eyes and the flames took them away. And in the last second before they were consumed, they cried. She cried too. Not because she was afraid, but because the faces were all saying good by, and she knew she would never see them again. Suddenly, someone took hold of her and lifted her up. She saw the face of her mother, glowing in that same golden light and she had tears in her eyes. That's when she knew, in the way only a child can know, that her mother was going away too. She was carried into the bed chamber, but men were fighting there. Her mother tried another door but there was fighting everywhere. Men were screaming and cursing and hurting each other and she was afraid. Finally, her Mother stopped and looked around her. She was holding her so tightly it was hard to breathe. Then, she kissed her on the forehead and put her down. She didn't want to let go. Her mother removed an amulet from around her neck. As it passed through the beam of sunlight shining through the tall, arched window, it flashed for a moment with a deep crimson fire. Her mother looked at the red stone for a moment. It was bound in a fine golden spider web at the end of a long, golden chain. She kissed it, and then she placed it over her head. She tucked it under the front of her dress and then held her by her arms and looked into her eyes. She was smiling, through her tears.

"Wear this always, Cristin. It will protect you. I love you so much, but you have to run now. Run and hide and don't let anyone find you."

She started to cry again.

"Go now. Go to your secret place. You remember? The place where you go when we're playing the game. Go there and don't come out until someone you know comes for you."

She kissed her again and then threw her arms around her and hugged her one last time. Then she let her go.

"Run baby. Run fast. I love you."

She did what her mother said, but she was afraid now and she forgot where she was supposed to go. Some men were fighting with swords and she saw a man fall down and she saw the blood making a big, red puddle on the floor. And then her legs wouldn't work any more. She knew what she was supposed to do but her body wouldn't move. She couldn't remember where she was supposed to go. She looked all around for someone she knew but there were only soldiers and the other men with the swords and she just wanted to close her eyes and make it all go away. That's when the boy came. She remembered seeing the boy before, but she didn't know who he was. She remembered he was nice to her. The boy smiled. He said, "Come with me Cristin. I'll take you someplace safe."

The boy took her hand and she looked up at him and he was still smiling at her and he wasn't afraid. And then she wasn't afraid either. They walked out of the room and down a stone staircase. They didn't run. It was as if no one could see her anymore. There was fighting all around them but the boy kept smiling at her and walking. They came to a place under the stairway where there was a small opening. The boy went in first and he could barely fit. He took her by the hand again.

"Come in with me, Cristin. We'll be safe here."

She went inside and it was dark, but she could see the light from outside in the stairway. The boy sat down and then he put her on his lap and held her in his arms.

"Don't be afraid, Cristin." He said. "Nothing bad is going to happen to you. I'm here to keep you safe. Just rest now. Rest and forget."

He put his hand on her forehead and then slid it gently over her eyelids. Suddenly, she felt very tired and she couldn't keep her eyes open any more. The boy draped his cloak around her to keep her warm. He rocked her gently back and forth and he was singing a quiet song but she didn't understand the words. She always awoke with that song running through her mind, but fading quickly like an echo from a distant time, into silence.

She closed her eyes and remembered her mother's face again, bathed in soft candlelight and in the love and kindness that was there always. The pain of that memory would never go away but she was no longer a child, and her mother was no longer there to comfort her. Gone also was the feeling of security she had known and her belief that everything would be made better by the light of the rising sun. Her father had become cold and distant and he barely spoke to her. It was as if the death of his wife had destroyed his ability to love anyone, even his own children. But it was more than grief that weighed on his shoulders and slowed his step. No one spoke of it openly, but she had heard the rumors. War was coming to Elmet and soon. In many ways it had already claimed its first victim, for all the joy had gone out of the city and a cold and insidious dread had settled on the land.

She looked through her window at the thin crescent of moonlight. Her mother told her it was the fingernail of God as he beckoned the sun to rise out of the ocean and spread light across the earth. The thought of it made her smile and brought back other warm childhood memories that ever so slowly, pushed away the fear. She lay back down and pulled the covers tightly around her. Her eyes became heavy and she had nearly fallen back to sleep when she heard a noise. It was the sound of the latch on her chamber door being lifted. She peered at the doorway, barely visible in the gloom, and prayed it had only been her imagination. Then, the door began to open slowly, groaning softly on its hinges. She tried to cry out, but no sound would come through her lips. And then she saw the figure of a man standing in the doorway. A dark silhouette against the flickering torches lighting the hallway. A chill ran through her body and she instinctively grasped the amulet that hung around her neck. He moved silently toward her, his moon-cast shadow creeping along the wall. As he came closer, she saw the glint of cold moonlight on the blade he held in his hand. When he had crept close enough to strike he slowly lifted the dagger in the air. She raised her arms to protect herself and finally a scream escaped her lips. The blow never landed. The man's head snapped sideways and his knees buckled. Something fell and rolled away across the floor as he collapsed onto her bed. Out of the corner of her eye she caught the glimpse of a shadow, moving swiftly across the room and out through the doorway, as if a night wing had passed before the moon. Seconds later, a guard rushed in, followed by her lady-in-waiting, and several of the servants, dressed in their nightclothes. The alarm was sounded, and soon the entire castle was alive with frantic activity. The servants stood together in stunned silence, unable to believe that someone had made an attempt on the life of their princess. The man was a stranger, unknown to anyone in the castle. He had the look of a foreigner and no one could explain how he might have gotten into the castle without being seen. More than that, they could not explain how the attack had been thwarted. It was as if he had been struck down by the hand of God.

When she finally returned to her chamber, the golden light of dawn filled the sky to the east. She shivered and walked over to put a log on the fire. There, lying on the floor next to the hearth, she found a round blue stone, clear like glass, and speckled with patches of white and brown. She held it in her hand for a moment. It was a thing from her childhood that she had not held in her hand for many years. She thought perhaps the man who had come to kill her had taken the stone, but why? It was not a thing of great value. She went to the bureau and opened her jewel box. The stone was still there. She removed it and held it next to the one she had just found. They were nearly exactly alike. She carried them over to her window to examine them more closely, holding them up to catch the light. There seemed to be no end to the strange events that troubled her life, and now here was a new mystery to ponder. As she rolled the stones around in the palm of her hand, she peered out over the castle walls to the valley beyond, trying to make sense of it all. Wondering if it was some omen of things to come. She heard the sound of dogs barking far off in the distance and of the city coming to life below her window. Dark clouds were gathering in the south. A storm was moving in.

-1-

The people of Elmet lived on a broad fertile plain between two mountains that reached up and scraped against the sky. The children knew that the white bonnets the mountains wore in the winter were bits of cloud torn off by the craggy peaks when the wind blew in off the water. The wide, fertile plain sloped gently upward from a great estuary that opened to the sea. After several leagues, it narrowed into a lush, green valley. At the head of the valley, where the feet of the mountains touched forming a cradle of hard granite, King Guallauc had built his castle. It had started as a simple timber palisade to protect the people from the wild men who lived in the forest. But the bones of the earth already formed the beginnings of a wall, and Guallauc built upon it, using the vast quantity of hard stone within easy reach. As the wall grew ever higher, the men were drawn by the power of it and by the pride in the hard work that created it. A pride that sealed their allegiance to their king and to their kinsmen and convinced many wild men of the forest to give up the old ways, and take up farming and life in the city behind the sheltering stone. So it was that in this time long before the Normans would cross the channel and build their simple motte and bailey castles, Guallauc already had his citadel. It had rings of broad high walls surrounding a stout keep faced in white limestone. Flag topped towers rose from the keep into the sky to such a height that a man with good eyesight could see boats out on the river on a clear day. That was many years before, and Guallauc was king no more. He had passed away, peacefully and in the fullness of his years, near a half century after the Romans abandoned Britannia. With the departure of the Romans, the country lay open to a host of raiders, jealous for the bounty of the land. His son, Certic, now reined over a kingdom that had become well acquainted with war and a people who once again feared for the future of their children.

For a score of years, since their defeat of King Edwin's Saxon army, the people had lived safely in the high, fertile valley; tending their farms and watching their families grow. But there was trouble on the land again. For two years the harvest had yielded less than the year before and the quality of the grain was poor. The farmers decided that the land had grown tired and needed time to rest and recover. The stores of grain behind the city walls were plentiful and so in the summer before the Great War, the fields lay fallow and men hunted in the woods and fished in the streams to feed their families. The women foraged in the forest for wild herbs and vegetables. They kept a watchful eye on the children who picked the wild berries that grew there in abundance and returned in the evening with half filled baskets, stained lips, and aching stomachs.

As the season wore on, men returned from the hunt with stories of armed strangers wandering in the wilderness and of sorcerers with long beards and bad tempers, staring at them from the darkness of the forest. They spoke quietly of it in the taverns and inns as they sat around the hearth and smoked their long clay pipes and sipped on their tankards of mead and barleycorn ale. Any man returning from the forest was probed for new information and many, desiring to hold the floor for a while and lacking anything of substance to report, made up some wondrous tales that left heads shaking in silent resignation. Bad times were coming, they all agreed. None of them imagined how soon it would be upon them. What they did know, was that a great wrong had been done years before by their king. A wrong that cried out for vengeance. A vengeance that would some day be visited upon his heirs and on the people of the kingdom. And even though they had been at peace for many years, there was a reason the walls of the city had been built so high. Inside the castle keep, the king could be heard pacing the floors of his private chambers late into the night. Even though many of his advisors did not believe a war was inevitable, his heart told him otherwise. He sensed that the hour was already late and preparations needed to be made but somehow he could not force himself to act. He waited while the snows melted away and the birds began to return to the forest and still he did nothing. Then, just when he had convinced himself that there was really no cause for worry, an assassin had gotten past his guard, and nearly murdered his daughter. No one knew how he had gotten in and there were fears that an enemy had put spies in the keep. Why and how his daughter was spared, no one knew. It was the most deeply unsettling thing that had occurred in the castle in many years. The assassin went to his death without speaking, but Certic knew he was a Saxon and he knew who had sent him. He also knew it would not be the last attempt on his children's lives. The king could not bear the thought of losing his son and daughter, as he had lost his wife those many years before. He knew he could wait no longer.

He sat at the head of the great oak table, speaking quietly to a group of men. He was not an old man, but his hair was nearly gray and his face deeply lined. A look of weariness was upon him always and his shoulders slumped as if he were carrying a great burden. His hands were soft from the lack of physical work, but there was strength in him still. Those he addressed were common men, dressed in plain tunics of wool and with sandals on their feet. Their hair was uncombed and there was dirt under their fingernails. They were not much accustomed to the grandeur of the great hall with its massive stone fireplaces and iron fire baskets lighting the dark corners. The table was lit by candles in alabaster holders and decorated with vases of translucent Isinglass, holding flowers from the princess's own garden. The walls were decorated with brightly colored tapestries and embroideries of the finest linen and the plates and dishes were of bronze and pewter, not the crude, wood-carved things they used in their homes. The ceiling was supported by massive beams of hewn oak and held aloft by pillars of smooth stone. Above the central hearth, the great wall, crown and crossed swords of the king's banner told them they were in the place of power and they felt honored and more than a little awed to be sitting at the king's table. The king spoke.

"I know that it is against everything you have learned and there may be some discomfort in it, but I must insist that the fields be allowed to lay fallow for another year. There are adequate stores of grain in safe keeping and it will be good for the land to rest a while longer."

"But what are we to do sire? We are farmers and not so skilled at the hunt as some may be."

"You were farmers last year as well, when you saw the need to let the fields rest. As I recall, your families fared quite well. There will be plenty for you to do. We will need every available man to scour the countryside for game to fill our smokehouses and to gather wild foodstuffs. Also we will need great stores of dry hardwood for the fires that will keep us comfortable against the cold winter. The mountain springs within our walls insure an abundant supply of water, but everything else must be gathered and the time, I'm afraid, is short."

"Yes sire, it was good for the land to rest, but two years is a long time to refuse the earth's bounty. If the weather is bad or the blight or locusts come, we may not have a good harvest when we return."

The king was silent for a moment, considering his words.

"You are good men, all of you, and you are all leaders in your own right. You are also not ignorant of the events that are likely to befall us.

You have seen the signs and heard the rumors. You know as well as I that war is upon us once again. Soon you may be asked to take up arms to defend our city. If you plant now, there is little likelihood you will be able to reap the fruits of your labor. If war comes, your lands and farms will be occupied by the invader. It is he who will eat the grain you have planted, as he lays siege to our walls. We cannot allow him that comfort. Within the next week or two at most, I implore you to take what belongings you can comfortably carry and move your families behind these walls where they will be safe. We can find you suitable lodging and there are adequate stores of food to get us through the next year. We will be outnumbered but our walls are thick and strong, and our people resolute. We will not be defeated."

"But sire, they will burn our barns and our houses and slaughter our livestock."

"I'm afraid this is true, but it is something that cannot be prevented in any case. Were you to remain, you and your families would no doubt be killed or taken captive. Houses and barns can be rebuilt. We have room inside the walls for enough breeding stock to replenish our herds and beasts of burden when the war has ended. Have your communities take stock of what beasts they keep and they will be compensated when the time comes. Those animals you have set aside for slaughter should be brought inside the walls. We will livery as many plow horses as our barns can bear. Take the remainder of the horses up into the high meadow where they can graze. I am sorry to be the bearer of this news, but it is the duty of the king to be forthright with his people and to protect them to the best of his ability. This is the best thing to do and although I feel your sadness at this, it is as it must be. And one additional thing. Although I will not order it, I would ask you this. Once the Saxons have landed on our shores and the battle is upon us, I would ask you to put your own barns and houses to the torch so that he will be denied the comfort of your labor. If you cannot bear to do this I will understand. Most importantly, do not wait until it is too late to retreat to the city."

After the men had left, the king sat silently staring into the fire. The worry on the faces of his people caused him physical pain, and he blamed himself for the horror they would soon be facing. They were not nobility, but they were men like him none the less. Men with wives and children and hopes for the future. He wondered if there would ever be a time when men could live on the earth and raise their families without the fear of war. In a while the great door to the hall opened and a soldier entered. He took a few paces toward the king and then lowered himself to one knee and bowed.

"Sire."

"Come sit with me, Martin. I seek your confidence."

The soldier, a man of high rank and with a fair amount of gray in his short, dark hair, came forward and sat next to the king. He wore a leather subarmalis, with gold braid around the neck and shoulders to indicate his rank. He was a tall man of stern bearing and forearms like tree limbs.

"How go the preparations?"

"They go well sire. Our smiths and fletchers are working late into the night and we will not be wanting for stout arms. If only we could make strong men as quickly. I think we will be greatly outnumbered in this fight."

"Yes, I'm afraid that's true, Martin, and it troubles me. I don't believe Edwin's forces can breach our walls, but neither do we have the forces to break a siege. We are well supplied and can hold out for a year at least, but we cannot prevent him from resupplying by sea while our stores wither. Without outside help, Edwin will succeed in the end. I must seek aid from my cousin, Uryen. If I can convince him to bring his forces behind Edwin's army, the siege will be broken and Edwin will be defeated."

"Are you convinced King Uryen will send help, sire?"

"I am convinced by no means, but he knows well that a defeat here will embolden Edwin. He knows he could soon be facing the same enemy if we are defeated, and with no help of relief from Elmet. I believe he is wise enough to see this as his best choice."

"How will you get word to him, sire? The sea routes are surely being watched. King Edwin will anticipate this move."

"I will send a party overland, through the Mernwood and the West Pennine moors."

"If I may say so sire, that is an arduous journey through hostile country. The men of the forest will not take kindly to an armed force moving through their lands. They may very well consider it a breach of the truce and throw in with our enemy. We also know the Edwin's spies are abroad and have been sighted in the Mernwood. Also we can ill afford to take a company of men away from our walls. Even if they make it safely through the forest, they will be faced with many miles through the Pennine which provides almost no cover."

"All of that is true, Martin, which is why I will not send a company of soldiers. I will send a small party only. Men who know the forest well and can move with stealth, unnoticed by our enemies. Such a party, if led by the right man would not seem like a threat to the Brigantes. I am sure it can be accomplished, but that is not chief among my worries."

"What troubles you sire?"

"We now know that there are spies among us. Long have our gates stood open to strangers who desired to trade with us. After the attempt on my daughter's life last week, we can assume that there are assassins among them. Edwin has sworn revenge against me and my heirs. I do not fear for myself, but for my son and daughter. Even if we can keep them safe for a time, if we fall they will be slaughtered. I have thought on it for many days, and I have decided they must escape from the city before the battle is joined."

"They will be in grave danger in the wild sire. I believe we can keep them safe here with us."

"I don't doubt your skills and courage and I know you would give your life for them and for me, but I must count on you to defend our walls. The battle will require all of your effort and the men will need your firm hand. I fear that while our attention is directed toward the enemy, treachery will come from behind."

"But who would you chose to lead such a party? Who would you trust to defend your own flesh and blood that you could spare in this fight? I know of no such man inside these walls."

"The man I would choose for this task is not inside these walls, Martin."

"Who then sire?"

"I will call upon Stephan for this task."

"Stephan? Forgive me sire, but how could you chose one such as he. His disdain for you is well known. He has no loyalty to you or to this kingdom. I know he is not a coward as many say. Far from it. But for my part, I would not put the care of my children into his hands. Why do you think he would accept such a task?"

"It's true Stephan has no regard for me, but he loves the people as much as I do. Even if he wouldn't admit it. Why do you think he has remained so close to these lands all these years, when he has been banned from entering our walls? You may not be aware of it, but he has long watched over this kingdom from the wilderness. He moves about these forests and mountains at will, and keeps them free from the treachery of those who wish us harm. He knows the men of the forest and they grant him passage through their lands. They even have their own name for him. They call him Sigurd. He has many friends in the wilderness that would come to his aid. Also, in the time before the first war when the princess was just a child, he was like an uncle to her. I was distracted, Martin. Concerned with my people. Focused on strengthening this fortress against this day that I knew would come. It is a heavy burden to be a king. I would not wish it upon you. I had little time to play with my children and I think their love for me is tempered by this absence when they were young. But Cristin has always loved Stephan and I know he would do what he could to keep her safe."

"If that is so, he may not wish to expose her to the dangers of the wilderness. He would know better than anyone the risk they would be taking."

"That is why I must speak to him, Martin. And I cannot delay in doing this. When he knows the truth of our situation, I believe he will agree to help."

"He will not come to you sire."

"We will see. I'll send someone to seek him out. Someone he trusts. Someone who will not fear to approach him."

"Do you know of such a man?"

"Yes, there is one I know Stephan will listen to. I believe he is currently a guest in our prison. He is called Liam of Keld. Please see that he is brought before me first thing in the morning."

"That is not a name I trust, sire, but I will do as you ask. I would prefer the man be guarded while in your presence sire, and not by just one or two. He is a giant of a man and capable of defeating many. Is there anything else?"

"Yes, the farmers have been given their fate. It is time to begin flooding the fields. I want you to send some laborers, protected by an armed guard to divert the river out of its course and down into the valley floor. We will make it as difficult as possible for Edwin's siege towers and mangonels to do their work, and cause his soldiers to slog through the mud to reach our walls. Also I would have you harvest the young, stout trees from the surrounding forest. We will use them to shore up our walls if they suffer a breach and also deny their use to the enemy. Spare the old growth and the saplings. Also see to our horses, Martin. In the end they may be the only advantage we have on our side."

-2-

He crouched just inside the tree line, at the place where the deer waited in their infinite patience for the first light of dawn. The two mastiffs lay next to him, silent save for their soft panting, their ears perked up and alert; their eyes watching the movement below them and waiting for their command. They began to growl softly, but the man reached over and scratched them behind the ears and patted them on their muscular flanks. He spoke to them with soft words in a language they shared and indicated with his hand the direction they should take. The dogs moved off quietly downwind of the assassins. They moved through the forest silently, as they had been taught to do on the hunt. It mattered nothing to them whether the prey were deer or elk, bear or men. They knew what to do, and needed no further words from their master. The man took up a position behind a broad oak and strung his bow. He was tall and fair skinned, but his hair was nearly black and it fell to his shoulders. He had eyes of a light blue color and they studied the hillside like a hawk riding on the wind. Although he was a man in his middle years, he was still young enough to bear the rigors of a life in the wild. There was a look of wisdom on his face that was rarely seen among men who lived their lives in the forest. It was a face that other men looked to when danger was upon them. The earth had told him of the coming war, long before the spies of the enemy had moved across the waters in the night to prepare the way. He saw the fear in the animals and he felt it in the air. Still, he had held out hope that the signs were wrong. Hope that no more blood would be spilled in the rich green valley and the mountains that had become his home. Now, as he looked at these men, creeping toward him in the dim light of dawn, he knew it had begun.

There were eight of them. Their dark green cloaks rendered them nearly invisible when they were still and they moved like shadows, one at a time in short burst from rock to tree. Creeping like a giant spider up the side of the mountain. There were still patches of melting snow among the trees where the sun was slow to penetrate and the thin air still carried the evening chill. They were coming for him. More than all of the men in the kingdom, even more than the king himself, they desired his death and humiliation. It would be the first thrust of their revenge and it would leave the southern approaches to the castle unguarded. He knew of these men. They were more than soldiers. They were King Edwin's assassins. Vicious, highly skilled and lacking any vestige of honor or compassion. He studied their movements and marked the position of the sun. They would not come for him until nightfall, after the moon had set and plunged the mountain into utter darkness. When they reached the top of their climb, they would take cover under their cloaks and wait in stillness for the time to move against him. They would never reach their destination.

His name was Stephan and as a young man he had been a soldier sworn to serve the new king Certic, son of Guallauc. By the time he had reached his twentieth year, he had already risen to the rank of captain. He was known and admired for his strength and agility and his fighting skill but there was something more. There was an aura about him that made men give him their trust. It made them want to follow him into battle and fight by his side. During the two year campaign against the wild men of the forest he had turned the tide of many a battle with his courage and his refusal to yield, no matter what the odds. He had once charged single handedly through a wall of flames, and with his hair on fire, slew three men to save the life of a comrade who had fallen. The wild men knew and feared him. They called him Sigurd, the warrior from the fire. When the war was over and the wild men had been forced to sign a treaty with the kingdom, they paid homage to the great Sigurd and welcomed him into their camps if he came upon them during the hunt. Few were allowed their hospitality. Although he did not count them as his friends, he often preferred their company and their honesty to the duplicity of the men of the castle. But that was long ago. Before the great betrayal that had sent him off to live in the wilderness alone. Before the great treachery had separated him from his king.

He checked the position of the sun again. It had now risen behind him and was flooding the forest below with brilliant shafts of light that would blind anyone trying to find him as he moved among the trees. He removed a small, carved wooden whistle from his belt and placed it between his lips and then selected an arrow from his quiver, notching it against the taught bow string. He blew softly into the whistle. It made no sound that a man could hear, but immediately from down the mountainside, below where the assassins were climbing, came the ferocious growl of the two mastiffs. The assassins turned in sudden alarm and as they did so, he let loose his arrow. The nearest to him fell, an arrow piercing his throat and preventing him from crying out. The dogs moved silently through the undergrowth. Now still, and now growling fiercely, and feigning an attack but staying out of sight. Always driving their prey toward their master. Two more men fell before the others became aware of the threat from above. They sought cover but they had become confused. The dogs pressed their attack, lunging forward and then quickly returning to cover. As the assassins moved to defend against the dogs they exposed themselves to his arrows and one by one they fell, until only one man was left. The dogs moved forward, ready on command to tear their prey apart, but Stephan blew his whistle again and the dogs sat back on their haunches. They would not attack now, unless the man moved. The assassin stood with his sword drawn, facing the dogs as Stephan made his way toward him. When he reached the last survivor, he spoke.

"Throw down and kneel or I will set the dogs on you!"

The assassin sneered.

"You will get no information from me, coward."

Stephan turned to the dogs.

"So my warriors, a snake who stabs men in the back calls me a coward. What shall we do with such a man?"

The dogs let out a sharp bark and moved forward. The assassin raised his sword but Stephan motioned with his hand and the dogs sat again and were silent.

"I will tell you once more only assassin, lay down your sword or die."

The assassin looked at the dogs again and then dropped his weapon on the ground.

"Now kneel as I told you."

The man complied.

"Even if you give me to your dogs, I will tell you nothing."

"You have already told me many things. There were eight in your party which tells me you have more to do here than to take revenge for your king. For that he would have sent one or two at the most. Such is his confidence in your skills, mistaken as it may be. You have come to scout the southern approach to the castle because your king knows he cannot win a quick victory unless he can put men inside the walls. Many have heard the rumors that there is a secret entrance into the city. Edwin has sent you to find it and to open the way for an attack from within the wall when the war comes. You have also told me that the attack will come soon but not too soon. Your king will want to hear your report before he moves his forces forward. He no doubt is hoping to mount my head on the prow of his ship when he launches his attack. For this reason, a single vessel now rides just over the horizon at the mouth of the river to the east, waiting for your return. Such a ship can remain in place for at most a week or a little more.

Already the winds turn from the south and the spring storms will not be far behind. So now you have told me that the ships holding your army will come over the horizon in no more than two or three weeks. Sooner if your mission had been successfully completed."

The assassin spoke.

"Why does a man like you fight for a king who has shunned you and given you to live in the forest like a hermit? What loyalty do you have for such a king?"

"Do you say your king would treat me better? This king who has sent men to kill me."

"You know the truth of it. But you can leave this place. You can escape before the battle is joined. I know what kind of man you have become. You need no king."

"You know nothing of me, assassin. But you are right. I need no king nor do I crave the comfort of the city or the security of the Castle walls. I have always known this war would come. What I do, I do for my own reasons. Now is there anything else you wish to tell me?"

The assassin said nothing.

"You do not wish to bargain for your life?"

"I know better."

"So what am I to do with you?"

"Do as you will. There will be others to deal with you. You will not survive this war."

"Perhaps you are right, but..."

In a sudden swift move, the assassin leapt to his feet and lunged forward, taking even the dogs by surprise. For Stephan the world had stopped turning and everything moved in slow motion. The assassin threw his cloak aside. His right hand reached to his waist and he pulled a lethal looking dagger from his belt while in the same motion his left hand reached out to grapple the wrist of Stephan's sword hand. Against a lesser opponent the attack might have succeeded, even as the dogs leapt forward for the kill. But even though Stephan appeared to be relaxed, he was prepared for an attack from this man who believed his life was lost no matter what occurred. Stephan slapped the assassin's arm aside and grabbed the wrist of his knife hand, twisting it above his head and locking the elbow. With a blindingly swift spin, he threw the man over his shoulder against the trunk of a tree. Before Stephan could stop them, the dogs were at the man's throat. He screamed, and then he moved no more. He searched each of the assassins for any information that could be useful and he collected their weapons. Because they were men without honor, he left their bodies as they lay for the birds and beasts to claim. He climbed back up the hillside with the dogs at his side and although he seemed calm, his mind was racing. He wondered if Certic knew how soon the attack would come and whether the city was prepared for war. He thought of all the families living out in the valley before the castle walls and wondered if there would be enough time for them to reach the safety of the city. They needed to be warned, and his mind turned on how it should be done.

As he returned to his dwelling he sensed a presence in the forest, the dogs sensed it too, and they wanted to rush down the mountain toward the castle. He held them back. Someone else was coming for him, someone not too concerned with being detected. It was either a very brave man, or a very foolish one. Or perhaps it was someone with news of the coming war. He walked a little distance down the hill and surveyed the forest. We will have some company for the afternoon, my warriors. I will need to put some meat in the kettle.

***

He was a giant of a man, more than a head taller than anyone he had ever met and as broad as an old oak. His thick, curly black hair and beard, along with his deep-set dark eyes gave him the look of a wild beast. He could carry a full grown man over each shoulder and still run a mile. The sword that hung from his belt was so heavy that most men could barely lift it, let alone wield it against an enemy. In his hands it was like a giant scythe, cutting great swaths through the enemy and causing such terror that most men dropped their weapons and ran from him. In his entire life he and been bested in a fight only once and that, in a friendly contest, by the man he had come to visit. For all of his power and ferocity in battle, he was a good natured man and true. A man who would never turn his back on a friend or harm a man who had fallen and begged for quarter, except at war. As he made his way up the steep trail to Stephan's dwelling-place he whistled a happy tune. Partly because he had regained his freedom after more than a month in the castle's dank prison and partly because it was not wise to travel in this place unannounced. He knew he was being watched, and he had seen Stephan's dogs at work. They were like ghosts. He had never known dogs to keep their silence like the two mastiffs. They did not bark unless Stephan allowed it and they hunted with such stealth that they would be at an enemy's throat before he even knew they were close. The dogs knew him, but it had been a while since he had been in their company. He did not want to be unhappily surprised. The north side of the slope, leading up to Stephan's lodgings had not yet felt the warmth of the new Spring. There was a chill bite in the air that was much to his liking during what seemed like an interminable climb.

He came to a place where the trail climbed even more steeply before it turned around a large bolder that looked as if it would roll off down the mountain if you leaned against it too hard. It was placed there for just that purpose. He was breathing heavily when he reached the top, and found a man standing in front of him, his arms folded and a sly smile on his lips. The man was tall and dressed in deer hide breeches and a woolen tunic under a cloak of forest green. His head was covered with a hood that kept his features in shadow. His leather boots were laced up the sides and reached almost to his knees. He wore a sword and dagger at his waist and a bow and quiver over his shoulder. The two mastiffs came silently and sat next to him, waiting for a command.

"You have slept too long in a comfortable bed, Liam, and you grow fat and lazy like an old bear."

The giant glowered at him fiercely.

"Fat you say! If you were not such a stick of a man I would roast you on a spit for saying so. Give me a moment to catch my breath and I will teach you some manners."

"Many would say your efforts to teach me better manners had been of little avail till now, but you are always welcome to try again, if you are so fond of wasting your time."

"No. I see now that I have been too easy on you. I think I will just take your head to decorate my hearth, and be done with it."

They stood staring at each other for a few seconds and then they both broke out in laughter and embraced.

"It's good to see you, you giant oaf"

"And you, you wisp of smoke."

"I have a tasty venison stew on the fire for us. I have been waiting for you."

"You were told of my coming then?"

"Not by men. You made such a din thrashing about on the side of the mountain that every creature within ten leagues knew you were on the way."

"Then they were wise to flee from me in fear."

Stephan's dwelling was an earth covered log structure built against a stone outcropping in the side of the mountain. It was a small, simple place built by a man who lived alone, and preferred to spend much of his time in the wild. But for all that, it was comfortable and spacious enough to accommodate his infrequent guests and built to hold the winter snows and spring rains at bay. The two men sat in front of the hearth, enjoying a tankard of ale. The flickering flames cast large shadows on the walls and illuminated the men's faces in dim, yellow light. The perfume of burning hardwood hung in the air.

"I was told you were enjoying the king's hospitality, Liam. I'm surprised you would give it up for a bed of straw in these mountains."

"The king's hospitality is not as you might imagine. In the last month I have become acquainted with a large number of rats, some of which were not men."

"Dare I ask for what reason you were invited to the king's dungeon?"

"I came upon a magistrate beating an old woman with a switch in the square. While I was discussing the issue with him, he somehow fell into a well. He is a very clumsy man I think."

"A magistrate, no less. I'm surprised you are breathing the fresh air so soon."

"I was released by the king himself, fearing no doubt that I would soon pull his castle down around his ears. He has sent me here to meet with you, Stephan."

"Since when do you carry messages for the king?"

"I have never done so until now, and only because you should know what is about to befall the kingdom."

"I know war is coming. I have already dealt with some of Edwin's spies. Their corpses are decorating my forest."

"It is worse than you might imagine. There was no harvest last year. The walls may well hold, but if the siege cannot be broken within the year the people will begin to starve. You know better than most of Edwin's resolve. I fear the outcome will not be good."

"And what message are you to relay to me."

"The king wishes to meet with you as quickly as you can come."

"Does he forget that he has banned me from the city?"

"He does not forget it. He also knows that it has never stopped you from your visits in the past. He holds no malice toward you Stephan. A king cannot allow men like us to openly defy his authority."

"So you defend him, Liam? You surprise me."

"I do not defend him, but I care for the people of this kingdom and I know they cannot stand alone for long. Although I was not told directly why the king wants to meet with you, I have heard he desires to send a party through the wild lands to the west to carry an appeal for help from his cousin Uryen."

"And he believes I would lead such a party?"

"I don't know what he believes, but I saw the desperation in his eyes. In spite of what has passed between you, he is not an evil king. Perhaps a better king than he is a man. He is just and he cares for his people. For my own part, I would be willing to join this party, although the wild men may wish to discuss our past dealings at some length, and not fondly."

"And what do you think I should do, Liam?"

"I think if the war comes, as you yourself say it must, this is not a good place for you here. Edwin would gladly expend half of his forces just to capture you. I also don't think you would be happy fighting behind Certic's walls. So it seems to me you have two choices. You can leave this place to stand or fall on its own, or you can join in this attempt to seek help."

Stephan was silent for a while. He stood and threw another log on the fire, showering the floor with glowing embers. He poked absently among the hot coals with an iron rod, lost in thought, his face illuminated by the glow of the fire. A look of deep concern was on him. In a while he returned to his chair.

Liam spoke again.

"I know you are torn by this news and I have always listened to your wisdom in these things. I'm happier when I only decide which head to detach next, but if you seek my counsel, I would say to at least meet with the king. Even if it is the last thing you do before you leave here forever."

"How do you think the people will fare if Certic is overthrown, Liam?"

"The way all people fare in war. Not well."

"But what about after? Do you think they would be murdered or enslaved?"

"I don't know. Probably they will be returned to the land to work, except they will be sorely taxed and perhaps harried by a hard overseer. Possibly even a tyrant. Do you see it differently?"

"No. I think as you do. But that is how the decision hangs with me. I don't hate Certic, in spite of our differences, but I have no love for kings. Especially, I have no love for the sons of kings or for their sons. The more generations that pile on one another the more kings forget what they're for. They begin to think that the people are on the earth to serve them and increase their wealth. Edwin is not so benevolent a king as Certic, but who can tell about their sons and their grandsons."

"No man can know such things."

"But you agree this is the choice we are making. We wager that the sons of Certic will be better than the sons of Edwin, and for this we would risk our lives to save his kingdom."

"I am a simple man, Stephan. If I were to think as you do it would fill my head with bees. I can only fight the battle that is before me. I can only choose from the kings I know."

"You're right my old friend. I spend too much time arguing with myself here in these mountains."

"Aye, and many wonder why you have remained here for so long. I myself expected you to move on years ago. What is it that holds you in a place where lies are told about you and where the king bars you from his gates?"

"That is a question I have asked myself many times. I don't have an answer, except that somehow I have always felt there's something unfinished here. This war that is coming to Elmet has always been as inevitable as the rising of the sun. It has always been only a question of when."

"And you remained here to join this fight?"

"I am some of the reason Edwin seeks revenge on these people. I feel a duty to stand with them."

"You were not to blame for what happened here all those years ago, Stephan."

"You and I and a few others know that, but many believe otherwise."

"Their foolish beliefs should not be a reason for you to risk your life."

"No, and that is not the reason. If I were to flee from Elmet to avoid this battle, Edwin would win a victory, even if he does not prevail on the field. The people can think of me what they want, but I will not be named a coward in the court of a king. Any king."

Both men were silent for a time, gazing into the fire and lost in their own thoughts. Finally Stephan spoke.

"And what of you, Liam? These are also not your people."

"Perhaps not, but since I have been made unwelcome in the country of by birth, I have adopted the people of Elmet. I like them Stephan. There is happiness here that I do not find in my travels to other places. Since the Romans abandoned their forts, most of the Britons have lived in fear and their lives are hard and short. Perhaps Guallauc's walls make the people here feel a bit better about their future."

"Let's hope the walls are still standing when this war is over."

"Aye, and what then for you? Will you remain here if the walls hold and Certic prevails?"

"I don't think so. I feel something pulling at me that I can't really explain. There is some destiny I need to find. I think when this matter is settled, it will be time for me to seek it out, wherever that may take me."

Stephan stood, walked over to the side of the hearth, and took hold of his sword. He removed it slowly from its scabbard and held it out in front of him, watching the light of the flames dancing along the polished edge.

"You know this sword, Liam?"

"Aye, I know it well. It has a voice like no other sword I have ever heard. When we fight, I know where you are by its song. It rings out on the field like a trumpet, calling men to your side. The sound of it has often lifted my spirits when the enemy has pressed us sorely, and I am not alone in this."

Stephan ran the blade lightly against the back of his wrist, leaving a thin red line on his skin, and a drop of blood that ran down the length of the blade and fell into the fire with a sound like a sigh.

"Through all, it keeps its edge like no weapon I have ever held. A wise man once told me this sword was forged of iron from the vast deserts far to the south. The iron is melted along with some charcoal from the fire and some fine, desert sand the color of blood, and bits of wolf bone in a sealed clay crucible. There is even a pattern in the steel that looks like drifting sand. After many hours in a great oven the clay is removed and allowed to cool slowly. The metal from within is given the name Damascus steel, from the far away place where it is made. It is carried by merchants through the long trade routes to the east along the river men call the Volga. In time, it finds its way to these lands, where it is traded to our peoples for animal skins and wool from the flocks. The smiths reheat the steel to the color of the sun and then hammer it for the length of one full day. As the sun sets, it is said they quench it in the blood of a bear and then listen to it cool in silence. If the steel does not cry out, they know it is good. This sword has never failed me, Liam. It is the sword of my ancestors and yet I don't know who they are or where they live. There is a strange symbol on the hilt which is a twice bent rod and two discs, like the sun and the moon. I don't know what it means."

"And that is the thing that eats away at you in the night?"

"I need to find them. I need to know who they are. That same wise man who told me about this steel, told me my destiny lies with them and that the time would come when I must find them and reenter the history of my people. I feel that time is near. It calls to me from afar, in some soft voice beyond words. I think this war that is now upon us, was what held me here all these years. I'm glad for it. Not for the blood or the killing, but because of the way it will make open for me."

Stephan slid the blade back into its scabbard and returned it to its place near the hearth.

"In any case, the hour is late and I will need my rest. I have argued with myself for too long. Tomorrow I will argue with a king."

-3-

The two men followed a winding deer trail down through the forest. They could see the castle through the trees as they made their way carefully across the rocky ground. The mastiffs patrolled the forest on either side of the trail as they had been trained to do. As they neared the castle, their ears were filled with the sounds of hammers on iron and of axes and saws. They stood for a moment and watched as a small herd of cattle was driven in through the main gate.

"They make ready for war, Liam. If only they could be spared what is about to befall them."

"Aye, it seems there is never an end to it. Those are good walls, but I would not be happy inside of them when Edwin's army draws near."

The rear wall of the castle ran parallel to a massive monolith that soared a thousand feet into the air. It had never been climbed in anyone's memory, nor could the top of it be easily reached from any other direction. Stephan stopped and took his bearings. The entrance to the cave was so well disguised that he himself often passed it and had to double back to find it.

"We will leave the dogs here. They will insure the way is clear if we have to leave in haste."

Liam looked around, a puzzled expression on his face.

"Perhaps a wisp of smoke could get through these rocks, I don't see a hole large enough even for a hare."

Stephan stood with his back to the monolith and laughed at his friend.

"Trust you to miss a crater large enough for an elephant. Now watch carefully."

Stephan flattened his back against the rock and smiled. He took a step to the right and disappeared completely. Liam stared at the place where his friend had stood a second ago and bellowed.

"By the gods you are an evil wizard I swear it. Where have you gone?"

A second later, Stephan reappeared.

"Over here you great oaf."

The huge man walked over to where his friend was standing. Next to him a long vertical crease ran up the face of the monolith. Because of its orientation to the sun it was always in deep shadow. At the bottom of the crease where it met the ground was a vertical slot, wide enough for a man to pass through. It was difficult to see, even if you were standing right in front of it. Liam looked at it doubtfully.

"I think I'll walk around to the main gate where the normal people enter. I would have to stop eating for a month to fit into this"

"Come on now. It's bigger than it looks."

"Perhaps, but so am I."

Stephan disappeared again and the giant man put his back against the wall and stepped sideways. His massive frame scraped against the walls as he inched his way through the gap. It seemed to get narrower as he moved deeper into the rock. Just as he was about to give up and go back he felt a hand grip his arm and pull. He lurched forward and found himself in an open space of indeterminate size. It was as black as night and he was disoriented. In a few seconds he saw the sparks of a flint and the beginnings of some embers glowing on the ground. Suddenly a torch burst into flame and it took him a few seconds to adjust his eyes.

"From here it is an easy trek, but stay close behind me. There are some deadfalls along the way."

"I will not ask you why they are called deadfalls. Please keep in mind my head, and most of the rest of me, is a bit closer to heaven than is yours. Kindly alert me if I need to duck."

They made there way down into the cave on rocks that resembled a crude stairway. After they had descended for several minutes the cave opened up into a deep grotto which was ringed by a ledge just wide enough for a man to walk. Stephan cast a small stone into the darkness and there was a long pause before the sound of it splashing into a pool. Liam shook his head doubtfully. Stephan led the way and Liam followed, trying not to look down into the void. They had gone perhaps a hundred yards when they came to a rock wall. Stephan waited for him to catch up. He held the torch low to the ground where it illuminated a passageway with a low roof hewn into the rock.

"Thirty feet above us the castle wall begins. We will need to crawl for a while but it is quite wide enough, even for a giant such as you."

"When we are through here I will look like I've been making mud pies with the children." Liam said.

"Then you will probably look no different than most of the men inside the walls. Preparing for war is not dainty work."

The passage was not long and it opened into a fairly wide chamber. There was a shaft of diffuse light coming from above. Liam was glad to be out of the darkness.

"What is this place, Stephan?"

"It was once a mine. Many years ago, when they were excavating for the walls they found a rich vein of copper. It was mined for a few years but it proved to be shallow. They cut the passageway we just traversed in the hope that the vein continued on the other side but when they came to the grotto they abandoned it."

"How did you find the way into this place?"

"I didn't find my way in. I found my way out. I was about to be made an unwelcomed guest in your recent lodgings."

"It must have been difficult. It is very confusing in there and not much to my liking."

"It's not so difficult if you have some light. The first time I had no torch."

Liam shook his head and marveled at the man standing next to him. They had fought side by side many times and there was no one he trusted and admired more than Stephan. There was some unnatural quality about the man. He would not accept defeat and no matter the danger they were in, he always seemed to find the way out of it. It was as if his fate was tied to some future time and until it arrived, nothing could touch him.

A wooden ladder, lashed to the bracing timbers, ran up the side of the chamber for a few dozen feet and then a long sloping passageway led up into the daylight. They emerged from the mine entrance which was located behind the stables. In a few minutes they had joined the masses of people going about their daily work. No one paid Stephan any notice. They were too busy marveling at the giant who walked beside him. It had been a while since Stephan had been inside the walls and he could see the concern on the people's faces. They made their way around the perimeter of the inner wall that protected the keep and then up the long stone ramp to the barbican where the heavy iron portcullis stood open. Two armed guards barred their way. They looked nervously at the giant and had their hands resting on the hilts of their swords. Above them the faces of other soldiers appeared at the murder holes in the roof of the chamber and they knew well that archers had them in their sights.

"What is your business here?"

Stephan spoke.

"I am here at the invitation of the king."

"And you?" They asked, looking at Liam.

"I am here to make sure you don't keep us waiting too long."

"Who are you?"

"I am Stephan and this man is Liam of Keld."

One of the guards turned and crossed the wide courtyard, stopping at the castle door. In a few moments a tall man exited the keep and crossed the courtyard with long confident strides. Stephan recognized him immediately. He had once been a captain of the guard like himself, but had since risen through the ranks and now commanded the king's army. He approached Stephan and after a pause, offered his hand

"It has been many years, Stephan. I can't say that you are entirely welcome here, but for my part, I give you my word you will not be held or harmed. I must ask you for your weapons before you sit with the king, are we agreed."

"Greetings, Martin. I'm pleased to see you well. For my part I would prefer to be out in the wilderness where I do not find the treachery of men. I know you to be a man of your word however and so I will comply, but should you betray my trust, your army will be in need a new general."

"That will not be necessary, I assure you."

Stephan turned to Liam.

"I must meet with the king in private, Liam. If I have not returned to the inn by nightfall, please knock down this wall and retrieve me."

"Gladly." He said, glowering at the guards.

He was sitting at the large oak table when the king entered the room. He stood, but he did not kneel before the king. The king crossed to the head of the table and sat, indicating that Stephan should do the same. He studied Stephan's face for a few moments before he spoke.

"You are looking well, Stephan. The years have been kind to you."

"It's one of the benefits of the life I live, even if I did not choose it."

"Yes, I have often envied your freedom. You have been in my thoughts often over the years. I know you have kept watch over our frontiers, even though you have avoided contact with the people. For your vigilance, you have my gratitude. A king is just another captive after all, trapped within the walls built to keep him safe. Much has passed between us, Stephan, and I do not wish to revisit it. I hold no grudge against you, and I wish to offer the freedom of the city to you once again."

"Such an offer comes late and at a time when you are in need of me. I would be less skeptical had you offered it in more peaceful times."

"I had thought to do so many times in the past, I give you my word this is true. You are not an easy man to find and, in truth, I didn't believe you would come to me nor forgive me for the wrong you believe I've done to you."

"So what is it you would ask of me now?"

"You know war is upon us. Edwin has amassed a great army. I am told it is three times the size of our own He has plotted his revenge for many years. He will lay siege to these walls and we do not have the strength to break it. I need to send a party through the wilderness to Craven with a message for my cousin, King Uryen.

Unless he offers his help we will not prevail here. We can hold the walls through the next winter perhaps, but then the people will begin to starve."

"You knew this time would come. I told you as much but you did not listen."

"That is a discussion I will not have at this time. What's done is done. I must look to the future and the safety of my people."

"There are many capable men who could carry such a message to your cousin. If they are careful and respect the forest they have a chance to reach Craven in safely."

"That is the case, and were it only a message I asked them to carry through the wilderness I would find such men."

"What then?"

"Edwin has sworn a blood vengeance against me and my heirs. Once the battle is joined it will not be possible to remove my children to safety. If the city falls, they will be slaughtered."

"If the city falls, many will be slaughtered."

"Some will die during the siege, I know, but I do not believe Edwin will take his revenge on the common people. It would be much more profitable to put them to work in his service, should the worst happen."

"Do you believe the prince and princess will be safer traveling through the wilderness? The forest harbors spies and assassins. I have already dispatched a number of them. The land is wild with few places to shelter. It will be an arduous journey beset with dangers, many of which are unknown, even to me."

"I am aware of the danger, Stephan. I wish this choice was not upon me but I cannot escape it. I have not slept for thinking about it. Even now there are spies inside our walls. Things have been done. Last week my daughter, Cristin, was nearly murdered while she slept. They need to be guarded at all times. My children are virtual prisoners here and it will only get worse. I believe the best thing is to attempt to get them to safety. Especially if you agree to help me. You don't know my son Brien well, but he is becoming a fine man. He is young, with the impatience of a young prince, but he is brave and a skilled fighter. It will be good for him to learn from a man such as you. As for Cristin, she has always loved you from the days when you were my confidant and had the freedom of this castle. She still asks about you sometimes. She blames me for your absence as do more than a few others."

"I would not be able to care for the needs of a child on a journey such as you are proposing. It would be very difficult for Cristin."

"She is no longer a child, but I will not send her alone. Since the death of the queen, she has been cared for by the Lady Emeline. She is devoted to Cristin and since the death of her husband in the last war, has been like a mother to her. She herself has a daughter, Ailis, who is near the same age as Cristin and they are fast friends."

"A woman and two girls along with a pampered prince? This is not a party I would like to take into danger."

"Nevertheless, it will be done. I hope you will agree to guide them because you are their best hope. I will also send one capable man-at-arms who will act as their personal body guard. His name is Eogan and his life is sworn to them. He would be under your command except that should a skirmish be joined, his only duty is to defend my children and he will not leave their side. There will also be a servant to the princess. One named Flann, who can help with the cooking and in the care of my children. You may bring others with you as you see fit."

Stephan sat in silence, staring absently at his hands. He remembered the little girl well, and the thought of her being slaughtered was not something he could countenance. Although he would not speak of it, he believed the city, at last, would fall. He knew little of the king's cousin Uryen, but there seemed not much hope that he would agree to join such a fight. He looked at the king once more, and saw the concern in his eyes. Both men were silent for a while as the decision hung in the air. Finally, Stephan spoke.

"How goes your treaty with the Brigantes?"

"There is an occasional dispute but nothing too serious. We have been a peace for many years now."

"And how do you think they will react if war comes?"

"That is something I'm keen to know. I don't think Danius would see it as an advantage to throw in with Edwin, but neither do I expect his support. The Brigantes are not known for their loyalty. It was they who betrayed Caratacus to the Romans all those years ago, in spite of their common blood. It is another reason I need you Stephan. Danius respects you. You will need to cross his lands. If you agree to this task, and have the occasion, it would be good for you to sit with him. I will give you a gift of value for him if you decide to seek him out."

"No one passes through his forest unseen and unknown. Whoever takes up this journey will have to deal with him."

"All the more reason I need you for this task. I would like to give you this night to consider my proposal, Stephan. Should you decline, I will not hold it against you and my offer to open the gates of the city to you will stand, though they soon will be closed to all. Think also on this. Our people and those of my cousin Uryen are the last of the Celtic blood south of the great Roman wall. The Saxon tribes are greedy for this land and they have no respect for those they conquer. Perhaps in the end it may be a struggle we cannot win, but if I am to be the last Celtic king in Britannia, I will not be remembered as the king who surrendered this land without a fight."

"How long do you think it will be until Edwin lands his army on your shores?"

"I think it will be soon. Perhaps two weeks at the most. Do you think differently?"

"No, that is also what I believe. Will you be ready?"

"I pray we will. Preparations are going well, but there is much remaining to do. Please return to me in the morning with your reply, Stephan. You must know it is difficult for me to ask you for this help. I beg you to take on this task."

-4-

The heavy wagons were built to carry timber. They could be seen early each morning departing the main gate, empty save for a party of woodsmen and their tools. Two pack horses were tied to the rear of each wagon to carry the saws and axes and tackle on the way home, when the wagons were piled so high with timbers that the teams of oxen could barely make headway. The wagons moved along the north road up into the forest, the drivers whistling commands and cracking their whips. The road branched in many places and soon the wagons had gone off in different directions to reach the many areas being forested. The last wagon in the chain moved off alone on the westernmost branch and soon was out of site of the rest of the woodcutters. A keen observer may have noted that the driver was an extraordinarily large man and that the two pack horses trailing behind were already laden. If they looked closer they may also have noted that this particular wagon was lined with a thick layer of straw, covered with a heavy cloth and that these woodcutters were armed with swords instead of axes. If there were spies in the forest, it was likely they had long since lost interest in the daily procession of wagons, but it was better to take no chances. The wagon made slow progress behind the enormous beasts, swaying their massive horns from side to side as they walked, like reapers in a field of barley.

After an hour the wagon crossed a ford and stopped on the other side. The large man jumped to the ground, causing the wagon to buck and sway. A muffled oath came from beneath the dark cover in the wagon. He put his fingers to his mouth and let forth a distinctive bird call. It was answered from a short distance with a similar call but with a rising note at the end. The forest went silent, save for the sigh of a light breeze blowing through the tree tops. Almost immediately, the two mastiffs came into the clearing and began sniffing at the legs of the men. The soldiers were startled and nearly drew their swords, but the large man greeted each of the dogs in turn, patting their broad flanks. In a few seconds two men emerged from the forest. They were clothed in woodland green tunics and carried bows and several quivers of arrows. One of the men was of middle age with a handsome but weathered face and the sharp eyes of a hunter. His hair and eyes were dark. He was not an exceptionally tall man but he was muscular and carried himself with the ease of a man at home in the wild. The second was a young man with the perpetual smile of youth upon his face. He was a bit taller than his father but not so stout and his hair, which he wore long, was a light brown color. They greeted the party and waited. The men searched the forest with their eyes, anticipating the arrival of the leader of this peculiar gathering. Suddenly, they turned and were startled to find Stephan standing behind them.

"By the gods I swear you are blown in on the wind." Liam said. "One day you will succeed in unnerving me."

"Let us move quickly, Liam. Rouse our travelers and have them make ready."

He untied the pack horses and then joined them together so that they could be led single file by one man. He handed the reins of the lead horse to Eogan. A woman emerged from under the cover first, followed by two girls in their late teen years. Stephan was pleased to see that they were well dressed for the journey with good boots and long riding skirts and covered by long woolen cloaks with hoods. One of the girls smiled at Stephan and then walked over and gave him a great hug. She was tall for a young woman and lithe with long blond hair and eyes the color of the deep ocean.

"I am so happy to see you once again, Stephan."

"And I you." He said, smiling warmly. "You have become a woman since I saw you last."

"Yes, it has been much too long. I'm so happy you will be with us on our journey."

"We need to make haste now, Cristin. We'll have time to speak this evening but now we must move quickly."

The last to come out from the cover of the tarp were Flann and the young prince. Brien brushed the straw off of his clothes and looked at the party with disdain. He was dressed in his royal crimson sagum that caused him to stand out in the forest like some traveling troubadour. He was nearly as tall as Stephan but not yet grown into a man's body. His hair was darker than his sisters, and his eyes were a hazel color. His face wore a condescending expression that Stephan did not like.

"Retrieve my weapons and belongings Flann, and brush my coat of this straw."

"Is this what you've brought to travel in Brien?" Stephan asked.

"It is what I wear for the hunt."

"It may be suitable for the hunt but you will not wear it on this journey."

"You do not tell me what to wear or not to wear."

Stephan took the young prince by the arm and pulled him down the trail so that the others would not hear.

"Unhand me, or I will strike you!"

Stephan pushed him roughly against a tree.

"You may be a prince behind your father's walls, young Brien, but out here in the wilderness you are less than a peasant. At least a peasant carries his own burden. Your very presence in this party brings danger to us all. There are men in this forest who would kill a prince for sport, and many more who would hold you for ransom. My task here is to seek help from your uncle Uryen. If I can get you to safety, I will do so. If I cannot, so be it. I suggest you draw as little attention to yourself as possible. Now you will get yourself into suitable clothing and these peacock feathers will be returned to the castle. Your father tells me that there is much to be admired in you. So far I have not seen it. Now do as I say, and if you ever threaten to strike me again I will remove your hand from your arm. A prince with one hand is no more useless than a prince with two."

Stephan returned to the party. The wagon had been turned around and the pack horses made ready. He took the Lady aside. She was a beautiful woman who had not yet reached her fortieth year. Her hair was long and dark with a long braid along the side of her face. Her eyes were green and he saw wisdom there and perhaps a touch of sorrow.

"I am told you are the Lady Emeline."

She smiled.

"My friends call me Emma. And you are Stephan."

"Do you believe these young women are capable of making this journey?"

"It matters little whether I believe it or not. Our fate is cast. But do not underestimate us. These young women are not the silly creatures you may have expected. They have learned how to hunt and to forage and they are stronger than you may imagine. They are both skilled with the bow and know how to defend themselves as I do. For my part, you will not hear any complaints. The only thing I ask is that you be forthright with me so that I can properly instruct them. I am aware there will be danger ahead of us. We will be less of a burden if you let me know what to expect."

The young girl walked over to them.

"This is my daughter Ailis."

Stephan smiled at her. She was a copy of her mother, except that her hair was blond. She was slightly built and shy.

"Hello Ailis. I'm happy to meet you."

The girl smiled and curtsied.

"I am pleased to meet you, sir."

"You may call me Stephan as everyone else does."

Stephan had never been in the company of three more beautiful women. He felt regret instantly, for the danger they would face on this journey. He turned back to Emma.

"I will do my best to keep you informed, Emma, although there may be much on this journey that I don't expect. For now I ask only that the girls speak quietly and not fill the forest with their laughter as young women are wont to do. We must get as far away from the castle as possible before nightfall and without being seen. There is a hunter's lodging along this road. If we push forward we will reach it by sundown and have a comfortable place to rest. If not, we will sleep under the stars tonight."

Stephan nodded to the remaining two soldiers whose job it was to return the wagon. The driver cracked his whip and the wagon moved off, crossed the stream to the other side of the ford, and was soon out of sight in the turn of the road. Stephan next spoke to the hunter and his son. His name was Cadman and his son Lucas. Stephan and Cadman had hunted in the vast wilderness together for many years. Cadman was a man of few words, but his skills at the hunt were unmatched, even by Stephan. He was a skilled bowman and was nearly invisible in the forest. He was also an expert fighter with the long staff and sword. His son was an intelligent lad nearing manhood. He was still a little uncomfortable around adults, but Stephan had seen courage in the boy, who had learned well from his father. Cadman and Lucas moved off along the road at a run. The prince rejoined the group wearing breeches, a leather tunic, and a cape of dark colored wool. Stephan glanced at him and then turned away. They waited for a while to give the hunters enough time to get well ahead. Cadman's job was to signal the party if he came across anyone on the road. It would provide time for Brien and the women to take cover in the woods. They did not anticipate an attack in this part of the forest which was secured by treaty with Brigantes. What they wished was to avoid any contact with travelers who might recognize the prince and princess. Aside from Martin, no one in the castle was told of their departure. It was hard on Cristin who desired to say her goodbyes to the many people she cared for, but she was mature for her age and she knew what was at stake. As Stephan prepared the party to move out, he noticed that Cristin was not with the other women. He looked around and found her nearby, standing on the stump of a fallen tree and looking back through the forest at the castle off in the distance. He walked over to her.

"Is anything wrong, Cristin?"

"No. I only desired to see Elmet one last time before I walk off into the wild."

"It will be here waiting for you when you return."

"Yes, I believe it will still be standing when these troubles are finally ended, but I don't believe I'll ever see it again with these same eyes. This journey turns a page in my life. It's the beginning of something new and there is some sadness in it. My heart tells me it will change us all."

"We cannot escape change, Cristin. We can't grow without it."

He reached out his hand to her.

"We need to be moving now. It's time to look to the road that lies ahead of us."

The party started off with Stephan and Liam at the front. The women followed along with Eogan and behind them the prince, walking alone with a sullen expression on his face. Flann trailed behind with the pack animals. He was small in stature, with blond hair and a turned up nose and large ears that gave him an impish look. He had the enchanted look on his face of a boy seeing the forest for the first time. The dogs immediately took up their flanking positions in the woods on either side of the road. The forest was beautiful and full of life in the early Spring. Birds flitted between the newly leafed trees and their mating calls echoed like music in the boughs. The underbrush was dappled with spots of bright sunlight and the air carried the sweet fragrance of fresh pine and the pollen of oak, ash and elm trees sparkled in the beams of light. They traveled quietly, speaking among themselves in muted voices. The girls were excited to be off on a journey, even if it was fraught with danger. For many months they had been sequestered in the castle and the sudden freedom was exhilarating. At one point, Ailis let go with a trill of laughter which was greeted by a stern look from her mother.

Stephan spoke quietly with Liam as they walked.

"Later this day I would ask you to spend some time with Brien. I had to be harsh with him this morning but he will do us no good sulking as he is. The king tells me he's a skilled fighter. I would have him show his skills to you if there's time."

"How badly does he need to be cuffed?"

"Not badly. Only enough for him to discover his limitations. If he is indeed as good as his father says, tell him as much. We will be in need of every able sword available to us and I need to know if he can defend himself or if he needs protection."

"Have you thought this journey through to the end, Stephan?"

"Only broadly. I've tried to plan it so that each day's march will end at a place that provides some refuge, but it may not be possible. Once we reach the Pennine moors there will be little shelter available to us. I'm afraid the women, at least, will suffer but I have no remedy for it. Tonight at least we will have a hearth to warm us."

"The hunter's camp is at the edge Certic's border, Stephan. From tomorrow on we will be on uncertain ground."

"Yes, the next three days will take us through the territory of the Brigantes. We will need to take care."

"Does Danius still grant you passage through his lands?"

"He has in the past, but then I traveled alone or with one or two others. I don't know how he will feel about a party such as this. If he learns we are traveling with Certic's children he could see it as an opportunity."

"We cannot pass through his lands without his knowledge, Stephan."

"Yes, I know. He will learn of our presence soon enough, which is why tomorrow I will locate his camp and seek a meeting with him. I will go alone."

"How do you know you'll be welcomed?"

"If he does not choose to decorate his spear with my head."

"Perhaps I should accompany you. It would take at least the two of us to defeat his entire tribe."

Stephan smiled briefly and then his expression turned serious.

"If it comes to fighting the Brigantes, there is little hope for any of us, and our mission will be lost. I don't believe it will come to that. I'll need you at our camp, Liam. The party will need to be shown how to stand an attack. Cadman you can depend on, but the rest know nothing of battle. Do you remember the tactic we used at Cana henge when we covered Guallauc's flank?"

"Aye, we held back half of the Lingran's army with fewer than a hundred men. I took many heads on that day."

"I think that is how we must fight if it comes to it. Show them what to do. The women will be of little help, but at least we can keep them protected."

"So we will wait for your return?"

"I will depart before first light. It will not take long for the Brigantes to find me in their forest. I will not make my presence a secret. If Danius has not moved his camp, I should be able to meet with him before noon. If I am back with enough time we may try to make a little distance. Probably we will need to remain at the hunter's camp for the day. We still have some time and enough provisions. What we need is safe passage.

Try to disturb the camp as little as possible. When we depart it must look like no one was there."

-5-

The camp had once been a border outpost. Now it was open to anyone permitted to hunt on the king's lands. It was located in a clearing within a half day's trek of a primary game migration route and beside a stream of clear running water. It included a smokehouse to preserve meat and, in addition to the main lodging, a stout log hut to keep the provisions safe from bears and other prowling carnivores. The camp allowed hunting parties to remain in pursuit of the herds of deer and elk without the need to return to the castle before the meat spoiled. Inside the lodging was a stone hearth with an iron kettle for cooking and a number of straw filled mattresses. It was kept well supplied with firewood and each departing hunting party replaced what they had used.

It had been an uneventful day on the road. They didn't come across any travelers nor were there any signs of pursuit. They were tired after the long walk but spirits were high. As Flann and the women prepared an evening meal, Liam came

71

through the door carrying two staves of yew he had cut to be used as sparring weapons. He gave one to Brien.

"I think we have enough daylight left for you to show me your skills, young prince. I'm in the mood for a friendly contest. How say you?"

"I'm ready enough."

The two combatants squared off in the clearing in front of the lodge. Stephan and the other men gathered around to watch. Brien opened with a savage attack that was at once, skillful and sly. Liam was well accustomed to facing smaller men who attempted to overcome his great size with speed and craft. Even so, he was impressed with Brien's skill. He held back his attack and offered several openings to see it Brien was skilled enough to take advantage of them. After a few minutes of close combat, Liam stepped back.

"Nicely done young prince. You can press the attack. Now let us see if you can defend as well."

Liam came forward like a bull, pressing forward but not hurrying. Although his thrusts were not as quick as his opponent, he moved with a practiced grace rarely seen in one so large as he. With his long reach he could make use of the openings his opponent gave him without overextending and losing his balance. Even with just part of his strength, his blows stung Brien's hands as he parried, and the last stroke hit him square across his thigh causing him to wince. The prince's face flushed red with anger and he charged at Liam swinging wildly. With one sweeping stroke, his feet were knocked out from under him and he landed on his back in the dust, Liam's weapon at his throat. Liam smiled, then dropped his stave and reached down offering his hand. Brien glowered at him for a moment and then took it, allowing himself to be pulled to his feet. Liam slapped the young prince on his back.

"You fight with skill and courage, young prince. Someone has trained you well. Remember to step forward when you parry to the left, so you keep your feet under you. That was how I was able to sever your leg."

The men applauded the contest and then returned to their tasks, leaving Brien standing alone and a little bewildered by what had just happened. Stephan approached him.

"Walk with me a while Brien."

Stephan took him a little into the forest and they sat together on the trunk of a fallen tree. Brien looked at him as if he were about to receive another reprimand.

"Have you ever seen the wild men whose lands the kingdom borders?"

"No, never."

"You know we fought a war with them before you were born. I was not much older then you are now. The men of the forest carry the same Celtic blood that courses through our veins, but they still follow the old ways and they keep to the old beliefs. The first time I saw them in battle I was nearly frozen with fear. In battle they seek death. They welcome it. It is the greatest honor they can attain, because they believe to die bravely in battle is to come back to the earth in a new life with greater wealth and power and glory. Even when at peace they wear the heads of their enemies on their belts. In war they fight completely naked except that their bodies are painted with a blue dye made from wode. They use this same dye to tattoo their bodies after winning a battle. Their druid priests give them something to chew before battle that makes them fearless and enraged. We fought a battle near here. It was my first and I will never forget it. They charged at us down a long hill, screaming like beings from the netherworld. It was all I could do to hold my ground. I did not fight well that day. I was lucky to have survived."

"How did you survive?"

"I had good men at my side, who had fought many battles with the Brigantes. They kept me unscathed until I could get my wits about me. I left that battle uninjured but with a deep sense of shame. Shame that I had let these wild men daunt me, but something else also. The shame of killing a man without mercy. When the battle was over and we had won, I looked about the forest at the dead and dying men. At the severed limbs and the blood staining the forest floor and it sickened me. I learned many lessons that day, Brien. Most importantly I learned how to defeat the wild men or any man who flies into battle in a rage. Rage can only serve a man for a short time. Even with the weed the wild men use, their rage abandon's them at some point and it is then that they are vulnerable. The wild men are not skilled fighters. More often than not they fly into battle, hacking with axes and clubs. Once they have spent their rage they thrash about without tactics and are easily dispatched by a skilled and discipline opponent. When you are in a fight, and you most certainly will be before this journey is ended, seek out an opponent who is enraged. If you see a warrior who is calm, almost serene as he fights, he is a man to be feared. You are a skilled swordsman but you lost your temper when Liam wounded you. As soon as you did so, the contest was lost. In battle, if you need to think about how to fight, you will fight badly. You must surrender yourself to your skill and training and as much as possible keep your mind calm."

"How do you do that?"

"Each man has his own way. For my part I see myself standing on the field of battle with my enemies at my feet, as if the battle is already won."

"I don't know if I can do that, Stephan. Not yet at least."

"That is the first step in learning to be a warrior. Admitting what you have not yet mastered and listening to those who can teach you. When the fight comes to us, you will be with men who will look out for you. Believe in your skills and you will fare well enough. You have courage, Brien. It is a daunting thing to face a man like Liam, even if you know he does not aim to kill you."

"I admit I would not wish to face him in battle."

"There are few who would. You will spend some time in his company over the coming days. Learn from him. Learn from everyone."

"I will do so."

"There is one additional thing I would ask of you."

"What is it?"

"I would like you to take up with Lucas during this journey. He is not skilled with the sword and I would have you instruct him. In return there is much he can teach you. He has courage as you do, and is an excellent hunter and woodsman. He is also skilled with the staff

76

and bow. If you do not talk down to him. If you do not make him feel inferior. I think a friendship could grow between you. It is something that will serve you both well, regardless of the outcome of this journey."

"After the way you spoke to me this morning, I am surprised you would trust me with such a task."

"I am not here to spare your feelings, Brien. I am here to get you and your sister to safety. On this journey we must all look out for one another. It must be so if we are to survive. Even your servant Flann may need to join the fight. Treat him less like a servant, and more like a man. If you become a king some day, it is how you will make your people love you."

Later that evening when the meal was completed, Stephan went outside and sat with the dogs, looking up at the stars. It was something he did every night and it troubled him that the peaceful times were ending. After a while, Cristin came and sat with him. She looked at the man she had loved so much as a child, and saw him for the first time with the eyes of a woman. There was a deep well of peace and kindness in him, as if he lived aside from the trivial cares of the world and all the things that distracted other men and made them less than they could be.

"It's a fine, soft evening, Cristin. I hope we'll have many more on our journey."

Cristin looked at him and smiled. She reached over and petted the dogs.

"These are beautiful animals. I think they do not like to be inside."

"They come and lie by the fire on the coldest of nights or when there is a deep snowfall, but no, this is their home out here in the wild. If they could speak, they would tell you every animal within half a league of this place, and what he hunts. They come from the same litter and they are joined to each other. Even if separated by large distances they sense each other and know if there's trouble. They also know where I am at all times and come to me if they sense I'm in need of help. They are my great, silent warriors."

"What do you call them?"

"This one is Lero and the other Baco, both gods of the hunt."

Cristin stroked the animal's smooth shoulders and they nuzzled against her. Stephan watched her with the dogs.

"They like you Cristin. They do not warm to everyone so easily."

She turned to him, and a look of regret crossed her face.

"I've missed you Stephan. It was such a joy to see you around the castle when I was a child. Not many come to know the children of a king or spend time entertaining them. It can be a lonely life. I was inconsolable when you left. "

"I wish it had not been so, Cristin. We cannot always control our destiny."

"Has the great rift between you and my father been settled now, after all these years?"

"It will never be settled entirely, but we have made a kind of peace with each other."

"I'm glad then. I only wish it had come sooner, before we had cause to flee the castle and seek refuge here in the wild. What will you do when this war is over? Will you abandon the forest and come live with us once more?"

"I don't know, Cristin. Everything hangs on how this war is settled. I too wish these times were not upon us, but bad times make good friends. We will have some time now to get to know each other again and I'm glad of it."

"Has it not been lonely for you? Living as you do out in the wilderness. Have you never missed the company of other people?"

"I miss those I count as my friends. I rarely crave the company of strangers. I don't enjoy the lies and the hollow boasting and the pretending. I think it takes many years to learn how to deal with such things and I have never had the time or the paticncc for it."

"You do not like our people then? That's a sad thing."

"I do like them, Cristin. I find that all people everywhere are the same in this and I don't hold it against them. I think these are skills a man needs to learn to live closely with other men and I don't think badly of them. I have learned that speaking honestly often makes more enemies than friends, but I don't know how to be otherwise."

"But you have fought in the army, closely with other soldiers. People say you are a great leader and that men rally to your side in battle."

"People will say what they want. I'm comfortable with the men who fight by my side. They say who they are with their courage and their skill. There are few lies told on the battlefield, save for when a man says he is not afraid."

They both were silent for a while, looking up at the night sky. A meteorite streaked overhead and Cristin reached out and touched him on the sleeve.

"Did you see it?"

"Yes. I'm out in the night often and I see many. Some say they are omens of things to come, but if they are, I don't know how to read them."

"When I was a child, my mother told me they were the gods' way of telling us to pay attention."

"To pay attention to what?"

"To whatever was happening when you saw one. She said too often we don't realize the importance of a moment until it has passed us by. The falling stars are like someone whispering in your ear, saying pay attention now, this is important."

"Perhaps she was right."

"I know you would wish to reassure me, but you cannot hide the truth on your face. This journey is fraught with great danger for us is that not so?"

"It is so, but don't despair of it. This is a good company we travel with. I could not find better men to stand with me."

"And women?"

Stephan smiled. He reached out and put his hand on her shoulder.

"I am told you have skill with the bow, Cristin. You will have to show me."

"I can shoot a bird on the wing, if that's good enough for you."

"Now that would be worth seeing. I must depart the camp early tomorrow and I would get some rest now. I'll enjoy getting to know you again. Tomorrow Liam will teach you all how to stand an attack. Listen to him well. When I return we will shoot some flies out of the air together."

"I'll look forward to it. Are you coming inside?"

"No, I'll keep my two warriors company tonight under the stars."

-6-

The moon had nearly set when Stephan departed the camp and the forest was dark and foreboding. The dogs did not want to let him go alone but he couldn't bring them. The Brigantes ran with wild dogs that would not obey the command to heal, nor hesitate to attack the two mastiffs and overwhelm them with their numbers. He made his way slowly through the wood, following his instincts and letting his memory guide him. Danius had located his camp on a high hill and Stephan knew if the ground was rising he was headed in the right direction. After an hour of slow going, the sky began to brighten in the east and the visibility improved. In another hour he began to pick up the scent of cooking fires in the distance. He moved cautiously now toward the west to be downwind of the camp. There would be sentries in the forest this close in, and they were known to slay intruders without hesitation. He didn't want to surprise them. He stopped and waited at the base of a large elm. In a few minutes he heard the sound of men moving quietly through the underbrush. He called out to them in their dialect.

"I am Sigurd, friend to Danius. I have come to share meat with him."

His call was met with a sudden silence and then quickly, by the sound of men running toward him through the brush. He leaned against the tree with his arms folded. Before they came into view a spear flew through the trees and imbedded itself in the tree trunk, not six inches above his head. He did not flinch. He did not move. Seconds later, two men emerged from the forest. They wore bear skin tunics and one had a human head hanging from his belt. They had sandals on their feet and large broadaxes in their hands. Bathing was unknown to these men and their faces were smeared with dirt and their odor strong. Their hair and beards were tangled and embedded with bits of brush from sleeping on the ground.

Stephan repeated his message. One of the men came forward and reached for Stephan's sword. Before he could grasp it, Stephan pulled his dagger and held it to the man's throat. He backed away. They would not harm him now that he had invoked their chieftain's name but they would take his weapons and possessions if Stephan allowed it. He did not.

"Put away your blade outlander, and follow. If you draw it again you will die."

They moved off through the forest, one leading, the other following behind. In a short time they entered a clearing and had to navigate through a series of concentric defensive ditches dug into the hillside. The wild men looked at him with interest. A few of the older men recognized him and a conversation followed their progress. The dogs growled and lunged at him but he paid them no notice. After some time they reached the center of the camp where a large, circular, thatch covered enclosure stood. The two pickets stopped him and they waited. In a while an old man emerged from the structure. He was short but thick boned and still well muscled in his advanced years. His long hair was silver and his face and body were decorated with many wode tattoos, indicating his success in battle. He had too many scars to count and an empty socket gaped where he had lost an eye in battle. He looked at Stephan but said nothing. Stephan spoke.

"Greetings Danius. I am pleased to see you are well."

The old chieftain grunted and turned back toward the enclosure. He raised one arm and moved it forward, indicating that Stephan should follow. The floor of the hut was covered with bear skin and a cooking brazier stood in the center.

The old chief sat by the brazier and Stephan sat across from him. He reached into the kettle and removed some meat on the bone, and threw it into Stephan's lap. A man entered with two wooden cups filled with a kind of mead that the wild men favored. Stephan lifted his cup to the old chief and then drank it down to the bottom, turning the empty cup over and dropping it in front of him. The old man spoke.

"I've been expecting a messenger from Certic. I did not expect to see you, Sigurd."

"I did not expect it either. These are strange times that have come upon us."

"Strange times always come before a great shedding of blood. The Saxon's will soon camp before Certic's walls, and I think they will remain as long as they please. I don't believe this king is strong enough to push them back into the sea. I trust he did not send you to ask for my help."

Stephan reached into his pouch and removed a silver chalice. He handed it to Danius.

"The king sends his greetings. He does not seek your help. He hopes that you will not rise up against him in this fight."

A smile crossed the old chief's face.

"I was told you and the king were enemies. Now you come bearing his gifts. What has changed you, Sigurd?"

"It is true I am no great friend of Certic, but at least he does not want my head."

The old man laughed loudly, and then he spoke.

"I care less even than you for this king, or for the seed throwers he protects, but our truce has lasted many years and I would not foul my honor by breaking it. It matters nothing to me who scrapes lines in the dirt, as long as they don't enter my forest. I am glad it is you who have come to me. I expected some forked tongued serpent. You can tell Certic I will not rise against him, as long as he keeps his bargain."

"I will tell him, but think upon this. This Saxon king is not a man who honors treaties. If he prevails, you may soon find yourself at war again. They wish to claim all the land south of the Roman wall and their numbers are large and there arms strong."

"So, you do think I should throw in with this king!"

"I would not think to advise you Danius. You will do what you wish and for your own reasons. I share my thoughts with you to consider or not."

"But this is also not the end of your journey, Sigurd. We have seen your party. I have never known you to travel with women before. Perhaps you have taken a wife since last I saw you. Or perhaps more than one."

"That is my second reason for coming to you. I wish safe passage through your forest with those who accompany me. We would take only what game we need to feed ourselves during the journey."

"And where will that journey take you?"

Stephan was silent for a moment as he studied the face of the old chieftain. Finally he spoke.

"Certic would not wish me to share this information with you, but since I seek safe passage I will tell you that we are bound for Craven with a plea for the king's cousin, Uryen to join in the fight."

"And how will that message be received, do you think?"

"I don't know Uryen. I don't know how he will respond."

Now the chieftain was silent as he stared into the fire. Stephan hoped he would not question him further about his traveling companions. In the end it didn't matter.

"You are an honest man Sigurd which is why I will allow passage for you and your friends. In truth, I expected such a move by Certic, except that I thought it would have come sooner. The time is late and the Saxons already have men in your way. We've found some already and their heads can be seen hanging from some belts. I will not question you further about your companions. I have my suspicions but I won't make you lie to me. You can tell that giant you travel with he still owes me an eye. I will let it be known among my people that you have been given passage and they will not attack you. Be warned that not all the men in this forest answer to me. Those who do will stay clear of you but there may be others who would hunt you. I cannot guarantee your safety. Our forest is deep and even though our enemies cannot hide from us for long, this will not be a safe journey for you."

"I do not ask for your guarantee. I am grateful for your hospitality."

"The druids have told me that a new branch is growing on the great oak tree of life. They foretell a time of great change and upheaval. I will not have a place on this new branch, Sigurd. My time is past. I will tell you that I would rather leave this earth swinging my axe than wasting away in this hut. We may yet play a part in this tale before it's over. Of those who would take my place when I die, there are some who prefer the hunt, and those who would take heads. I cannot tell who will take the power when I'm gone, or whether they will honor my treaties. We will see how things unfold. Now, is there anything else you wish to discuss?"

"No, I believe the matter is settled."

"Good, then if we have finished here let's walk together a while. You have won a place in the legends the men tell at night around the fire and there are some who may wish to meet you. I will decorate my belt with Certic's gift so my people can see how a king lives."

He slapped Stephan on the back, and laughed.

"Besides, it is good for an old chief to be seen walking with a legend."

***

Flann awoke at first light and began to prepare the cooking fire. He spoke to no one unless asked a question. He was polite but not overly friendly and he kept to himself. Liam watched him moving about the lodging as he lay under his cloak. He had never known such a man and he was curious about him. He was small of stature and not built for soldering, but still, he thought a man should not accept the yoke so readily. In a moment the women awakened. They moved about silently arranging their things. In a while they made for the door, carrying soap and combs and potions that Liam had no knowledge of. When Cristin exited the lodging, the dogs immediately went to her and nuzzled against her. It was as if they had been given a silent command by Stephan to protect her. The women, followed by the dogs, went through the forest a short distance to the stream where they would care for themselves. Eogan followed at a distance and waited in the forest out of sight, but within earshot. Cadman and Lucas had spent the night under the stars. They were hunters, and they did not wish the scent of the fire to be on them as they stalked their prey. They had strung their bows and were preparing to depart for the hunt when Brien exited the lodging and approached them.

"Are you off to find our dinner?"

"We are." Cadman answered.

"Would you allow me to accompany you? I would like to learn your skills."

Lucas was clearly not pleased by the request and he turned away.

"You are welcome to hunt with us, Brien." Cadman answered. "Only stay behind us a little when we begin stalking. The smell of the castle is on your clothing and the game will flee from you. Do you have a bow?"

"I didn't bring it."

"Lucas. Let Brien try your long bow. It's built for larger game than we hunt today and it has a strong pull but it also has great range."

Lucas retrieved the long bow and a quiver of arrows and handed them to the prince. Brien smiled at him.

"Thank you Lucas. I'll care for it well."

"Can you string it?"

"I have strung a bow before. Perhaps not as stout as this one."

"Try it."

Brien braced the bow against his boot with the string secure in the notch on the bottom and looped around the shaft near the top. He took hold of the bow and pulled down with all his might but was unable to get the string into the top notch. He tried again and his face was turning red with the effort. Lucas watched him and was secretly pleased, but his face showed nothing.

"Let me show, you Brien. It is not a matter of strength. Even my father could not string this bow as you are trying. Place your knee against the shaft of it and as you pull, lean your knee into the bend."

Brien tried it and was able to string the bow easily. Lucas nodded to him.

"Are the bows your soldiers use to man the walls not as stout as this one then?"

"They are stout but not so long as this one. It would be too difficult to maneuver them among the parapets. We have bows of this kind but I have never strung one as you have seen."

They set off into the woods, Cadman in the front and the two young men walking together behind.

You fight well with the sword, Brien. I have not had much occasion to use one."

"I have another with me. I'll let you carry it if you wish. If there is time we can spar a little. Perhaps I can instruct you in its use."

Lucas smiled.

"I would like that."

As the hunters disappeared into the forest, Liam exited the lodging and went to check on the pack animals. He untied them and walked them off to the side of the smoke house where there was a small meadow. He hobbled their foreleg pasterns and set them free to graze. It seemed to him the party was carrying too much baggage and had one too many animals. He walked over to where the bags had been piled and began to look through them. The women had since returned from their bathing and Emma walked over to him. She could see he was annoyed.

"What is all this chattel? Are you thinking to furnish a castle with this?"

"The girls packed as little as they needed as did I."

"We cannot carry all of this."

"But the horses carry this load, surely they are not overburdened."

"Where we travel it will be difficult enough for one horse, let alone two. There are wolves in this wilderness, great packs of them. They do not generally attack men, but these horses will draw them to us. If we are attacked, either the horses will bolt or a strong arm will have to hold them. There are too few of us to spare a strong arm. Even if we succeed in driving them off, the horses will certainly be wounded in an attack and we will have to put them down. I would rather have no horses at all, but for now I will permit one. There may well come a time on this journey when we will have to abandon it also."

"Very well. I will go through the bundles and see what can be left behind. Do you think our belongings will be safe if we leave them here?"

"Whatever you do not bring we will burn. The horse will be turned loose. It will find its way back to the castle."

Emma stiffened and glowered at the huge man.

"I will not burn the princess' clothing nor my own. How could you ask such a thing?"

Liam looked at the woman, and shook his head.

"Perhaps Stephan has been too kind and did not wish to give you nightmares. But I will tell you now what we face on this journey. For the next three days we cross the Mernwood. It is the land of the Brigantes as you may know. Stephan has gone off this morning to meet with their chieftain. They respect Stephan and will likely allow passage for us, but the matter is by no means sure. Even if we are permitted to pass, it does not bring us safety. The Brigantes are fierce brutes and have no respect for women. Their smell alone is enough to sicken a man. I have fought them and I know what they are capable of. But as bad as they are, they are the best of what we may come across in this forest. There are other wild men who know no tribe. I have known them to capture men and roast them alive over a fire and then eat them for their evening meal. If you and the young women do not carry daggers, I suggest you do so from now on. It would be better for you to take your own lives than to be captured by these beasts. The packs of wolves I have already mentioned and now, in the spring, the bears with their young have emerged hungry. They too normally avoid men, but if we are unlucky enough to come across females with cubs they will attack us. They can break a man's back with one swipe of their claws and unless you place your arrow perfectly they will not stop attacking until they are dead."

"This is not my first time traveling in the wild. You do not scare me with these tales."

"Then let me tell you this, and listen well. We may be lucky and avoid the wild men and the beasts, but we are pursued. They have not found us yet but it is likely they will. They are assassins sent by King Edwin to prevent us from seeking help from the king's cousin. If they find us, and we can not defeat them, they will kill the prince and princess and bring their heads to Edwin on a pole. This is why we cannot leave the princess's clothing behind for them to find. So go through these things carefully and without sentiment. Bring only what will keep you alive, and pray we will not have to abandon the rest as well."

The men returned from the hunt with a brace of rabbits and two fat pheasants. They were in high spirits and Brien and Lucas had already started to forge a bond, as young men finding their way in the world are wont to do. They gave the game to Flann and he took them inside to prepare them for dinner. Liam greeted them and asked that the party assemble in front of the lodging with their weapons. When they had done so, Liam spoke.

"We will be traveling together for many days and you all know we will likely be facing some danger on this journey. If we are attacked, our best chance is to stay together and to fight as one. If we stay together, we are strong enough. It is important that no one is separated from the party."

He took one of the yew staves and drew in the dirt.

"If we are in the open we will arrange ourselves in two circles, one inside the other. Each will protect the other."

He looked at Emma.

"Stephan tells me the three of you have some skill with the bow, is that true?"

"It is." She said "With an edge in her voice that everyone noticed, but Liam ignored."

"Good. Then the three of you and Lucas because of his skill with the bow will form the inside circle. I don't know if Flann has any fighting skills but he will be in the inner circle and help as is his ability. At the very least he can wield a dagger if that becomes necessary. Eogan will also be on the inside with his sword in case the outer circle is breached and an enemy gets through. The outer circle will consist of myself, Stephan, Cadman and Brien with our swords. We fight for each other. The archers will prevent our swordsmen from being overwhelmed by more than one opponent. The swordsmen will concentrate on anyone who attempts to reach the inner circle. It is the same whether our foe is man or wolf. It is important that we keep our formation but we will not stay still. At all times we will move toward higher ground so that it will become difficult for our enemy to get behind us, and to avoid being easy targets for a bowman. When we reach a good slope at our back, our formation will flatten into two arcs so that we can concentrate our defense. Does everyone understand?"

"But we will be traveling in the forest." Lucas said. "How do we arrange ourselves then?"

"The principle is the same but even better for us. The archers can take cover behind trees as they pick their targets. We move through the forest as one. Anything else?"

"What of the horse?" Emma asked.

"The horse will bolt. We cannot tie it or it may be slain. If we're fortunate, the dogs will find it when the skirmish is ended or it will return on its own. It will prefer our company to being alone in the forest. More questions?"

"Very well, then let us see how it will work. Please arrange yourselves as I have shown you."

The circles were formed and Liam began the instruction.

"The size of the circles will depend on the size and deployment of the attackers. Each archer will watch the back of one swordsman. If the battle is joined, say out loud what swordsman you protect. Now move off to the left."

The group moved sideways. Ailis stumbled and fell.

"That's all right Ailis. Remember to watch where you move. Archers who are skilled at this tactic will notch an arrow while concentrating on the ground and stop only to set their feet, aim, and shoot. Never let go your bolt if you do not have a clear shot at your enemy. It's better to be accurate than fast. If you shoot in haste, you may end up shooting one of us. Take your time. Lets try again."

They practiced for an hour and at the end they were moving as a cohesive unit at Liam's command. Just as they were breaking up to go about their separate tasks, the dogs suddenly sprang off into the forest. In a short while they returned, walking with Stephan who was wearing a deer hide amulet marked with Celtic runes. A token of passage from Danius. He greeted them and then took Liam aside for a conversation.

"How did they do?"

"As you said, the women will be little help to us."

"I know it, Liam. The point is to give them weapons to hold and to make them feel they have a part in their own defense. If nothing else, if they are thinking about fighting they are less likely to break and run. We cannot protect them if they panic and run loose. I think they may do better than you expect. Cristin has some strength in her and all of them if threatened may find the strength to shoot the arrow that will save their own lives. Encourage them, Liam, and teach them when you can."

"How did it go with Danius?"

"Well, I think. He knows more about us than I would like but I do not sense treachery from him. He has found Saxons in his forest and he knows this war is coming. If he were casting the stones I don't believe his bet would be on our survival. He says you owe him an eye."

Liam laughed. "Well, I'm using both of mine at the moment. I'll see if I can find him one."

After a few minutes he called to Cristin.

"Come forward princess and bring your archers. Show me how you can shoot a fly out of the air."

***

That evening they all gathered around the hearth for dinner. Stephan was glad to see the group coming together and bonds being formed. Liam's training session had lifted their confidence and Stephan had learned that the women could shoot quite well, at least at targets that were not shooting back. Ailis was the weakest of them but she was also not without skill. He hoped if they were to be tested it would not be too difficult at first. Something to prepare them for what might come later, as the journey took them into unknown lands. The women sat together next to a pile of garments that they would be sacrificing to the fire. To ease their pain at giving up their valued possessions, Liam had opened a small cask of ale. It was to have been poured out and donated to the fire as well, but Liam said it would come with them even if he had to carry it himself. By the end of dinner the women were a bit into their cups. Cristin suggested a game of riddles. Stephan had been watching her and he was amazed by this woman whom he still thought of as a little girl. She had qualities of empathy and leadership that her brother did not possess and she had grown into a beautiful woman. She had accepted the loss of her possessions with grace and understanding and had set an example for Ailis and Emma. The men listened in silence, unused to the company of a group of high-born women.

"I will go first." Cristin said. "Ailis. Throw another dress on the fire will you. I feel a chill." Ailis giggled and nearly went into the fire herself. Emma steadied her.

"All right, here is the first riddle. The more I dry, the wetter I become. What am I?"

"I know it." Ailis said.

"Wait. Let's ask our giant. Are you good at riddles sir giant?"

"I am good at everything. I think the answer is a drunk."

The women laughed. "That is not the answer, sir giant. What say you Ailis?"

"It is a towel."

"I liked my answer better." Liam said.

Ailis spoke next.

"My turn now. It cannot be seen, it weighs nothing, but when put in a barrel it makes it lighter. What is it?"

Cristin looked over at Lucas.

"How about you, sir hunter. Do you know the answer?"

"Perhaps hot air. A lot of it."

They laughed again.

"A good answer, sir hunter, but not the right one. The answer is a hole."

Brien groaned.

"When do you have time for these games, Cristin?"

"You know well the answer to that question, Brien."

"I will go next." Emma said.

"My life is measured in hours. I serve by being devoured. Thin I am quick, fat I am slow. The wind is my foe. What am I?"

They all looked at each other.

"No one?" Emma asked.

"A candle."

Everyone turned. Flann was smiling back at them a little sheepishly.

"Well said, sir Flann. Cristin said. Come sit with us. You are good at this game."

Stephan stood and stretched.

"I will see to my warriors"

He went outside into the night. The stars were brilliant but there were clouds moving in from the east and there was just a light chill in the air. He had some meat for the dogs. They followed him, slavering at the jowl. Stephan looked down at them.

"Do you want what I carry, my warriors?"

They barked in unison and danced around his feet. He gave each of them a fist full of meat and they gulped it down greedily. He sat with the dogs under the stars, letting them lick his hands until they were clean. He guessed this might be the party's last comfortable night and perhaps their last without fear. It was good to hear their laughter. The sound grew briefly louder as someone exited the lodging. He turned and saw Liam walking toward him.

"We will have some unhappy women traveling with us tomorrow. I don't want to be the one who rousts them in the morning."

"Aye, and I think there will be some weather as well. Later in the day perhaps."

"How do you feel about them, Stephan?"

"It's better than I'd hoped. I think Brien can hold his own and Cristin has surprised me with her strength and ability. I think we have a chance, if we are not overwhelmed."

"Certic will be distraught when the horse returns to the stables."

"I'll send a message with it. Certic will want to know that Danius will not take up arms against him."

"What if Edwin's spies intercept it?"

"The message I send will be marked in runes. There is only one in the castle who'll be able to read it. An old man who was in that place since the early days. He is an old friend and I have made this arrangement with him in case we were able to get a message through."

"Do you think the horse will find its way back?"

"I think so. Or it may be found by a hunter or woodsman. It bears the king's mark so unless an enemy finds it; it will get to the king's stable eventually."

"How do you think it will go tomorrow?"

"I don't have a feel for it yet. Danius says he has found others, not from his tribe, in his forest. Sooner or later I expect we will be discovered and then it will turn on how many they are and how good the ground we are standing. Perhaps we will get through tomorrow without an attack, but I am not confident of it."

"Have you thought what may happen if we are overwhelmed and unable to save everyone?"

"If that happens then my life will end at that place. I will not abandon them no matter what. Did you think otherwise?"

"No. I know you well Stephan, and you know also I will stand with you if that fate befalls us, but what if we can save only one or two. How would you choose? Will you save the princess and the prince and leave the others to their fate?"

"I will save all, or I will save none. There will be no choosing."

"I knew as much, I ask only because I see how the young princess looks at you. There is some love between you if I am not wrong."

"I've known Cristin since she was a child. I do have a great love for her but I'm bound by my honor to all in this party. It cannot be otherwise."

"And where will the end of the day find us tomorrow?"

"I know a place if I can find it. It is a cave that the bears like in the winter. I think they'll be out of it by now. It will keep us out of the weather and we can have a fire. Cadman and Lucas will set out ahead of us again and they will hunt for our dinner as they go. In the morning let us bury our ashes and leave no sign that we have been to this place."

-7-

When they awoke the next morning a heavy mist clung to the trees and the sky was thick with cloud. Stephan tied a deer hide strap around the horse's neck. He rubbed its withers and spoke into its ear before swatting it on the hindquarters, sending it running off the way they had come. Liam attended to the other horse, making sure the packs were secure. He filled the water skins and made himself ready for the trail. From this point they would leave the road which curved around to the south and eventually found its way to the river. The trail they would follow was rough but the land was still mostly flat and not too difficult. It was heavily wooded with dense thickets in places. The women moved about silently, and the men knew better than to talk to them. In an hour they were ready to start off. Flann sifted through the ashes in the hearth to make sure there were no buttons or shards of fabric, and then he buried it all behind the cabin. Liam took one last look around the camp. He took a branch and backed through the area erasing their footprints. The rain would do the rest. There would be no sign of their passing.

Cadman and Lucas were ahead by fifteen minutes when they started out. Stephan looked at the party as they moved through the mist. The women in their dark, hooded cloaks and with bow and quiver on their shoulders looked like wraiths following behind a giant and leading a woodland elf with a pony. It was a strange company indeed, and one he knew was headed in harms way. Stephan led them steadily through the forest along the game trail. For the most part, they walked in silence. The weather was damp and chilly, and memories of the pleasant evening around the hearth were rapidly fading. Stephan and Liam spoke quietly as they walked.

"I thought I might see some of the Brigantes in the forest this morning."

"They watched us depart the camp. They're gone now."

"You have better eyes than me, my friend. I saw nothing."

"I didn't see them, but I felt their presence."

"You've told me such things before, Stephan, but I swear I have no understanding of it."

"I don't understand it myself, but I've come to trust it, and it has served me well. I think they've lost interest in us now that they know who we are. I'm sure there are more than a few who would like to take us out here in the forest but Danius would have their heads for it. They are not my worry."

"Yes I know. The forest is thick here and an enemy could easily lay in wait for us."

"My dogs would find them long before they could surprise us. As long as they are quiet we will not need to fear an attack close in. If we find them, they will be in front of us."

"Do you think we are on a fool's errand, Stephan? I mean besides finding safe haven for Cristin and Brien. Do you think Uryen will offer his help to Certic?"

"Danius asked me the same question and I will give you the same answer. I do not know him. I'm told there is some jealousy between them and their relationship is not warm. Also it would be a gamble for Uryen to throw his army into this fight. If the war is lost he will not have the strength to defeat Edwin."

"I am told that his army is not half the size of Elmet's. He must know if Certic falls, there will be little hope for him."

"If he does not throw in with Certic and the war is lost, he will no doubt sue for peace and throw his gates open to the Saxon's to avoid being slaughtered. Either way will be a terrible gamble for him and I do not expect him to be happy to see us. I hope he has the courage to fight, but as I said, I don't know him."

They had traveled for several hours when they came upon Cadman and Lucas at a place where the trail forked. When the party stopped, the dogs came in and joined them. Cadman spoke.

"I don't know which fork to take here Stephan."

Stephan looked around the forest, trying to get his bearings. Liam came up behind.

"This is new to me, Liam. This trail did not fork before. Do you remember it?"

"I don't have the memory of places as you do, Stephan. If you are not sure, I can't help you. Without the sun or stars to guide me, I am easily put off my course."

Stephan removed a small black stone from his pocket. It was wrapped in a piece of yarn. He loosened the yarn so that the stone hung freely. The stone spun around at first but then became still. Stephan moved the stone in an arc but it turned as he did to face in a single direction.

"What piece of sorcery is this, Stephan? Some magic charm a witch gave you?"

"It's a lodestone. They can sometimes be found near where lightning strikes the earth. They always point to the north."

He dropped the stone into Liam's huge hand and the giant held it by its string, moving it about.

"How is it I've never seen you use it before?"

109

"Because I usually know where I am and where I'm going. The animals have changed their direction here. Can you think why they might do that, Cadman?"

"They often do this when the land is disturbed. Sometimes by fire or flood. Sometimes by men. By the look of it, they stopped using the left branch at least a season ago. I don't know what it means."

"Stay with the party, Liam. It's a good time for them to rest and take some food. I'll follow this trail a while to see if I can find some landmarks."

Stephan started down the trail with the dogs. The party sat on the leaf covered earth and took some water. Liam went to the pack horse and retrieved some salted meat and bread. Flann gave the horse some water and tended to its hooves.

"Could we have a small fire, Liam?" Cristin asked. "We are chilled to the bone."

"We can't risk it here, in the open. The food will help even though it's cold. Would you like a bit of ale?"

The women cringed at the suggestion and Liam laughed.

"I thought not."

Eogan circled around the party, peering into the forest and listening for sounds of approaching danger. Brien and Lucas stood off to the side comparing their experiences. The conversation, in time, came around to Stephan.

"No one has ever told me how the rift developed between Stephan and my father. I think they are both good and strong men."

"You've not heard about the first war with King Edwin then?"

"I know there was a war and that we prevailed. That's all I know of it."

"You must have heard that Stephan was the great hero of that war?"

"I do not hear his name used in the castle."

"Well if you sat in the taverns you might hear that Stephan single handedly defeated Edwin's army and the king was jealous and cast him out of the city. Of course, that is not to be believed."

"So what is the truth of it?"

"I will tell you what my father told me. He fought with Stephan in the war against the wild men. That's where they became friends. It was shortly after that war and soon after your father became king. A hunter came hammering on the city gate late one evening. He had run hard all night and was nearly too exhausted to speak. He told the guard that a large force of armed men were landing their boats on the riverbank and were preparing to march on the city. Your father realized that it was Edwin, come to take advantage of his depleted army. Because Stephan had fought so well and was a natural leader of men, the king had already made him his military advisor, in spite of his young age. The king sent him out in the night to judge the size of the army and to decide on the best way to defend against it. He reached the camp and circled it, observing the soldiers and what arms they carried. He noticed that no sentries had been placed to guard the camp's provisions. What he did next was something no man had ever thought of and it was the beginning of his legend. He went into the forest and gathered some bear scat. Fighting in the wild had taught him what drinking fouled water will do to a man. He silently overcame one of the sentries and took his uniform and arms. Then he circulated through the camp pretending to take a sip of water from the bladders, but instead he dropped some of the dung into each bag, except for Edwin's own, which was inside his tent.

When he had finished, he returned to the castle and told the king what he had done. The king was elated. They both knew that within a day, anyone who drank the water would become very ill. Your father wanted to press the advantage and slaughter Edwin's army. Stephan argued that they should be stripped of their weapons and provisions, but be allowed to return to their homes. He believed that killing defenseless men was against his honor and would only bring a terrible retribution in time. Stephan believed that he left the meeting with your father with an agreement to spare Edwin's army. The king claimed later that no such agreement was ever reached. In any case, by the end of the following day, most of Edwin's army lay out on the field, lying in their own filth. Your father's army charged out from the city gates and attacked them without mercy, slaying them where they lay. All except for Edwin and his guards who escaped. When Stephan saw what was happening he refused to join in. He angrily confronted the king on the battlefield and was banished from the army and from the city. They have not spoken in all the long years that have passed since then. Although now that Edwin returns. It seems they have put the matter aside."

"My father was right to slay Edwin's army. He knew they could be rearmed and press the attack again while his forces were still too weak to defeat them."

"Perhaps. Stephan believed that by showing Edwin his mercy, the beginnings of a peace between them could be forged and a future war avoided. We will never know who was right. What is certain is that Edwin is returning. This time he will guard his camp well."

They were interrupted by the sight of Stephan running toward them with the dogs.

"To your feet and prepare to defend yourselves!"

The women appeared to be in shock but Cristin took charged of them. She pulled Ailis up by her arm and put the bow in her hands. They formed their circle as they had been shown and they each notched an arrow. Their hands were shaking but they stood firm.

"Who attacks us?" Liam shouted.

"They are wild men, not Brigantes."

"How many."

"More than a few. The dogs will come first."

Within seconds it seemed as though the forest had grown snarling beasts. Ailis fainted and fell to the ground. Cristin let fly an arrow and killed one of the dogs in mid leap. Liam and Brien wielded their swords along with Stephan and Cadman. Lucas and the women let loose their arrows. Eogan stood with the women and dispatched any of the beasts that came close. The mastiffs fought together, tearing apart any animal that dared to confront them. In a couple of minutes it was over, but already the cries of the wild men could be heard. Liam shouted.

"Regroup. Stand your ground."

They could not maneuver without leaving Ailis exposed, but the wild men did not use the bow and they were well positioned to defend against them. In seconds the battle was joined. Spears sailed through the air but landed harmlessly. The wild men burst upon them, screaming their war cries. Liam swung his great sword and decapitated the closest enemy. Others fell with arrows in their bodies. Brien was suddenly confronted by a pair of huge men swinging their axes. Lucas saw it and put arrows into both of them. Stephan moved as if in a dance, ducking and swinging low and then high. Cutting the legs out from under them and then thrusting under the ribs. The battle raged but the wild men did not know how to fight together. Cristin stood next to Lucas, fighting without hesitation, her arrows flying straight and true, and finding their marks. Soon the bodies of the wild men littered the ground. The last turned and ran, but before he could escape, Lucas's arrow pierced the back of his neck and he fell. The forest went silent. Emma fell to the ground crying. Cristin looked to Ailis who was just starting to be aware of her surroundings. Stephan spoke.

"That is the last of it. Are you hurt? Is anyone injured?"

"A dog has tasted my leg, Cadman said. It's nothing."

"Clean your wound, Cadman. Put some moss in it."

Stephan looked around at the party.

"Where is Flann?"

Suddenly everyone was concerned. The horse was gone and Flann was nowhere to be seen.

"Brien, Lucas, come with me."

The three men fanned out to the rear of the group. They had gone a short way when Lucas cried out.

"Over here! I've found him."

Flann was lying on the ground covered in blood. A dog lay on top of him, its throat cut and still oozing. Stephan pulled the carcass away and knelt down. Suddenly Flann opened his eyes and smiled.

"I guess I'm not dead then?"

"Does any of this blood belong to you, Flann?"

"I don't know. Are there any holes in me?"

Stephan pulled him to his feet. He was still clutching the carving knife he had used to dispatch the animal.

"So you can defend yourself after all, master Flann." Stephan said.

"I know how to cut meat at least. I was sorry to kill the dog but it would not listen to reason."

He looked around. "Where is the horse?"

"Don't worry she'll return to you. She doesn't want to be alone in this forest. Let's join the others. We can rest for a few moments, but not for long."

They sat in a group on the forest floor. The women were badly shaken and although Stephan felt the urge to get moving, he knew the women would need some time to recover. Emma had regained enough control of herself to attend to Cadman's wound. They were all exhausted and Ailis was distraught.

"I am worthless. I fainted dead away."

"Don't fret about it Ailis." Stephan said. "Young women should not have to see such things, or fight such battles. No one thinks badly of you."

"I don't think I hit anything with my arrows." Emma said. "I've never been so frightened. It was the noise and the screaming I was not prepared for. My knees were shaking and I thought I would fall. Those men are like wild beasts. I couldn't have imagined it."

"Now you know what to expect and you will do better if we need to fight again. The first time is the worst. Everyone was frightened." Liam said. "Even me. I feel the fear at the start of every battle. It has become an old friend. It leaves me as soon as I sever a head."

Stephan addressed the group.

"So now you have seen the truth of it. We will not face the wild men in greater numbers then we have seen today. Not while we are in Danius' forest. I think we will not see them again on this journey. This was a raiding party, probably out to collect some Brigantes' skulls. You see how they fight. They are no match for us if we fight as we did today. We could have defeated a band twice their numbers. No one was badly injured. You should all take heart from this skirmish. You have done well today."

Cristin looked at the dead men lying about them and shuddered.

"Should we not bury the dead?"

"We have no time for such things." Liam said. "In any case, we want anyone coming upon this place to think it was done by Danius, and the Brigantes do not bury their enemies. I may sever another head or two before we move on."

Ailis looked like she would be ill. Lucas and Cadman stood and set about retrieving their arrows. Stephan talked to the woman to see if they were able to carry on. As he was talking the horse came out of the forest and trotted up to them. It whinnied and then nudged Flann with its head. Everyone laughed.

"Kari thinks we should be getting along." Flann said.

"You have named her Kari?" Cristin asked.

"Yes, because that's her job."

Everyone broke out laughing. It was the release they all needed.

"We do need to get moving again." Stephan said, when the laughter had subsided. "We have some way to go before we can rest for the evening. We will take the trail to the left."

"I'll catch up with you." Liam said. "Brien and I have some business to complete here. We can leave no sign this work was done by our party."

They started off along the trail. Stephan took them at a fast pace. He knew the best thing for them was to get moving and to get away from the site of the battle. Everyone seemed to have recovered at least for the moment. Stephan knew there would be bad dreams on this night. He wanted more than anything to get them around a reassuring fire in a place of safety. When they had traveled some distance, Liam came up from behind at a run.

"How did you leave it?"

"I removed the heads and dropped them down a ravine, except for one which I hung from a tree as a gift for Danius. I left an eye in it to repay my debt to him."

119

"He'll appreciate the humor in it. How did Brien fare?"

"He was reluctant, but he did as he was asked. Now he knows what it takes to detach a man's head. It's useful information if he ever needs to remove one that is still talking."

"Good. There is some strength in him, as his father said. He held his own today."

"I didn't think to see so large a band of Danius' enemies in this wood." Liam said.

"It surprised me as well. I found them in a hollow just ahead of us. This place has been used for some time by the looks of the bones lying about. It is why the game now avoid this path."

"There is something else Stephan, I found some gold coins among the dead. I have never known these barbarians to carry coins. At least not into battle. What do you think it means?"

"Perhaps they waylaid some unlucky travelers before we came upon them. The other possibility is not a happy one?"

"Which is?"

"Which is someone paid them to hunt us."

"Why do you think Danius didn't find them by now?"

"He grows old, Liam, and fond of his bed. He doesn't have much time left, I think, and there will be a struggle for power when he's gone. Also, I believe he fears Edwin and wants to keep his men close. He's happy that Certic will face this army before he needs to deal with it, which is a part of the reason he did not stand in our way. He would not admit it to me, but I walked through his camp. They feel this war coming."

"Do you think his successor will honor the treaty?"

"I don't have a feel for it. Let's hope Danius does not depart this life before this war is settled. We will continue on this trail for a few hours more. Take the lead, Liam. I want to talk to our travelers a while."

Stephan stepped off the trail and let the woman catch up. They smiled at him bravely and seemed to be over the worst of it. He walked with Ailis a little."

"Are you all right, Ailis?"

"I suppose so. I still feel a little weak."

"If you need to stop and rest just say so and we will give you some time."

"No, I'll be fine. I only wish I had done my part today."

"I don't need you to fight, Ailis. I need you to stay with the others and not become   separated from the group. If we are attacked again I would like you to stand with an arrow notched and ready, but do not shoot it. I want you to save that arrow in case someone comes at you that we have not stopped. Do you think you can do that?"

"Yes, if I don't faint away."

"I don't think you will. Take heart, Ailis. You are with people who will look out for you."

Stephan stepped aside again. He nodded to Eogan. He was a man who knew his duty well and Stephan respected him for it. Still he had little to say, and Stephan wondered if he had been forced against his will to accompany the king's children. He remained silent for the most part, and when the party stopped to rest, he often wandered off by himself. Stephan guessed he might think it improper to talk to the prince and princess on familiar terms. He fell in beside Brien who was walking alone.

"You fought well today, Brien."

"I confess my knees were trembling as badly as Emma's. Liam is right though, once you are engaged the fear is less. It helped that you told me about your first battle. I didn't feel so bad about myself as I might have."

Stephan patted him on the back.

"I would fight along side you any time, Brien. How goes your friendship with Lucas?"

"It goes well, I think. He helped me today when I was nearly overwhelmed. He is a deadly shot with the bow."

"Yes, nearly as good as his father, and he keeps his wits about him in battle. He will be good company for you. I see he carries one of your swords."

"I'm working with him when there's time. He is agile which helps but he has a long way to go, I think."

"Keep at it with him. The time may come when the bow does him no good."

"That was a nasty business just now with Liam. I hope I don't have to do it again."

"War is a nasty business, Brien. Liam is trying to prepare you for it. A king cannot avoid the things he asks his subjects to do in his name."

He waited again and let Lucas and Cadman pass. He fell in beside Flann walking next to the horse. As the journey progressed he had become more and more curious about Flann. There was a quality about him that Stephan liked. He wanted to find out more about him.

"You do not have a lot to say, Flann."

"I was taught that servants should talk little and listen well."

"Who taught you this?"

"My mother was a servant to the queen before she died."

"Your mother or the queen?"

"Both. My mother passed away soon after the queen was killed. She had served her for many years."

"And what of your father. Did he not teach you?"

"I didn't know him well."

"It's an honorable labor to be a servant in a royal house, but did you never think to try another profession?"

"As a young man, I wished to join the army, but they wouldn't have me because I'm too small. I grew up inside the castle walls and know nothing of hunting or fishing or the other things that men do. I suppose every man must find what suits him. It's not a bad life you know. I found I like to cook and I am told I'm good at it. I live in a castle. I have good food to eat and a warm place to sleep. This king and his family are kind to me. Especially Cristin who often speaks with me. She has taught me how to read and write. I hear intelligent conversation every day that I would not find in the fields and taverns. I have come to enjoy what I do."

"And what of the prince?"

"I'm a servant to him, nothing more. But he is not cruel to me."

"So it must have come as bad news that you were chosen to come on this journey."

"No, I asked to come. It's an adventure for me and to be truthful, I wanted to be sure that Cristin was well cared for."

"Did you think you would end up in a fight and need to slay a fierce beast as you did today?"

"I knew there would be some danger. I'm not afraid of dogs. Just because I'm small in stature, does not mean I am a coward. I would protect the princess with my life."

"I believe you. If we are attacked again, let the horse run and go to Cristin's side. Do you have skill with any weapons?"

"Well, I know how to use a knife. Also, I have some skill with a sling. I have killed more than a few rats with it. It's not much of a weapon perhaps, but at close range it can drop a man to his knees. I have seen it done. I have also shot a bow, although I would not say I'm very skilled with it."

"Perhaps there will be the opportunity for you to practice with us. We could use another comrade in arms. Here on this journey, Flann, you don't have to hold your tongue. Your opinion is as good as any man's. Let me know what you're thinking if you wish to do so."

"Since you have offered, there is something."

"What is it?"

"It's not good to eat only meat every day. We are passing by many things in this forest that would be good for our dinner. I can not forage and lead the horse at the same time. Perhaps someone could take over this task for a short time each day, so that I can collect what the forest offers."

"A good suggestion. I will see to it."

"Also, I'm curious. Could I ask you if you marked our trail back where the path divided?"

"No, why would I so such a thing?"

"I can think of no reason, but someone did. I noticed a strange marking on a tree a short distance down this path we are on. I could be wrong, but it looked like a new marking to me."

"What did it look like?"

"It was a vertical line with two horizontal lines crossing it. I believe it is the rune Onn."

"You know the Ogham?"

"Not well, but Cristin has shown me what the runes look like, even If I don't know their meaning."

"And you are sure it was a fresh marking."

"It appeared so to me."

"There is more to you than meets the eye, Flann. You have done well. Don't hesitate to tell me if you find anything else of interest."

"I will do it."

As Stephan returned to the front of the party, the rain began to fall.

-9-

It was nearly dark when they found the cave entrance. Stephan and Liam went in first with a torch to make sure it wasn't inhabited. In its deep recesses there was evidence of recent bear habitation, but they were gone now. There were loose rocks and rubble lying about the floor and it took a while to make it suitable for sleeping. Everyone pitched in to collect firewood and by nightfall they had a good fire going. They arranged their cloaks on the rocks to dry and set about scraping the mud from their boots. Flann tended to the horse and then began preparing a dinner for them while the others found places for themselves and saw to their belongings. The cave was not large but it accommodated everyone. The rain had stopped, and Stephan took the dogs out some distance from the cave. They sat quietly in the dark forest, listening. The attack earlier in the day was wearing on him. No one knew their exact route even if they knew the destination. In the end, there were only a few overland routes to Craven and the passage over the Rossendale Fells was the most direct. He had chosen to travel through the Brigantes forest because he believed there would be a minimal chance of an attack such as the one they had suffered. The more he thought about the wild men being found with gold coin, the more he was convinced they were paid by Edwin's men to intercept the party. Edwin's assassins would be reluctant to enter Danius' forest, at least so close to his camp. He wondered how many more attacks would be launched against them if they continued along the game trails. It also meant that their mission was no secret and somehow, Edwin had learned of their departure. It was likely someone from the castle had given them away. Also, there was the matter of the mark Flann had seen. He hadn't had time to go back to examine it. It was possible the wild men marked the tree for their own reasons. They were not literate men, but they knew the tree-runes of the Ogham. The alternative was not something he wished to consider. He decided to discuss the matter with Liam and Cadman. The forest was quiet and he didn't expect another attack on this night, but for the first time since the journey began, he was unsure of how to proceed.

Flann prepared a stew with some rabbit meat and some scallions and herbs from the forest. Everyone was grateful for the warm food and the fire. The men had a bit of ale but the women had brewed up some herbal tea from some crushed leaves they had gathered. The flames cast diffuse shadows on the walls of the cave, like flickering ghosts from the underworld moving inside the rock. There was not a lot of conversation while they ate. Flann tried to lift everyone's spirits by singing happily while he tended the fire, but after a while he gave up on it. The women were still unsettled and they sat quietly talking among themselves. None of them had ever experienced anything so frightening as the attack by the wild men. They all realized that they could easily have been killed and the excitement of going out on an adventure was now replaced by a deep feeling of dread. Even though they had known there would be danger, nothing could have prepared them for the reality of it.

After Stephan had eaten and fed the mastiffs, he asked Liam and Cadman to join him outside. The sky had cleared and the stars were beginning to appear from behind the clouds. The men sat together some distance from the cave entrance, listening to the sounds of the forest. Cadman lit his pipe and watched the smoke drift straight up on the still evening air. They were all veterans of many skirmishes like the one they had stood on this day and they had recovered quickly from it. Still, the attack had come sooner than they expected and they knew it would not be the last.

Stephan spoke.

"It's possible we have been betrayed and our route discovered."

"That thought occurred to me as well." Liam said. "The attack today did not look like a thing of chance."

"How could anyone have found us so quickly?" Cadman asked. "We took great care."

Stephan was silent for a moment before he answered.

"It's possible we have been discovered in this forest, in spite of our care. Once our general direction is known, it would not be difficult to predict our route. They would expect us to follow the game trails. But I am troubled by something Flann told me today."

"Flann? Our cook?"

"There is more to him than you might think, Liam. He noticed a marking on a tree back where the trail forked. It was a Celtic rune. He believed it to be a freshly made."

"A message for the wild men perhaps?" Cadman said. "It is their writing."

"That is probably the right answer. There is one other possibility however."

"Which is what?" Liam asked.

"Which is that there is a traitor in our party. Someone who is marking our passage so that the pursuit can find us."

"I can't believe it." Cadman said. "Who would profit from such a treachery? Besides, the attack was waiting for us. They were not following."

"That's true, but perhaps when the attack failed someone left this mark to let others know our route."

"Perhaps it's Flann himself." Liam said. "If he is devious, he may have brought your attention to it to direct suspicion away from himself."

"He does trail behind us with the horse. It would be a simple thing for him to do." Cadman said.

"I don't believe it's Flann. The party had already passed. No one would have seen the mark if he hadn't told me about it. Besides, I have spoken to him. He is devoted to Cristin. I do not see treachery in him."

"Who then?"

Stephan answered.

"Emma and Ailis are always with the princess. Obviously the prince could not be the one. The only other from the party I do not know is Eogan."

"But he is the kings own man." Cadman said.

"Yes, it would be difficult to believe, but I think we need to be watchful. We will have a chance to test him tomorrow. I plan to take us off the trail and into the wild."

"That will make for hard travel, Stephan."

"It will be difficult but I think we have no choice. If my suspicions are correct there will be another attack tomorrow before the day is past. I don't think it will be from the wild men this time. I think we will see Edwin's assassins tomorrow if we stay to this trail. They are skilled fighters and I fear we will not escape unscathed. In any case, even though the going will be slower, the route will cut some miles form our journey. This trail we are on bends around to the west and we will reach it again by going over the foothills."

"So, you have traveled through this wood before?" Liam asked.

"Yes, many years ago. I went to visit one who lives here. If he's still alive, I hope to see him again tomorrow night or the next. I hope he will offer shelter for us."

"I know of no one who dares live in this wilderness."

"His name is Timan."

Liam looked shocked.

"Timan? Timan the sorcerer? You can't mean it. You actually know that witch?"

"I know him as well as any man can know him, I suppose. He was my teacher for a time."

"Your teacher? Did you learn how to turn men into serpents or bring down fire from the sky?"

"Men such as Timan are misunderstood. It is true they can do some wondrous things, but they are not gods and they are not evil. At least Timan is not. He's a bit bad tempered I will admit, and he will not like to see so many strangers in his wood. But I believe I can prevail upon him to help us."

"Do the wild men let him live here?" Cadman asked.

"The wild men flee from him. He lives by no mans leave and he goes wherever he wants to go. He has powers that men do not understand and they fear him."

"Well if you say we must, I will follow you. I saw him once before and I can't say I trust him entirely. If this wizard turns me into a newt, I will have a grudge to settle with you."

Stephan laughed.

"I will have a hard time now getting a vision of you as a newt out of my head. In any case, before we find Timan, I have a plan which may tell us if Eogan has betrayed us. Here is what we will do..."

***

The party arose early. It had been an uncomfortable night and there were more than a few sore backs. They took some bread and tea but there was little conversation. Since the attack, all of the joy seemed to have gone out of the party. As they started out down the trail, Stephan could see fear on the women's faces. He wished to reassure them, but he knew this would be a difficult day for them all. When they had been on the trail for an hour, Stephan stopped. He studied the forest for a moment, and then spoke to the party.

"I have decided we must leave the trail and take to the forest. Since the attack yesterday, we can't be sure the trails are not being watched. Stay together and mind your footing. If any of you need help, ask and it will be provided."

Liam watched Eogan's face when Stephan gave them the news, but he showed nothing. Stephan led them off through the forest and in a short distance the land began to rise. Everyone had to watch their footing and they kept their heads down. The horse struggled under the load. After a while, Stephan took the opportunity to step away and hide behind a tree. He let the party pass. As they moved away, the forest went still. He waited for a while, but all remained quiet. He had hoped he was wrong about Eogan, but in a few minutes after the party had passed, he heard movement in the forest and he saw the soldier heading quickly down through the trees toward the place where they had left the trail. Stephan, followed him, keeping out of sight. Eogan stopped at a tree just off the trail and

Stephan watched as he carved the rune into the tree trunk. When Eogan turned to rejoin the group, Stephan confronted him.

"I thought you a soldier and an honorable man, Eogan. Why have you betrayed us?"

"I am an honorable man. I owe my allegiance to my king Edwin."

"Allegiance or not, what you have done here is the act of a coward. You would visit treachery upon innocent women."

"I avenge my father who was slaughtered before the walls of Certic's castle after you performed your own treachery many years ago. I came to your city as a boy and I vowed that one day I would repay that injustice. I have waited many years, rising through the ranks, working my way into the confidence of Martin so that I could gain free entry to the castle. I would have finished my work by now except that Certic decided to send his children on this fool's errand. When I found out about this journey, I begged Martin to allow me to join the party. There is no hope for you now. Many are hunting you and soon you will be overwhelmed. Your prince will meet the same fate that Edwin's son and my father suffered at your hands all those years ago. The princess will be used and then sold into slavery. You cannot prevent it."

Stephan drew his sword.

"Perhaps not, but you will not be alive to see the outcome."

Eogan drew his sword and attacked. He was strong and a skilled fighter but he was no match for Stephan. The sound of clashing swords rang through the forest. Eogan fought well, but soon enough it was over and he was lying on the ground. Stephan searched his pockets for anything that might inform him about his enemy, but he found nothing. In a short while, Liam joined him, along with the two mastiffs. The dogs sniffed at the fallen soldier. Liam carried the body off into the forest and they buried it in a fold of the earth. Liam took his sword.

"He has already made his mark, Stephan. They will know where to find us."

"I allowed him to make it. I know where we are and there is a place ahead of us where we could hold off an army. I only pray there's time."

"Did he tell you why he has done this?"

"He told me his loyalty was with Edwin. His father fought for Edwin in the Great War and was killed. He came to Elmet as a boy and worked his way up through the army. It's hard to comprehend someone planning such a thing. Nearly an entire life dedicated to revenge. There is much hatred for Certic among the Saxons and soon he will feel the brunt of it. Certic told me there were spies in the castle. One of them who made the attempt on Cristin's life and now there is Eogan. If I had more time, I would have questioned him further, but I fear an attack could come soon and we must make haste. There is no way to get word to Certic now. We need to get moving."

-10-

Stephan gathered the party together.

"Where is Eogan? Cristin asked. He said he lost his knife."

"Eogan has betrayed us. He lies below us in the forest."

Everyone gasped.

"Betrayed us how?" Brien asked.

"Eogan has been marking the path we have taken so our enemies will find us. It's thanks to Flann that I discovered this."

Flann looked at his feet, not wanting to show his embarrassment.

"Surely there's another explanation." Brien said.

"I caught him in the act and he admitted it to me. We can discuss it later if you wish but we have to get moving now. There is much to do and I don't know how much time we have. I'm certain we'll be attacked again on this day. I chose this stretch of forest because above us, at a few league's distance the ground rises sharply. There are many rocks and boulders and the approaches are steep. I had a skirmish with the wild men at this place long ago. We'll climb and shelter among the rocks. From there we can hold off a large force of men. It will be difficult work getting there, but once we reach it you will be able to rest."

"What about the horse?" Flann asked.

"We'll let her climb with us as long as she's able. When she can go no further we'll unburden her and carry the packs with us to our place of shelter. There's an area to the north of us where you will find a small clearing. Tether her and let her graze. She should be safe there. Give her some water first and then return to us as quickly as you can. If you return and find the battle joined, shelter in the woods and keep out of sight until we come for you. Do you think you can do this?"

"I will do it."

The need of urgency was upon them and they moved quickly as Stephan had asked. As they moved along, the ground became steeper until they needed both arms and legs to climb. It took them the rest of the morning and they were exhausted. They could see the place of shelter above them but it seemed like they would need wings to reach it. They paused to catch their breath. In a while, Stephan spoke.

"We will unburden the horse here. Lucas, you are a climber, are you not? There is a good length of rope in one of the packs. Would you find it and bring it to me?"

"Everyone helped with the packs and in a few moments Lucas returned with the rope coiled over his shoulder."

"I will ask you to climb here, Lucas, and when you reach the top, tie the rope off and come back down to us."

Flann departed with the horse. They watched Lucas climb and took heart at the sight of it. It seemed no effort to him at all. When he reached the top he secured one end of the rope on a boulder and threw the coil down to Stephan. He tested his weight on it and then returned to the bottom quickly.

"I would ask you to go first, Lucas, along with Ailis. Next will be Emma and Cadman, and then Cristin with Brien. When you've all reached the top, Liam and I will attach the packs and you can haul them up. We'll come up last with the dogs."

Lucas started off with Ailis. Her feet were slipping out from under her but the young woodsman kept her from falling and at last they reached the top. Emma was not much better a climber than Ailis but Cadman steadied her and they also reached the top without incident. Cristin and Brien came next and it was difficult to see who was helping more. There was a natural sibling competition between them and it seemed in the end that Cristin was the better climber. When the three pairs had reached the top, Stephan and Liam attached the packs and they were hauled up one at a time. Liam went next but they were unable to get the dogs to climb. Finally Stephan took the dogs aside and held them. He stroked their backs and talked to them before letting them loose to run free. They would do well enough on their own, but he was worried that they might join in against the attack and be slain. There was nothing for it. Stephan went last and they hauled up the rope behind him. They all sat for a moment to regain their strength. There was a flat area in among the rocks and boulders and they were glad to have the protection the place offered.

When they had rested a while and had some water, Liam surveyed the ground below them.

"This is a good position, Stephan. I can see why you chose it."

"Let's deploy ourselves so we can use it to our best advantage."

Stephan arranged the party to provide clear lanes of fire. Only Liam was without a bow but he had a selection of very large rocks to choose from and some boulders that, if he managed to move them, could take out a dozen men if he placed them well.

"These will be your positions if an attack comes. Keep your weapons close and be ready."

"When do you think they'll come?" Cristin asked.

"It could be at any time or not at all today. There's no way to know. In any case, we will not move from this place this day unless the fight comes to us. We may have to sleep here tonight as well, so find places for yourselves. If anyone wishes to get some sleep, do so now. Take some food if you wish. You will be awakened if the enemy is sighted. Above all, make as little noise as possible. I don't want them to know we're here until they are too close to avoid our arrows."

Stephan was surveying the forest below them when, suddenly, the dogs come bounding in over the rocks above him, followed by Flann.

"How did you come here, Flann?"

"The dogs found me in the woods and they showed me the way."

"I confess I didn't know there was another way but how we came." Stephan said.

"There is a ledge. It's not very wide. It was easy enough for me since I'm built for small places."

"Well done Flann."

Liam looked around him at the trees that clung to the hillside.

"Brien, Lucas, come with me and brings axes. I would make some stout levers to help me move these boulders."

***

The attack didn't come until late in the day. The party was growing restless, sheltered as they were in a fairly cramped place. Stephan had started to wonder if it might have been better to press on but he didn't want to be caught out in the open. It was a pleasant afternoon and some of the party had dosed of. It was Cadman who saw them first and he hurried over to Stephan's side. Liam joined them. They peered out from behind the rocks, keeping their heads low. They were Edwin's men and they were armed with bow and sword. They came up through the forest on a wide front watching the ground for sign. There looked to be at least twenty men and they moved with caution. They would know it was a good place for an ambush. Stephan made the party ready. He spoke quietly and again arranged his archers to take the best advantage of the attack. The sun was beginning to set behind them and would be in the eyes of the attackers if they came within range soon enough. The dogs began to growl softly, but Stephan steadied them. When the front rank of the enemy reached the place where the party had gathered for the ascent, they read the signs in the earth and then looked up with alarm. It was too late. The archers stood as one, and let fly a fusillade of arrows. Six men fell at once. The remainder sought cover but

Cadman, Lucas, and Stephan were able to draw again and each of them found their mark. They had cut the enemy nearly in half but the remainder would not be so easy. Arrows began to rise up at the them and these were skilled archers. Cristin took an arrow through the sleeve of her cloak, but it did not wound her. Stephan had the women move behind cover. Edwin's men fired from behind the trees and although they were at a disadvantage shooting up hill, they were also difficult to hit. Cadman managed to pick one off as he exposed himself to aim. The skirmish continued sporadically, and the sun was now behind the mountain. Darkness would soon be upon them. Liam came over to Stephan at a crouch.

"We have no advantage now Stephan. They can keep us pinned down here. It could take a week to finish them off. If you have an idea, we should try it now before we lose the daylight."

"There are four of them sheltering in that copse, almost directly below us. Do you think you can dislodge that large boulder by the lip, without taking an arrow in your thick head?"

"I will need some help, but yes, with the levers I prepared it can be done."

"How many will you need?"

"Perhaps one other."

"All right, take Brien and get ready to push it. Cadman, Lucas, and I will make ready to shoot. When the boulder is dislodged they will have to break from cover and we may catch them on the run. Prepare to move on my signal."

Liam took Brien and they crawled over behind the boulder and made their levers ready. It was the size of a full grown ox. The archers took up their positions. Stephan nodded to Liam, then they peppered the copse with arrows to keep the enemy's heads down. Liam and Brien put their shoulders into the levers and strained against them. Liam pushed with all of his impressive strength. At first the boulder would not budge. They stopped for a moment to recover and readjust the levers, and then pushed again. Flann ran over to join them and he pushed with his hands. The boulder suddenly broke free and careened down the slope. Flann nearly went over the edge with it, but Liam caught him by the back of his shirt and dropped him safely behind a rock. They thought it would roll down through the forest like a ball, and it did for a short time but then it hit a hard rock imbedded in the hillside. It made a sound almost like a bell being rung and then it bound into the air. It traveled in an arc and then crashed down into the trees, snapping huge branches like twigs, before it landed with a mighty thump that shook the earth below their feet. The archers in the copse were slow to react. One was crushed and the others shot as they ran.

"Well done Liam."

"How many are left, do you think?"

"Perhaps four or five. They've gone to ground."

"Shall we go down and root them out?"

"There's not much light left. I think we'll have to shelter here for the night, and see how things look in the morning."

"I don't suppose we can have a fire." Cristin said.

"Let me think on it, Cristin. The remainder of Edwin's men will not leave this place. They may try to come at us in the night, but the dogs will warn us. At the very least they may let loose a bolt if thy see someone moving. If it's any consolation, they will not have a fire tonight either."

The sun set and the hillside was plunged into darkness. A damp chill began to settle through the woods. The women huddled together for warmth and they were all uncomfortable. Below them they could hear the moans of dying men, but there was nothing they could do for them. It was going to be a long night. Flann came over to Stephan.

"I'm worried about the horse, alone and tethered as she is. I would like to go look after her."

"We don't know were the enemy lies, Flann. It is a dangerous thing to attempt."

"Still, I think I have to try. There may be wolves about. I would go out the way I came and stay with the horse tonight."

"I won't stop you Flann, but take great care. I don't know when we'll depart in the morning but it may be early. We will be traveling north by west. If we are not here when you return head in that direction. You will come to a broad expanse of heath with few trees and in the distance you will see a tall peak. Keep it on your left shoulder as you cross. You'll come to a stream. It is wide but shallow enough to cross. In time you will see the beginnings of an old forest. Do not enter the forest. We'll wait there for you by its edge, or you for us."

Flann nodded and started to leave, but Stephan caught him by his arm.

"Here is Eogan's sword. I think you may feel better with it at your side tonight."

"Flann held the sword in front of him and then slashed it through the air."

"Now our enemies have one more to fear." He grinned at Stephan, and then he was gone.

Stephan moved over to where the party was huddled together and spoke.

"I'll leave it to you. There will be danger if we light a fire but the night will be long without one. If we light one, no one must stand or walk around it for the rest of the night, so you will have to make ready before it's lit."

They immediately agreed and set out to gather wood and tinder. Stephan kept his eyes and ears on the forest below but heard no movement. In a short time a small fire was going and Emma set a tea kettle warming on the side. It improved everyone's mood. They spoke softly but the fear of the previous night had been replaced by a kind of quiet optimism. It seemed to them all that Stephan had some magic about him and as long as they walked with him, they would survive. For Stephan's part, he knew they had been lucky and, although he would not say it, the worst was yet to come. In time everyone had fallen to sleep except the watch.

-11-

Brien took the first watch. It was past midnight when he rousted Liam to relieve him. He was soon joined by Stephan and Cadman. They spoke quietly.

"Cadman and I will go below to see who remains in the forest. We'll rig the rope to help our descent. Pull it up when we've reached the bottom. I'll signal you when we need it let down again."

Liam nodded. "Good hunting."

The two men moved silently. There was no moon, but from many years of stalking prey in the night, they were able to see well enough by starlight to navigate a forest. Especially one they had seen in the day. They moved through the trees like spirits in a repeating arc, moving soundlessly through the trees and descending slowly toward the trail they had left on the previous morning. There were no more injured lying on the forest floor. All had gone silent and they found only dead men as they moved. Cadman retrieved all the arrows he could find. As they approached the trail, they began to hear a noise and they made for it. As they got closer they realized it was the sound of a man snoring. They lay their swords quietly on the ground and then moved through the trees like a vapor, toward the sound. There were four of them lying in a copse, wrapped in their cloaks against the evening chill. They had gone to sleep, never imagining that the party they pursued would dare to come for them in the night. They would never reawaken. Stephan and Cadman pulled their daggers and crept forward silently.

The two hunters were heavily laden with arrows when they reached the bottom of the climb. It was nearly dawn and Stephan put his hands to his lips and made the call of a dove. It was answered from above and in a moment the rope came down to them. Liam was waiting at the top. He greeted them; taking note of the many quivers they carried.

"It would seem hunting was good indeed."

"We found only four alive. There are no more in this part of the forest at least. We did not go beyond the game trail. Still, I want to move before the sun rises much higher. Let's wake everyone and have them make ready. We'll have to distribute the packs among us. Whatever we cannot carry will have to be left behind."

They came down as they had climbed, but found the descent much easier. They went through the packs and prepared themselves to take up the load. It didn't look as if they would be able to carry everything on their backs, but just as they were debating what to leave behind, Flann came through the woods with the horse. They were overjoyed to see them both.

"How did you fare last night, Flann?" Stephan asked.

"We were fine. Kari was mad at me for leaving her alone and at first she pretended I wasn't there. I told her I would leave her alone again unless she forgave me."

"You talk with horses, master Flann?" Liam said, laughing."

"I talk to all manner of men and beasts. The horses, at least, are smart enough to listen."

Cristin laughed. Liam just shook his head and walked away. They started off again through the forest. They traveled north but swung around to the west as soon as the terrain allowed it. Cadman and Lucas now traveled in the rear of the party to pick up any signs of pursuit. They were still climbing but the slope was not so difficult as it had been. The forest began to grow less dense with openings in the canopy and fewer thickets. After more than an hour, Cadman believed they were in the clear and they caught up with everyone. Just before noon, the forest opened up into a broad expanse of heath. They paused at the edge of the clearing while Stephan took his bearings. Liam looked out across the flat plain.

"I do not like this crossing, Stephan. There's no place to shelter."

"Yes, we'll be exposed, but to go around would cost us days of travel. Edwin will know soon enough that his assassins have failed him. The more time he has, the greater the chance he'll make ready a new attack. In any case, this land is not as flat as it appears. About half way across there is a sunken creek bed. The water is shallow and it bends to the west and follows in the direction we need to the wood beyond. We can reach the creek in less than two hours from here. Once we are on its banks we will not be seen as we travel. Stay here with the party for a moment. I'll cross a short way and see if I stir some interest."

Stephan walked out into the open with the two mastiffs. The dogs sniffed about and soon picked up a scent. They were keen to follow it but Stephan kept them back. He put his fingers to his lips and let forth a sharp whistle. A herd of red dear broke from cover in the distance and darted away, finally bounding off into the forest. The sky was clear and blue with towering white cloud sculptures gliding on the wind. Stephan stopped for a moment to take it in. The dogs wanted to hunt but Stephan held them. He motioned to the party to follow. Friendships were beginning to form as the journey continued. Emma and Cadman were walking together and Brien walked next to Liam as they discussed fighting with the sword and tactics to be used in battle. When Cristin left Ailis's side to walk with Stephan, she fell in next to Lucas. Since the previous day when Lucas had helped her climb, Ailis seemed to have taken an interest in him. Lucas was a bit awkward with her, but he was happy for her company. The close quarters of the last two evenings had broken through some of the formalities that separated men from women in normal times. For his part, Flann seemed content to chat with the horse and for all anyone could tell, the horse was listening intently. He now wore Eogan's sword proudly in his belt. It nearly reached to the ground. Cristin looked up at Stephan and smiled softly. He showed nothing of his feelings but she could read what was inside of him.

"This journey has been hard on you already, Stephan."

"The fighting I am used to and I'm accustomed to caring for the men that I lead, but this is the first time I have had women in my charge."

"I'm sorry we are a burden to you."

"You are not a burden, Cristin, nor are the others. You have carried yourselves well. Much better than I expected. Once I saw your courage and resolve, I felt better about it."

"We have not seen the last of the fighting though, have we?"

"It's difficult to know what faces us, but no, I don't believe we have seen the end of it. We still have a great distance to travel and Edwin is determined to stop us. To be truthful with you, if I had known we would be attacked so often and by so large a force, I would not have taken you on this journey."

"My father believed there was too much danger for us to remain in the castle."

"He would know better than I, but he didn't imagine what we would face out here in the wild either. I don't know if I would have made his choice, but none of that matters now."

"How far will we travel this day?"

Stephan pointed out across the heath.

"Do you see where the forest begins again out in the distance?"

"Yes, I can see it."

"In that forest lives a friend that I have known for many years. I hope he will provide his hospitality for us tonight."

"He lives alone out here in this wilderness?"

"He is always alone except for his wolf and whatever animals he is taking up with these days."

"Is he a hermit?"

"Some would call him that. Many others would call him a sorcerer or a wizard. His name is Timan."

"I have heard of him! When I was a child we heard tales about him bringing down lightning from the sky and turning men to stone. We were all afraid he would come and find us and turn us into rabbits."

"I don't know that he can do those things, but I have seen him do other things that I would not have believed. I've seen him light a fire just by pointing the staff that he carries at a pile of wood, and uttering words from some tongue I have never heard used by any other man."

"You are having fun with me now!"

"No, Cristin. I saw him do this with my own eyes. I have seen him wave his staff and cause fierce men to cower and run away from him. He is joined to the earth in some way. I spent some time with him when I was a young boy. He wished to teach me his craft but I wasn't with him long enough to learn much of it. He did teach me to listen to the earth and to understand what it's telling me. It's a skill that has served me well."

"How does the earth tell you?"

"Men speak with their voices, but the animals have no voice to speak of the world around them. They communicate in another way. Just like they know when a storm is coming or that it's time to move to a different place, they know when there is danger, and they all know it at once. Just like the animals, I often know when there is danger near me. I can stand in the forest and know if I am being hunted, by man or beast and from which direction an attack will come. I can't explain it better than that."

"I'm excited to meet a man such as Timan."

"I hope you're not disappointed, Cristin. He is not always a pleasant man to be around and he yells a lot, at everyone. He will not like having so many of us in his lodgings but I hope he'll help us. Don't worry. I won't let him turn you into a rabbit."

When they reached the creek bed they stopped and had some food. The water was clear and they filled their water bags again. The horse drank deeply, and then splashed about in the stream. When they started out again they followed the streambed, sometimes walking on the bank and sometimes in the stream itself where the bank was too difficult. It was a clear day and very warm for so early in the spring, but walking by the water kept them cool and the sound of it lifted their spirits. Soon the attack of the previous day was just an unpleasant memory.

In two more hours, Stephan stopped them and climbed up the bank to mark their progress. He walked out of sight but returned shortly.

"This is a good place to resume our crossing. The stream does not go our way from this point."

They all climbed up to the heath and saw that the forest, indeed, was nearby. It took less than an hour to cover the remaining distance and when they entered into the wood Stephan stopped them.

"You will need to wait for me here a while. I'll find Timan and see if he'll shelter us tonight. Flann, I would ask you to keep the dogs with you until I return. No one must light a fire or disturb any of the trees and by no means harm any animal in these woods."

They sat just inside the wood line, chatting among themselves. Liam was loudly recounting some of his adventures and the audience was humoring him with their rapt attention, in part to be kind to a friend, and in part because they already had seen what this giant was capable of. The first sign that anyone was approaching made the women scream in alarm. An enormous black wolf came bounding out of the woods toward them. The two mastiffs stood as if to attack but when they came together they bounded upon each other in play. The three animals charged off into the woods, tackling each other and stalking as if they had known each other for many years. Soon two figures could be seen walking toward them. One was Stephan. The other was a slightly taller man wearing a long hooded cloak, of a color that seemed to change with the light, and blend with the background so that for an instant he appeared to be a disembodied head, floating along through the forest. He wore only sandals on his feet and carried a long staff with a wolf's head carved into the top of it. His hair was long and gray and his face weathered with a long prominent nose. His eyes were also gray but clear, like a child's, and he did not walk like an old man. Soon the party could hear him chastising Stephan.

"A giant you bring, and women, three of them who shriek like mice! You strain our friendship to the limits, Stephan. It would serve you right if I let you sleep out in the..."

He stopped suddenly when he saw Flann. His whole demeanor changed and a smile came upon his face. He walked over to him and bowed.

"Greetings, elfson. Welcome to my forest. It is long since I have seen your kind in this place."

"Greetings elffriend. There are too few of us remaining. I thank you for your kindness. The party stood, staring at the two of them with their mouths agape. Timan ignored them all and started walking back through the forest with Flann at his side, and the horse trailing behind, as if it were part of the conversation. Suddenly Timan stopped, as if he had forgotten something. He turned and stared directly at Cristin. In her head she heard a voice say, 'welcome, daughter of the light'. Then he turned and continued on.

Stephan smiled at them.

"We have been invited to spend the evening here. Timan is in a good mood. Please try not to upset him."

"I hope I don't ever see him in a bad mood then. I would try not to anger him if I knew what it was that upset him." Cristin said. "What on earth just happened?"

"I suspected it when I first met Flann but I couldn't be sure. His father was an elf."

Brien scoffed.

"There is no such thing."

"There are none remaining, Brien, but Timan told me there once were as many as there are men on this earth. Nearly all left long ago when the wars of men started to destroy the land, but some out of great love for this place remained behind. A few joined with the daughters of men, and some of their children still reside with us."

"But how could that be. Flann is not much more than a boy."

"He is not as young as you may imagine. The lives of elves were three times or more the lives of men. It's possible Flann's father was more than a hundred years old when he was born."

"Surely this is all nonsense. Do the rest of you believe this?"

No one spoke.

"I would suggest you keep such thoughts to yourself, Brien and observe. What you see may surprise you. Show no disrespect to either of them while you rest here. Timan is not a man to make angry."

-12-

Timan's lodging was a strange and wonderful place. Part stone, part earth and part timber with an earthen floor; it seemed to be thrown together with no plan at all. One part of the structure was actually built as a stable, and was open to the inside of the living quarters so that the animals could walk around inside if they chose to and go right up to Timan's table. No animals were using it when the party arrived. The rooms were connected in odd ways so that one could never be entirely sure where he would end up when he went through a door. Baskets of herbs and other unknown things were hanging from the low ceiling. Statues and carvings were everywhere and some of them were likenesses of strange beings the likes of which they had never seen. Along one wall was a long table, occupied by a large mortar and pestle and dozens of earthenware jars containing powders and liquids and indistinguishable things of various colors and consistencies. The hearth was large with a

161

great, copper cooking kettle hanging from an iron hook, and a smaller iron vessel for heating compounds. There was also the largest collection of books and scrolls any of them had ever seen. Many more than in the castle. Some were in Latin and some in Greek but many more were in languages they had never seen or heard. Stephan had them all sit on the floor off to the side of the hearth. Even Liam did not object. They didn't know what to expect and they were all a little in awe of this strange man of the forest. Timan was still carrying on an animated conversation with Flann and he didn't seem to be aware they were there at all. It was late afternoon and not a lot of light entered the two small windows on either side of the entrance. There was a good fire going in the hearth but the atmosphere was more like a barrow than a house. Suddenly the con-versation stopped and Timan turned to peer at them from under his bushy eyebrows. He looked at each of them in turn and they all felt like he was staring directly into their hearts. None could look away. Finally he spoke, in a voice that seemed to come from some hollow place inside of him.

"Because you are in the company of an elfson, I invite you to share my lodgings. There is a price I would exact however, and it is this. I expect each of you to sit with me for a while and account for yourselves. I will know who is in my house. If you do not wish to pay this price, you are free to leave and spend the night under the stars. I do not permit any fire in my forest so measure that in your decision. And do not attempt to lie to me or you will invoke my anger. Does anyone wish to forego my hospitality?"

No one answered.

"Very well. Flann has agreed to make dinner for us all. I hope you all appreciate what an honor this is. There must be some great value in each of you for him to show you this kindness. You are also fortunate in the season. My animals enjoy the evening outside now that the snow has left us, so you may make yourselves comfortable in their lodgings. There is clean straw there for you. It is a better place than you have slept for the last two nights, I wager."

At that he turned and resumed his conversation with Flann. The travelers carried their belongings over to the stable and made places for themselves. After a while they began to talk quietly. They knew at least they were safe for the evening, even if it might not be a pleasant one. After a while, Flann stood and began to prepare their meal. The women came over to help but they all suddenly felt awkward around him. He looked at them and smiled and then bent his head close and whispered.

"I am still Flann; Timan likes elves, is all."

"You never told me your father was an elf." Cristin said.

"I did not know him well. He was away when I was a boy. I was grown before I finally met him, and we didn't spend much time together."

"You met him? When? Where?"

"He visited me in the castle a few times, right before my mother died."

"How is it he came into the castle and no one saw him?"

"If an elf does not wish to be seen. He is not seen."

Timan took Stephan aside.

"It has been too long since we sat and talked together, Stephan. For this I blame myself. I have been immersed in my dreams and I've ignored my friends. I'm glad to see you are well."

"I am well, but I am also troubled. This is a difficult task I've taken upon myself."

"Difficult it is indeed, but it is something you were meant to do. Many forces are being brought to bear in the world in these days. The signs have been conflicting for many months, but lately things begin to take shape. A time of great change is upon us. You are where you were meant to be."

"Danius told me the same thing. I'm glad you believe so, at least. The future seems very uncertain to me, and it's hard to know what is the best thing to do."

"This is an interesting party you've assembled. I have not seen the like of it in many years. You keep good company, Stephan."

"Yes they are good companions, and yet I take them into harms way. I wish it were not so."

"And it would seem that Certic trusts you with the lives of his children. This is an unexpected turn of events indeed."

"He is a desperate man, Timan and he doesn't know who he can trust."

"So for this journey he chose an old enemy who he respects, rather than someone close to him who may have been turned by Edwin. A wise decision, and one that took a good deal of courage. I have more respect for him with this news."

"You know a war is coming, Timan."

"Yes. I have seen it in my dreams."

"Certic sends me to seek help from his cousin at Craven. His children travel with me because there is treachery inside his walls. He hopes they will find safety with their uncle."

"Be wary, Stephan. I sense there is more treachery afoot than just behind the walls of Elmet. In any case I am glad you stopped to visit me. There is something I want to discuss with you later. For now I would become acquainted with your traveling companions. Cadman and Liam are known to me from the war. I would like to speak to the mother and daughter."

Emma came over to the table with Ailis. Ailis was trembling with fear but Timan looked at her kindly. He reached over and touched her face.

"There is nothing for you to fear here, daughter. You are a gentle soul and such are always welcome at my table. Please forgive the ranting of an old man."

He bent over to her and whispered.

"I only pretend to be ill humored. Except when I actually am ill humored, of course."

Ailis laughed. "How would I know the difference?"

"If you see fire coming out of my ears, then run and hide somewhere. There's a good place under the bench where I never look."

He smiled at her again. "Join your friends now Ailis, you may talk with me any time you wish. For now, I would chat with your mother a while."

He studied Emma's face for a short time and she met his glance without looking away.

"You carry great sorrow in your heart, Emeline. It weighs heavily on you."

"How do you know my name?"

"Flann has told me about you. He holds you in high regard. You have great love for your daughter but as much also for the king's daughter. You have taken up the hardship of this journey for their sake and you fear for them but not for yourself. Why?"

"My story is written. I hope to weave a happier tale for them."

"Your story is not half written. The better part of it unfolds ahead of you. No life is without sorrow. This journey will test you like you never thought possible but there will be an end to it and much that is good for you when it is finished."

"Perhaps. We shall see."

"It's important that you believe it, Emeline. Believe on it and it will be so. Is there anything you would like to ask of me?"

"Do you see the future then?"

"Sometimes I have visions in my dreams. These things do not always come to pass, but often they do. I can never be entirely certain. Sometimes by seeing an outcome I change it somehow. I have not fully mastered this mystery but I continue to study it. Really, it is a gift of seeing. When I look at someone, I see a little of what progress they've made in their journey, even if I do not know the end of it."

"How do you see this?"

"I see the light around them. Life is in the light, Emeline. I can tell if they're on the right way or not. Some go so far astray that it's no longer possible in this life for them to set it right. Some just need a little help to get back on the right path again. You need to learn how to put aside your sorrow and allow yourself to feel joy again. Let me know if you are in need of anything while you're here. I'll provide it if I'm able."

He smiled and put his hand on her shoulder, then he stood and stretched himself. He walked over to the hearth and tasted the stew.

"I have something for it, Flann, if you will not be insulted."

"Of course. I don't have my spices here."

The wizard went over to his bench and started sorting through his powders. None of the jars had a label, so he had to taste each one. As he did so, he had a conversation with himself. He wetted his finger and put it into a jar and then tasted it. Ailis was watching him, and trying not to laugh. He made a terrible face and shuddered.

"Ugh, No that one is for growing mushrooms. Wait, I think I have some mushrooms somewhere. Now where did I put them?"

He tasted another and smiled.

"Oh, I forgot I had this one. I'll rub some on my feet tonight."

"Ah ha!" He said, finally. "This will do nicely. Add some of this, Flann, but no more than a thimbleful or everyone's skin may turn a bit green. Just for a day or so. Nothing to worry about."

He turned and found Brien staring at him.

"Come outside with me, king's son. I would talk with you a while."

Brien followed him out the door, not knowing what to expect. Night was beginning to fall in the forest and stillness had settled over the earth.

"You have reached the end of your youth, Brien. Too soon perhaps, but such is the fate that befalls a future king. Two roads stand open for you. The question is, which will you take."

"The only road I see is the one that takes me to Craven and my uncle Uryen."

"That is the road that you see with your eyes. It is the road that you see in your heart that is the important one."

"I don't know what you mean."

"It is the road that takes you to the kind of a king you will be. One branch leads to a place of great pride and arrogance and the desire to be served and to be worshiped and to cover yourself in riches. The other leads to wisdom and kindness and the desire to see your subjects grow and thrive under your rule. The choice is yours alone."

"I would desire to be a good king."

"Of course you would, but that is not enough. This is not a decision that can be made once and then all the good will follow on. It is a decision you will need to make every day of your life. Few kings set out to be a tyrant but in time the power takes hold of them. It is like a tall tree. If you continue to make small cuts on one side alone, eventually it will fall that way. The road to tyranny is the easy way. Often in the heat of the struggle it seems like the best way. If you learn to listen with your heart and not with your pride, you will know the right way. Then it will be a matter of having the strength and the courage to choose it. It is hard to be a king."

"And how would you know this?"

"I have known many kings in many places. I have sat with some of them through the darkest nights of their souls."

Brien looked away, into the forest. Finally he spoke.

"I hope these things do not come to me too soon, at least. My father is not an old man."

"We will see how fate unfolds for us all. This journey at least is good for you, even with all of the hardship and danger. At least you will not be handed the crown without seeing what it costs to wear it. Dark times are upon us, king's son. Learn your lessons well."

Liam came out of the house to tend to the horse. Timan walked with him a short distance to where the animal was grazing.

"How is it with you Liam? When I saw you last you were chasing some of the Brigantes through the forest and roaring like a bear."

"Aye, and I caught them too. I didn't know you saw me."

"How could I not? There are few giants left in this land and no dragons at all. Well, except for one perhaps. I think you may have finally stopped growing though."

"And a good thing too. I find it a bit harder to reach my boots these days. I am well, considering. And you?"

"I am not as good as I was, nor as bad as I will be."

Liam laughed.

"That answer tells me nothing."

"I give it to save you a long discussion of my aches and pains, which I'm sure you do not wish to hear. When will you tire of taking heads and find a comfortable chair before a good fire?"

"Not soon, I'm afraid. Perhaps when we see the end to this struggle. If there is an end."

"There will always be struggle. At some point you will have to decide it is no longer your fight."

"I think when that happens, I will end up being as grumpy as you are. Severing a head does wonders for your temperament."

"Then I think you will be in good spirits indeed, by the time you reach Craven."

While they were talking, Lucas joined them.

"I found some oats in your stable, sir. I though the horse would like some if it's all right with you."

"By all means. And you may call me Timan."

"Thank you sir. I mean, thank you Timan."

Lucas started to walk away, but Timan stopped him.

"You know, young hunter, the girl Ailis is quite taken with you. She is a fine young woman."

Lucas blushed and looked at his boots.

"I don't... I mean I haven't... I mean..."

"I know what you mean. Now go get the oats as you have asked."

Lucas hurried off to the house, and the men both chuckled.

"I am surprised Ailis would confide her private thoughts to you like that, Timan. She hardly knows you."

Timan laughed. "She has not told me if she likes the boy or not. But now he thinks she does, and that's all that matters."

He winked and walked back toward his house.

-13-

They gathered around the hearth for dinner. The fire had been reduced to coals for cooking and the room was very dimly lit. Timan had managed to talk with everyone except Cristin and she wondered why he was ignoring her. They all felt a little more at ease and there was some laughter in the conversation. Liam complained that it was too dark to see his food. There was a chandelier with six candles hanging above their heads. He spoke to the wizard.

"Can we make some light here, Timan? I cannot see what I'm eating."

"I don't see why that should trouble you Liam, since you would eat anything, but very well, if it will make you hold your tongue."

He flicked his fingers at the candles and they burst into flame one at a time. They all gasped, Ailis clapped her hands and laughed, but the wizard acted as if nothing had happened and continued on talking to Flann. Midway through the dinner the dogs showed up at the door and were let in. The wolf was curious and began investigating the visitors, but one look from Timan and he sat before the hearth and was quiet. The mastiffs greeted Stephan and he took them outside and fed them. When the party had finished eating, the women cleaned up and then decided to take the air. Brien and Lucas joined them. It was a pleasant evening and they felt safe in this forest. Timan asked Flann and the men to join him at his table. It was the first time Flann was included in their conversations, and Stephan was interested to hear his opinion.

"So what path will you take to Craven?" Timan asked.

"The most direct one, over the Rossendale Fells and then across the Pennine moors." Stephan said.

"You would be ill advised to take the horse across the moors. You will find little cover there and you may have to go to ground to avoid being seen. It will be three or four days travel on foot beyond the Fells to Uryen's castle and you will be exposed to the weather which is often quite cold there at this time of year."

"That's all true; Timan, but I don't see another way."

"I have hunted the moors." Cadman said. "Game is difficult to find there. We may have some luck, but we will have to carry enough food on our backs to get us through."

Timan nodded his head in agreement.

"You will be two or three days on the moor, and then you will be back in woodland again for a day or more until you reach Uryen's castle. If you carry food for four days, that should be sufficient. You probably will not be able to risk a fire, so anything that needs cooking will be of no use to you."

"Is there fresh water on the moor, Timan?" Stephan asked.

"There is, but not all that you will find there will be safe to drink. Do not drink from still waters. There are several small rills that run with fresh water if you can find them."

The men were all silent for a while, contemplating their journey. Timan broke the silence.

"You know also that Edwin has likely not given up on stopping you. His men will be in your way, and in larger numbers even than you have seen. They will try to take you out in the open where they will have the advantage."

"I know that's a possibility, but it appears to be our fate. I have thought of nothing else since we were attacked by Edwin's assassins but I know of no remedy for it."

"What say you, Flann? Do you have an opinion?"

"I don't know these lands, but neither I think, does our enemy. We have some skill moving about in the night. Stephan and Cadman can stalk in the darkness, and perhaps Liam also. For my part, I can see quite far in the night and my hearing is quite good also. A gift from my father, I suppose."

"Why did you not tell us of this gift before, Flann?" Stephan asked.

"We haven't traveled by night so far. I didn't think it was important. In any case, perhaps we should seek cover by day and see how we fare under the stars."

"I can fight in the darkness if I must, but I won't tell you I like it much." Liam said.

Timan sat lost in his thought, stroking his long beard and staring into the fire. They were all silent, unhappy at the choices that faced them. Finally Timan spoke.

"I think it would be wise to listen to Flann in this matter, although it may not be enough to save you. There is shelter to be had at the Fells, and I don't think Edwin would attack at that place. He will know now what you are capable of when fighting from a position of strength. Also, the moors are not as empty as you might think. I know several places where you may shelter in the daytime without being discovered, though they are a bit difficult to find."

"We will not find them traveling at night, I think." Stephan said.

"You likely would not find them even by the light of day. In that task you will need my help."

"How can you help us, at so great a distance?"

"I have decided to join you in your journey, Stephan. I find I am in need of a good walk."

The men were visibly pleased at the news.

"Your company is most welcome. I couldn't have asked for better." Stephan said.

Timan nodded and then looked around the table.

"This journey will try all of you more than you can know. But it is as it must be and you have many good qualities among you. Better than I have seen in many years. Do not lose heart. Now if you gentlemen would be so kind as to excuse us, Stephan and I have some matters to discuss."

They walked outside under the moon. Timan took him to a grotto of tall oaks surrounding some sitting stones. They sat facing each other. The clearing seemed to be enveloped by a fine mist and looking out beyond the grotto; it was easy to imagine spirits moving among the trees. They were both silent for a time. Stephan knew that this was a sacred place and he had learned that Timan would speak when he was ready to do so and not before. It was as if the world had stopped turning and the moon was a giant eye, staring down into his soul. It sent a shiver up his spine. When Timan finally spoke, it was like the voice in a dream.

"Your time has come, Stephan, and I know you sense this is true."

"Yes, I feel it more everyday, like something pulling at me."

"And yet you fight against it."

"I do not fight it, but I don't know what must be done so I do what is in front of me."

"Yes. It is something that has puzzled me as well in the past and I have spent many an evening in this place, thinking on it. In recent days the veil has been lifted a little, and I begin to see more clearly. I was preparing to come for you when you arrived in my forest."

"And what do your visions tell you now?"

"They tell me there is no future for the Celts here south of the wall. No matter if Certic succeeds in this war with Edwin or not. The Saxons will soon take this land, but even they will not be able to hold it for long. Years of war and bloodletting are upon this place, Stephan. It is time for you to go north. That is where you will find your people."

"This you have told me before, Timan, but it does little to guide me. What am I to do? Of what people do you speak? I know there are many tribes and that they often war against each other. And If I find those who are my people, am I to emerge from the forest and declare myself the heir to their kingdom? I can think of few better ways to be separated from my head. In any case, as much as I would like to find my people, you know I have no desire to be a king."

"No, that is not how it will be done, but a king is what you are and you cannot hide from it. When you find your people, you will see that they are in need of you and they will soon discover you for what you are. The way will be made open for you."

"So, am I to abandon Certic and his people now, in their hour of need? Am I to run from this battle and prove to Edwin that what he has said of me is true? That I am a coward."

"You should not worry yourself about what Edwin thinks of you. He is not someone who will be long remembered. I do not believe he will survive this war. You may choose to turn north once you've delivered your message to Uryen, if that is what you wish. Your promise to Certic will be fulfilled. Your absence or presence in this battle will not turn the tide, but in joining with Certic, you may shorten the fight and save the lives of many. Your presence on the field of battle will give the men courage. I don't know if the road to your destiny goes through this battlefield, but you will find it in any case, no matter what you choose. Follow your heart in this. There is no wrong answer. Above all else, look to the safety of Cristin while you can. More than the outcome of this war, is her importance to our race."

"How so?"

"That is a story for another time, Stephan."

"We will all be in danger on this journey, but I will do whatever I can to protect her and the others."

"Your best is all that I ask and is always what you have given."

Timan was silent again and Stephan also became lost in his thoughts. There seemed to be no end to his questions and no answers he could find. In a while, Timan spoke again.

"I need to be alone here for a time, Stephan. There is more that I hope to see before we set out on this journey. Go and take your rest while you can. I will return in due time."

***

Later that evening, Cristin awoke suddenly from a dream. In the dream she was on an island, standing in a tower of glass. The wizard Timan was calling out to her across the waters from a distant shore. All in the party were sound asleep, grateful for a place of warmth and safety. The room was dark, with just a single candle burning on Timan's table. When she looked over at it, she saw the wizard looking back at her in the flickering, yellow light. She arose quietly and went over to him.

"Welcome, Cristin. Long have I desired to speak with you."

"I've been here with the others. You didn't seek me out."

"This conversation has waited not on the affairs of this one evening, but for years since I became aware of you."

"You confuse me. I don't know what you mean."

"You don't remember, perhaps, but we met long ago when you were a small child."

She looked at him for a moment, a puzzled expression on her face which suddenly turned into a smile of recognition.

"I do remember! You gave me a small round stone. I though there was something familiar about you but I could not place it."

He smiled and pulled out a chair for her.

"I gave away two such stones on that day. The other to someone I value as much as you. They are called echo stones. The druids say if you give one to someone as a gift, that person will always return to you in time."

"I found another like it in my room on the night the assassin came for me. Is that the one you speak of?"

"Someday I will tell you about the second stone, Cristin, but there are other matters to discuss tonight. Will you sit with me a while? I have some excellent tea. Would you like a cup?"

"Yes, that would be kind of you."

Timan poured from his kettle and handed a cup to Cristin. She took a sip and immediately felt a warm, peaceful energy flowing through her body.

"Who was your mother, Cristin?"

"She was Ayleth of Tintagel."

"And her mother?"

"She was Peronell of the same place. Before her I cannot tell you."

"Before her were Bairbre and her mother Breyanna. And before them Cerdwin. Your lineage is known to me going back to the beginning of memory through Rhoswen and Rhiannon and to the first who was Arianrhod. Each of them after Breyanna wore the amulet that you carry next to your heart. The bloodline of the Celts is pure in your veins."

"You know about my amulet?"

"What you wear around your neck is a precious thing. More precious than you yet know, but that is also a tale for another day."

"Why do you tell me this?"

"As I have already told Stephan, this war that is coming to us heralds the end of our time in Britannia."

"Do you say that my father will be defeated?"

"That is not known to me. The end of this story is yet to be written, but soon enough the Saxons and the Viking hordes will overrun these lands and hold them. Much blood will be shed on this ground before there is an end to it. In your lineage lies the hope of mankind on this earth. The Greeks still knew that there was life in the earth, in the living rock and in the clear waters. The Romans, who followed them, did not honor the land. They carved it up with walls and roads and delved into it for riches for their amusement. To them and to most who will follow them through the mists of time, the earth is dead. They do not hear the music in it or feel the rhythm of its seasons. This world that you know exists in our minds like a dream that we all share. If somehow over the three score generations to come we lose this knowledge, then the time of men on this earth will be ended. If they cannot change, men, in their greed for power and wealth will become a greater and greater burden on the earth. I have seen it in my dreams. Great machines will tear the earth apart. Horrible weapons will be used to kill thousands and destroy entire cities. All because of greed, and pride and the hardness of their hearts. The time will come when the earth will no longer be able to withstand the assault and it will turn on mankind. When those times are upon us, there will be great suffering and many will perish.

There will be a few, when the time comes, who will have it in their power to cross the barrier that separates the worlds. People of like mind will join with them, and cross over to a new world, where men will overcome greed and envy and all those things that make us less than we could be. It is a place where all the generations may live in peace. Your descendents will hold the key that will allow that knowledge to be passed on through the ages to come. Your brother may be a king some day, but you will be the mother of kings and in your blood, the hope of the people lies.

"All of this is too much for me, Timan. I don't understand it."

"I'm sorry to lay this weight on your shoulders. For many in these times the sweet dreams of childhood end too soon. But this is your fate, Cristin. You cannot run from it. Already I have seen in you the strength and the courage you will need. There are difficult times ahead for all of us, but either by chance or by design, you have surrounded yourself with some of the best of this world and they will love and protect you. I will be walking with you on your journey, at least until you're safe. Do not be afraid."

"And where will this journey take me?"

"That I cannot say. If your uncle Uryen will shelter you and it is a safe place for you, then you will reside at Craven until this war is settled. If you do not find safety there, then another way will be made open for you to reach the place of your destiny."

"But where is that place?"

"That I also cannot say, Cristin. I have not seen it in my dreams. I can only tell you that we have come into a time of change. Many things will no longer be as they were. At times such as these there can be great danger, but without these times, we cannot fulfill our destiny on this earth. Be wary. There are others who understand what I have told you. They see you, and those like you as a threat to their ambitions. They will be watching you, and hoping for a chance to keep you from your destiny."

"But who are they?"

"They are men who have fallen into darkness. Some are very powerful, with skills that are equal to mine or perhaps greater. Some are ordinary men who do evil out of greed and the darkness of their hearts. In time, you will learn to see them for what they are so that you can protect yourself. Not everyone who walks this earth, Cristin, is of this earth."

-14-

In the morning when they awoke, Timan was already tending to the kettle.

"I've made something to give you strength on the journey today. It may not make you forget Flann's excellent cooking, but I think you'll like it well enough."

It had been a comfortable night, and again a feeling of optimism was in the air. When they found out that Timan would be traveling with them they were overjoyed. He acted annoyed with them but Ailis, at least, knew he was secretly happy for their company.

When they had eaten, Timan joined Stephan and Liam outside.

"We'll be able to take the horse to the Fells at least. It will lighten our burden through the forest anyway. My wolf will bring her back here and she'll be quite safe while I'm gone."

"We should decide now what to bring and what to leave behind, and divide it up into bundles for each of us to carry." Liam said.

"I'll ask Emma to join us." Stephan said. "She'll be able to tell us how much the women can carry."

As the party made ready to depart, Timan went back into his house and returned in a few minutes with an armful of garments.

"I have kept these cloaks for many years. They were made by elves, spun from spider silk. They're too narrow for the men but they should suit Cristin, Emma, and Ailis quite well. And Flann of course. I think you'll like them. They are as light as air but warmer than the thickest wool in the winter and cool like the shade of a tree in the summer. Water runs off of them. They do not tear and I have been told they offer some protection against weapons of various kinds, although I have not seen this myself. They also take the color and texture of the world around you, and make it difficult for you to be seen if you're not moving. The women tried them on and were immediately happy with them. They were nearly impossible to see against the surrounding forest. When they had taken up their bows and quivers they truly did look like a company of elves. Timan took the lead with Stephan and the rest of the party followed along in no particular order. There would be no danger while they were in Timan's forest and they were all in good spirits. The dogs ran together among the trees, never far from Stephan. After a moment, Timan stopped by a large rock. He turned and looked at his house. Then he raised his staff in the air and uttered the words, 'Tuatha De Danann'. He struck the rock and the house wavered in the air as if it were made of smoke and then it disappeared. The party all gasped out loud. Emma's knees began to buckle and Cadman steadied her. Timan turned and continued on his way. Ailis ran after him.

"Where did your house go?" She asked, finally, unable to contain her amazement.

"It didn't go anywhere, my dear. You just can't see it any more."

They moved off through the forest at an easy pace. Emma and Cadman struck up a conversation.

"The things I have seen with my own eyes these last few days, I would not have believed if someone told them to me." Emma said.

"Timan can do some wondrous things. I'm glad for his company."

"How is your wound healing?"

"I hardly feel it today. Thank you for your care."

"It was nothing. You seem at home in the forest. Do you have a lodging somewhere?"

"There is a place that was built by my father. My sister and her family live there now. Lucas and I have a room there when we need it."

"Have you been alone for a long time?"

"I am not alone, but if you ask about my wife, she passed away when Lucas was a young lad."

"What happened to her, if I may ask?"

"A sickness took her. She became unable to eat and soon, unable to walk even. She suffered badly."

"I'm sorry."

"Yes, it was a difficult thing."

"Did you never think to remarry?"

"I don't meet many women out here in the wild. Those that I meet back in the towns want a man who will be home to keep them warm at night."

"Do you think you will always be a hunter?"

"It's what I do best. I know nothing else, unless you include fighting. I have had too much of that and more to come it would seem."

"Are there not men who make their way hunting but come home to their families at the end of the day?"

"That's how I hunted when my wife was still alive. I would be away for several nights but then I returned home when I had enough to carry. When she passed, I could not bear to stay in our house anymore. This has become my home out here in the wild."

"But what of Lucas? Does he choose this life also?"

"He has not made his choice. I've kept him with me to teach him what I know, and he has learned it well. It will be up to him to decide how he wants to make his way."

"He has become a fine young man. You must be proud of him."

"More than you can know."

"Do you fear for him when we're attacked? I can't bear the thought of Ailis or Cristin being harmed."

"I don't think about him being wounded, but I do look out for him. When we fight, I know where he is at all times and I try to make sure he is not overwhelmed. The rest, I leave to his destiny. I cannot do more."

"And if he decides to leave you and perhaps takes up with a wife of his own. Will you stay out here in the wild alone?"

"I don't know, Emma. It depends on how the future unfolds. I find it is better not to think about these things before I have to."

It was a pleasant day and the ground was not difficult. They stopped for some food by a stream that seemed to be singing to them in many voices. Timan's forest was an enchanted place and many of the party wished they could remain for a while. After they had eaten they continued on. The earth was soft under their feet. Ailis and Lucas were walking together and seemed to be unaware of everyone else. After a while, Cristin fell in next to Timan.

"The things you spoke of last night. How do you know them?"

"It is given to me to know things, Cristin. I carry the history of our race in my memory, as do a few others who live as I do. There are no books to remember the great tale of the Celtic peoples, so it is for us to remember and pass along to the generations that follow. The druids do not allow our history to be written down, just as they have their ceremonies out in the open where they are not enclosed by walls. They live in the natural world and mistrust the devices of men."

"Yes, but what of the future. You spoke of the future of mankind on this earth. Where does that knowledge come from?"

"It comes in dreams. Not normal dreams. We call them dreams of light."

"What are they like?"

"They are much like normal dreams, except that I am aware of myself in these dreams. I am aware that I am traveling in time and I have some ability to manipulate things. If I see a book, for instance, I can open it and read from it. Sometimes they go on for what seems like days, and yet when I awaken, little time has actually passed. I have seen many things which I do not yet understand. I have seen houses that reach the height of mountains and wagons of many bright colors that move without horse or oxen to pull them. I have seen great winged carriages that carry people through the air and ships that move without oar or sail."

"Is that not frightening?"

"In the beginning it was unsettling, but no longer."

"I think I experienced a dream something like that last night. Before I awoke and joined you at your table."

"Tell me about it."

"It felt different than a normal dream. It didn't last very long. I was in a strange sort of tower made of glass or mirrors and it was very bright. The tower was on an island somewhere and I was surrounded by water. I heard you calling to me, and then I awakened."

"That was the beginning of a lucid dream, Cristin. The story of the glass tower is part of the ancient tales of our people. If you have more dreams like these, do not be afraid of them. Follow them and see what you can learn. Concentrate on your hands, and soon you will be able to do things with them. The dreams will not hurt you, and if you become frightened you will awaken, none the worse for the experience. The druids say the amulet you wear around your neck can open the doors of time. These dreams will help you understand your place in this world."

"It hardly seems like the same world anymore. If seems very different than it did only a few days ago when we left the castle. Somehow I feel that I've become older by years."

"You begin to see the world with different eyes. I hope we'll have time to talk more of these things as we travel on."

"I see some of you in Stephan. Does he dream as you do?"

"There was a time when he did. I think you must desire to dream in this way to make the dreams come. I don't know if he wishes for this knowledge."

"He told me you were his teacher once. Could I ask you about him?"

"What would you like to know?"

"Well, for instance where did he come from? Of what tribe is he?"

"No one knows the answer to that question, not even Stephan. Some say he was born with a sword in his hand which is not far from the truth. Years ago, after the Roman emperor Honorius decided to abandon these lands; there was a period of great unrest. The tribes south of the wall, like the Brigantes, had made peace with the Romans and depended on them for trade and defense. When the Romans left, there were a number of battles fought among tribal chieftains for dominance. There were also many barbarian raids. It was nearly forty years ago that my wanderings brought me to the site of a great battle just north of the Roman wall. The ground was littered with dead and dying men. I moved about the field, rendering what help I could. I had no idea even who fought in that battle. Among the dead and injured I found a small boy, not more than six years old. He was covered in blood and sitting, with a sword in his small hand, next to the decapitated body of a warrior. When I asked him who he was, he pointed to the warrior lying next to him, and he said, 'this man killed my uncle'. For all I know he himself slew the man who killed his uncle, although such a thing would be hard to believe. Knowing him as I do now, it does not seem as impossible as it did at the time. That little boy told me his name but it was a long and difficult thing to say, so I named him Stephan. I asked him where his father was and he said he went up into the sky. I believe he was the nephew of a king or chieftain. Only the tribal chieftains bring their families with them on campaigns and there is a tattoo on his back the likes of which I have never seen. As there was no one there to care for him, I brought him with me to my home. He became my student for several years."

"What did you teach him?"

"Many things, but mainly an understanding of the world as it truly is. It is knowledge that allows him to do things that ordinary men cannot do. He is bound to the earth much like the beasts of the forest and he shares their unspoken language. He knows some healing and he is a great reader of men. And of women I would suppose."

"How old was he when he left you?"

"Perhaps fifteen. There came a time when he became restless for the company of others. Few men can live as I do and it is not good for one so young as he to live in isolation. I brought him to your grandfather, King Guallauc, who was my friend. He agreed to look after him, and to have him trained as a soldier. It was not long before Guallauc could also see the strength in him. He rose quickly through the ranks and distinguished himself over the course of many battles. He was your father's trusted advisor before they came to odds."

"It seems such a lonely life for him. Has he never had a woman?"

"That, me dear, is something you will have to take up with him. If you will excuse me for a moment, there are some things I have to attend to."

-15-

They emerged from the forest and the ground began to climb steadily. It was rocky and uneven under foot. The Rossendale Fells, a low mountain peak that bordered the Pennine moors, stood before them. The ascent was steep but they did not need a rope to get them to the top. The horse was beginning to have difficulty.

"It's time to unburden the animal and send her back." Timan said.

"How will she find her way to your house if it can no longer be seen?"

"You cannot see it, Ailis, but the animals know how to get home."

They took the bundles that had been assigned to them and slung them on their backs. It didn't seem like so great a weight but they knew each mile would make them feel heavier. Flann tended to the horse, and spoke to it before he let it go. The horse neighed and then trotted back down the hill with the wolf at her side. The party watched her go with some regret. They knew the way ahead would be difficult. Liam shaded his eyes and looked toward the sun.

"Something is amiss here Timan. We have been traveling more than half a day, and yet the sun tells me it is still mid morning."

"Time does not feel the same in my forest as it does out here in your world, Liam. We will reach the edge of the moorland near noon and rest for the remainder of the day. When night falls we'll start off across the moor. I think some weather is coming upon us. It will add to our discomfort but also obscure the moon so we'll be less exposed."

The climb was long and they stopped several times along the way to regain their energy. As before, Cadman climbed with Emma and Lucas with Ailis. Cristin seemed determined to show her brother she could fend for herself and she refused any help at all. As Timan had told them, they reached the edge of the moors by midday. They found shelter among the rocks and took their rest, all except for Flann who climbed to the top of a tor and peered out across the wide expanse of wilderness. In a while he climbed back down and approached Stephan.

"There are riders out to our south, far in the distance."

"Horsemen? Are you sure?"

"I can see them clearly."

"I'll wager there are searchers to our north as well then, and perhaps others between ourselves and the castle. They know we will have to cross the Pennine now to get to Uryen and they know we are on foot. Let's hope they don't hunt by night."

Late in the day, Stephan allowed them a small fire to warm their food and brew some tea. It would likely be the last warm meal for several days. As they ate they looked out across the moor which was as flat and featureless as any land they had seen. It seemed like an endless sea of purple moor-grass and heather with patches of golden furze. There was an occasional copse of stunted trees but little else to break up the landscape. They could not see to the other side of it. The wild beauty of the place was tempered by the knowledge that they would have to trek across it in the night. A Peregrine Falcon sailed high overhead, riding a thermal rising off the Rossendale Fells. A flock of plovers flew in the distance and Stephan pointed them out to Cristin.

"There may be a chance for you to bring down a meal for us, Cristin."

She looked in his eyes again and saw the concern there.

"This place has a kind of beauty even in its emptiness. Still there is danger for us here, is that not true."

"It is Cristin, but we have Timan with us. The things he can do I would not trade for a hundred soldiers."

Timan pointed out across the moor.

"In this direction there is a ravine, at perhaps five league's distance. It is marked by a large rock that resembles the head of a snake. Can you see it, Flann?"

Flann looked in the direction Timan was pointing.

"Yes. I can just make it out."

"That is where we will shelter during the day tomorrow. We'll need to keep a good pace to reach it before sunrise. The moor is not difficult to travel to that point, but the ground is more broken from there on. I don't think we will be hunted tonight but we should stop at intervals and listen for the sound of pursuit."

As the sun began to set, a chill fell over the place and the women clasped their cloaks tightly around their shoulders. They waited until the sky in the west lost the last of its glow and then they made ready to depart.

Timan addressed the party.

"Sound travels a great distance in this place. If you must talk, do so at a whisper and don't let anything you carry rattle about."

Cadman and Flann led the way followed closely by Timan and Stephan. Liam and Brien walked at the rear to make sure no one fell behind. The dogs walked next to Stephan. Dark clouds covered the moon and soon they were having difficulty seeing what was in front of them. The only sound was the soft brushing noise of their cloaks rubbing against the heather, and the movement of the mastiffs as they sniffed the ground for scent. When they had traveled a while, Stephan stopped them. He joined Flann and Timan at the head of the party and pointed to the south.

"I see the glow of a fire in the distance. Do you see it Flann?"

"Yes, and there are some horses there as well."

"So it would appear our enemy will rest for the evening, but they are not too far off. No more than a league I think. They still could have dogs or riders out on the prowl. We'll need to take care."

The party was now well used to walking long hours, but the packs they wore dug into their shoulders. With nothing to look at except the shrouded moon, the time moved slowly. After several hours they stopped again and rested. The cold wind blowing down the moor whistled in their ears and there was some light rain to add to their misery. No one had much to say. They continued on through the night, stopping at intervals to rest and then forcing themselves to stand and travel on. A feeling of dread was upon them and although they did not speak of it, they all feared that they would be attacked before they made it to the safety of the forest beyond. Finally, as the sky had just begun to lighten in the east, they came to a place where the ground lay open. A narrow ravine cut into the earth. There was a small stream running at the bottom of it and it was strewn with rock and gnarled, stunted trees. It was a difficult descent and Stephan wanted to wait until there was more light. He was debating it with Timan when Flann raised the alarm.

"Three riders are approaching from the south. They are nearly close enough to see us!"

The party scrambled down into the ravine. Lucas fell trying to steady Ailis and Cristin slipped and went to ground. They all managed to survive with only some scraped elbows and knees. There was not much cover, but a rock overhang prevented them from being seen from above. Liam, who had come last, just made it under the rock ledge when they heard the sound of horses above them. They crouched in hushed silence, their backs pushed against the wall of rock. Stephan held the mastiffs and quieted them. Cadman and Lucas strung their bows. The horsemen dismounted and began talking to one another. Flann whispered to Stephan.

"They have seen our tracks. What will we do?"

Stephan readied his bow and spoke quietly to Cadman and Lucas.

"We will have to take them now, or they may raise the alarm and bring the others."

He picked up a stone and threw it into the water. Immediately, a voice came from above.

"Show yourselves. If we have to come for you we will spare no one."

Timan stepped out into the open.

"It's only an old traveler, come for a cool drink of water. I am no danger to you."

"What are you doing out in this wilderness?"

"I am traveling to visit some friends. Nothing more."

"Climb up here, old man. Let us see who you are."

"I'm afraid I cannot. I find it was easier to come down than it is to go back up. I will need some help."

Two of the soldiers started down into the ravine while the third watched from above. It was over in an instant. Cadman and Lucas took aim at the two who were descending. When they came into view, Stephan stepped out from cover with his bow drawn and took the third man who was waiting above, while Cadman and Lucas took the other two.

"Go quickly and steady the horses, Flann. We can't allow them to run."

Flann scrambled to the top with remarkable agility. Liam took the two fallen soldiers and carried them under the cliff where they couldn't be seen.

"Flann, if you are able, push that man over the edge."

In a few seconds a body came crashing down and landed in the stream. Ailis started to scream but Emma held her hand over the girl's mouth. Liam quickly retrieved the body and placed it with the others. Stephan called up to Flann.

"Do you see any more riders, Flann?"

"There are none close." Came the answer.

The men huddled together and spoke quietly.

"It may not be wise to stay here now, Timan." Stephan said. "These men will be missed at some point."

"If we leave this place we will be in the open if more riders come." Liam said.

Timan thought for a moment.

"Perhaps we can use this to our advantage?"

"What are you thinking?" Stephan asked.

"I'm thinking a gift has been given us and we should make use of it. If you and Cadman and Lucas can dress in these soldier's uniforms, the three of you can mount the horses with one of the women each behind you. Liam, Flann, Brien, and I will walk beside you. From a distance we will appear to be three riders as would be expected. If luck is with us we will reach another place of shelter before our ploy is discovered. We can let the horses run from there and their track will be hard to understand. We will be some distance away from this place if the bodies are discovered."

They all quickly agreed and while Liam and Brien helped the women climb back to the moor, the three men quickly donned the tunics and helms of the fallen soldiers. They all assembled at the top of the ravine and made ready to go. Emma climbed up behind Cadman and Ailis behind Lucas. Cristin rode behind Stephan. They moved off toward the west at an easy pace. After a while the excitement of the skirmish had warn off and fatigue began to set in. For his part, Timan seemed remarkably energetic and Liam never seemed to tire and he never faltered, regardless of the hardship they were facing. Brien was young enough to take the long hours and Flann moved so effortlessly that it seemed sometimes that he was floating across the ground. The women dozed with their heads resting on the shoulders of the riders. They traveled in this way until the sun was high in the sky and came across no more riders. They had been without sleep for many hours and at last Stephan stopped them.

"I don't know how much more distance we can make today, Timan. We will need to regain our energy in case we're attacked."

Timan shaded his eyes and peered out across the moor. In a moment he spoke to Flann.

"In this direction you may see a small hill standing alone out on the moor. It is shaped like an inverted beehive and is the height of a half grown tree. Do you see it?"

Flann looked in the direction Timan had indicated and he strained his eyes.

"I see something, Timan. I cannot make out its shape very well. It appears to come and go with the wind."

"Your vision is indeed good, Flann. What you are seeing is a Sidhe mound. There are few in this world who can see it at all. We will head in that direction."

"What is a Sidhe mound?" Cadman asked.

"It will be much easier to show you than tell you. I will only say that you will be one of the few remaining people who walk this earth that has ever seen one."

-16-

They rode for nearly an hour in the direction Timan had indicated, but none other than Flann could see anything. At length, Timan stopped and addressed the party.

"We have arrived. Please wait here for a moment while I announce our presence and ask for permission to shelter here."

They all stared at one another in confusion. All they could see was an endless stretch of moorland with the edge of a forest far to the west.

"Do you see anything here, Flann?" Brien asked.

"There is something here, but it is like a ghostly image. It is a small hill as Timan described and not built by nature I think."

They watched Timan walk off a short distance and were alarmed when he stooped down and suddenly vanished into thin air. They were accustomed now to seeing Timan do some amazing things, but this was the first time they had seen him disappear completely. Ailis giggled and pointed to where Timan had disappeared. He was gone for a considerable time and the party began to feel a bit anxious. Finally he reappeared, as if he had crawled out of a hole in the ground.

"We can shelter here for a time. When I take you inside I would ask you to be silent and to sit and be still."

"What magic is this, Timan?" Liam asked. "I see nothing here."

"You will see it soon enough."

He walked over to the horses and spoke to them for a moment and then he lifted his staff in the air. The horses reared and bolted to the east at a gallop.

"With any luck they will be far from this place when they are found."

"What place is this?" Cristin asked.

"It is a Sidhe mound. The Daoine Sidhe inhabited this world long before the elves even. They walked in two worlds and their burial mounds were portals between the two. Their spirits still inhabit these mounds. They are neither good nor evil but they will not harm you as long as you do not disrespect this place. They can be a bit mischievous, so don't be alarmed if strange things occur. Now if you will take up your belongings, I will take you inside. Leave nothing behind that would betray our presence."

"You are having a joke with us, surely." Brien said.

"If it's a joke, Brien, it is a joke that may save your lives."

He raised his staff in the air again and uttered an incantation in some strange tongue. Suddenly an earthen mound appeared in front of them. They all gasped in amazement.

"Hurry now, I don't want this to be visible for any longer than needs be. The entrance is here."

They followed Timan to a low doorway in the side of the mound. They had to stoop to enter it. Liam had to crawl on his hands and knees. The mastiffs did not want to go in, but Stephan pushed them through the entrance. It was pitch black inside but Timan struck his staff against the floor and the wolf's head carving at its end began to glow with a dim, golden light. They were inside a chamber of stone with a circle of stone pillars in the center which appeared to support the roof. At the center of the ring of pillars was a dark hole leading down into the ground.

Timan spoke to them in a soft voice.

"Sit with your backs against the wall of the mound and say nothing."

He waited for them to get settled.

"Are you ready?"

They nodded. He lifted his staff again and uttered another incantation. In an instant the chamber disappeared and they appeared to be sitting out on the moor again. They gasped in spite of themselves. Although they appeared to be outside, there was no wind and the sun did not feel warm on their skin. Lucas began to stand, but Timan stopped him.

"Be still and say nothing."

In a moment came the sound like the drone of a thousand bees. A beam of soft light came up out of the earth in front of them and resolved itself into the shape of a man, but smaller even than Flann. It moved among them. Cristin felt something touch her face and then as they watched, it stood in front of Flann and bowed. It hovered for an instant in front of Stephan and it seemed to speak to him. Finally, the light hung for a moment in front of Timan, and he spoke some words to it. In an instant, it disappeared back into the earth.

Timan spoke.

"We are welcome here, but if you value your lives do not move about this place. If you wander into the portal I am not sure I will be able to retrieve you. We are sheltered here from the weather and you may take food and drink but we cannot have a fire. Once you have eaten you should get some sleep. We have a long way to travel tonight and I don't know what awaits us."

"But surely we are back out on the moor, Brien said."

"If that is so, what are you leaning against?"

He reached behind his head and rapped his knuckles against what appeared to be nothing but air, but was in fact a stone wall that could not be seen. They opened their packs and shared some smoked meat and bread. They were nearly too weary to eat. When they had finished they stretched out and tried to make themselves comfortable. Suddenly Cadman turned and then stood with a look of alarm on his face. He reached for his bow, but Timan stopped him.

"Hold Cadman. You will not need that."

They all turned and then scrambled to their feet. Some riders were bearing down on them. They were riding hard and coming straight at them. Brien glanced at Timan who was standing still, watching the riders approach. There was no alarm on his face. The men stood with their hands on the hilts of their swords. Emma and Ailis stooped to the ground and covered their heads. Cristin moved over next to Stephan and held his arm. The riders came nearer but there was no sound of the horse's hooves pounding on the earth. Just an eerie silence. Then, just as it appeared the horses would run right over them, they parted with some passing to the left, and some to the right. They came together on the far side of the mound and then galloped away across the moor. Everyone turned to Timan, unsure of what had just happened. Ailis spoke.

"Why did they not collide with us? Are we here or are we not here?"

"We live in a river of light, Ailis. Think of this mound as a rock just below the surface of a fast running stream. If you approach the rock in a boat, even though you think you must collide with it, the current will take you to one side or the other even though you did nothing to change your course."

"So they never saw us?"

"They saw neither you nor the mound we are in. Neither were they aware that their course deviated or that for a time they rode apart. You were never in any danger."

"I wonder what else is in the world that we don't see."

"Many things, Ailis. Some that are better not seen at all."

They all managed to get some sleep, even Timan. In a few hours, the light gradually faded and darkness fell across the moor. Timan awoke and roused Stephan and Flann.

"Here is where we are in some danger, Stephan. We cannot close the distance between here and Uryen's forest in one night. The first light tomorrow will find us exposed on the moor. I know of no place of shelter between here and the wood. We will have at least a half day of travel on the open moor in daylight before we reach the shelter of the forest."

"Aye, and if my guess is right, they have found the men we left back in the ravine by now. They know we are on the moor."

"Then there is nothing for it but to press on." Flann said. "Fortune has been with us so far. I do not fear for us."

"Your optimism is a fine quality in a man or an elf, Flann. I hope you carry some magic with you that I have none of."

The roused the rest of the party and made ready to depart.

"Leave nothing of your own behind. Any refuse you have must be buried out in the moor before we depart. You may leave the enemy's helms and tunics for some future travelers to marvel at."

When everyone was ready to go, Timan raised his staff and they were immediately enclosed within the stone mound again. They moved in single file toward the entrance and assembled outside.

"Do you have all of your belongings?" Timan asked.

They all nodded. Timan once again raised his staff in the air and spoke in the same strange tongue. The mound disappeared once more. Ailis walked over to where it had been and tried to find it with her hands. She looked back at Timan with a mystified expression on her face, but Timan had no more to say about it. The party headed of to the west at a good pace. The rest had restored their energy and their burden was made lighter by the provisions they had used. The ground was less flat then it had been and there were ruts and gullies to be avoided. Flann led the way and guided them around any obstacles. They made steady progress. There were no fires in the distance and no sound of riders our on the moor. The night was clear and the sky strewn with bright stars. They looked up at the constellations as they traveled, remembering the tales of Orion the hunter and Hercules the warrior and they noted the signs of the zodiac in their silent transit through the night sky. They stopped once more just before dawn and took some water and a bit more food. When they had finished, the sun was just peaking up over the mountains behind them and they could see the forest ahead. It didn't seem like such a great distance, and they were anxious to reach the shelter of the trees after traveling so long, exposed on the moor. They moved off quickly, keeping an eye out for signs of approaching riders. In spite of their pace, the trees did not seem to be getting any closer and there was an urgency to their step. There was no more than half a league remaining when they suddenly stopped and their hearts sank. They watched as a company of mounted soldiers came out of the tree line and faced them. There were at least two dozen riders. They paused for a moment as if to let their quarry feel the fear of their overwhelming force. Then, with a shouted command, they came forward, with their horses at a walk. They could take their time against an enemy on foot and their slow, deliberate pace was calculated to cause despair in those about to be run to the ground.

"Make ready." Liam said. "Hold your arrows until they are nearly upon us."

-17-

The horsemen came forward slowly, holding their line, their silver helmets gleaming in the morning sun. When they had crossed half the distance they spurred their mounts and began coming forward at a trot, the riders posting in their saddles. The party held their position bravely. The archers knelt in the bracken with arrows notched and ready to draw. The horsemen came on like an irresistible force. Soon, they heard another command and the riders goaded their mounts once more until they were coming forward at a full gallop. A sound like thunder rumbled across the moor, growing ever louder as the riders approached. The ground shook beneath their feet. Emma and Ailis were trembling in fear but they did not run. The horsemen drew their swords as one and held them above their heads. It was a mesmerizing site, awesome in its precision and designed to render fear. Timan shouted above the din.

"Courage now, have no fear! We will not be defeated on this field of battle today."

The distance between them closed, the archers drew back on their bowstrings. Each in the party held their ground in the face of what appeared to be certain death. Their mouths were dry and their knees shaking as the terrible charge grew closer and closer but they did not falter. When the horsemen were not more than twenty yards in front of them, Timan raised his staff and swung it over his head. For a moment, time seemed to stand still. There was a blinding flash of light, and then the horses slammed to a halt as if they had hit a stone wall, throwing their riders violently to the ground. A few of the knights were killed instantly by the violent fall and many more were injured or in shock. Stephan, Liam, Brien and Cadman ran forward with their swords drawn and leapt into the mass of fallen men and panicked horses, cutting the riders down as they tried to untangle themselves. Lucas and the women fired their arrows as targets came open to them. Ailis had found her courage and she fired with the others. Timan moved into the fray with his staff. He pointed it at the enemy and great flashes of light blinded them as they tried to attack. He brought the staff down across their heads, knocking them to the ground. The two mastiffs stood by Stephan and leapt on any man who came near him. Flann moved about the battlefield like a whirlwind, swinging his sword and suddenly coming to the aid of any of the men who were in danger of being overwhelmed. His speed and agility were such that none of the enemy was able to strike him.

The battle raged on the moor to the sound of screaming horses and dying men; the snap of bowstrings and the clash of honed steel. One of the enemy leapt onto Liam's back but the giant threw him to the ground with a shrug of his massive shoulders. One of the soldiers broke through and ran at the group of archers, now standing to take better aim at their targets. Emma let loose an arrow that caught the soldier just above his breast plate, dropping him instantly to the ground. Cristin looked over at her and nodded. The women had lost their fear and their arrows flew straight and found their marks.

These were trained soldiers and they fought bravely, but they were unable to recover from the sudden loss of their mounts and they had never before encountered such skilled and fearless fighters. At last, there were none of them standing. Stephan looked around at the field of battle, his chest heaving from the fight. Cadman lay on the ground. He had taken a blow to his left arm and it was bleeding badly. Brien was cut on his leg but it was less severe than Cadman's wound. Aside from some minor cuts and scrapes, no one else was injured. Cristin tended to Brien's wound. Emma and Lucas rushed to Cadman's side. Lucas cut through the sleeve of his tunic with his dagger. Emma looked at the wound and a look of great concern crossed her face. She tore a strip of cloth from the bottom of her riding dress and pressed it against the wound to try to staunch the bleeding. It didn't seem to be helping. Timan hurried over and inspected the injury. He opened his pouch and removed a vile containing a white powder. He sprinkled some into the wound and it seemed to have an immediate effect. The bleeding slowed down at once. Emma wrapped the wound tightly.

"That will need to be sewn closed, Cadman, but we cannot stop to tend to it now. I only hope we make it to the castle in time. It is still a long trek."

"We will not need to walk, at least." Flann said.

They turned and saw him standing, holding the reins of several horses.

"Well done, Flann." Timan said. "Let us leave this place now, in case there are more riders nearby."

The party mounted hastily, the women riding as they had before. They galloped off toward the tree line, glancing behind themselves for signs of pursuit. The crossed the distance quickly and once inside the forest, they slowed to a walk. Stephan took the lead and they moved cautiously through the trees, wary of another attack. The forest was silent and foreboding but they did not encounter any more soldiers. In time they came within sight of a road leading off to the west.

"Let us take some rest here." Stephan said.

They dismounted. Emma immediately went to Cadman's side and redressed his wound while Flann attended to the horses. Stephan asked Timan and Liam to walk with him.

"There is something troubling here, Timan." Stephan said.

"Yes I feel it also."

"I have never known the Saxons to fight on horseback, and why are Edwin's soldiers roaming freely so close to Uryen's lands? Those riders were sheltered in his forest and we have entered this place unchallenged. Surely he watches his borders."

"They did not look like Saxon's to me and they did not fight like them either." Liam said.

"Perhaps the king is fearful of angering Edwin. Perhaps he doesn't want to risk a skirmish."

"That's one answer. Still he would want to know who enters his forest even in peaceful times. We should have been challenged by his outriders by now. The other answer is not to my liking." Stephan said.

"You think perhaps Uryen has been overcome? Or perhaps he has thrown in with Edwin, or entered into some agreement with him?" Timan asked.

"I don't like to think it, but there is that possibility."

"I have been told there is no great love between Certic and Uryen. Certic believes their common blood is reason enough to stand together, but perhaps Uryen has been offered something that Certic could not give him. Maybe he believes he cannot stand against Edwin and has made his bargain."

"If that's true. Why would they waste their time trying to stop us from reaching Craven?"

"I don't have an answer for you, Liam. It could be that Uryen is unaware that Edwin is preparing an attack on Elmet, although that does not seem likely. Or maybe there has been an offer made but not yet accepted. Perhaps Uryen wishes to see what Certic offers him."

"Or perhaps Uryen wanted to have done with Brien and Cristin out of sight of his people. In any case, if Uryen and Edwin are in league, you will be taken the minute you enter the gates." Timan said.

"Well this is a pretty fix we're in, and no mistake. We can't go forward and we can't go back."

"I could be wrong, Liam. Perhaps Uryen has merely underestimated the danger facing him and is unconcerned with his borders."

"I think it may be time to disband our party, Stephan." Timan said. "I would stay back in the forest for a while with Flann and perhaps Liam while you take the rest of the party to the gates. Cadman will need care for his wound or he may lose his arm. We will come to the gate this evening as travelers seeking shelter. I am not well known in this place. If you are detained, we will be of more use to you if we are not your neighbors in Uryen's dungeon."

"Perhaps you should hang back with us, Stephan." Liam said. "If your suspicions are true, some of Uryen's bargain will no doubt be your head in a sack."

"No, I will see this thing through as I have sworn to do. I pray that I'm wrong, for Cristin and Brien's sake."

"I doubt that Uryen would allow them to he harmed." Timan said. "If he gave them over, his people would hate him for it."

"So what is our plan if you are taken?"

"That is something that will have to wait until we discover our fate here."

Stephan took Brien and Cristin aside and talked to them.

"It's possible we have come too late. You may not be as welcomed here as you have supposed.

There could also be danger for you and no help for your father from Craven. I fear Edwin may have already made a bargain with Uryen, or perhaps he is under duress and not free to act as he would like. I won't know until I talk to him."

"Surely you are wrong about this." Brien said. "You should not doubt my uncle."

"I hope I'm wrong Brien. Just be aware that these things could come to pass. If you are detained, submit quietly and meekly. I know that will be hard for you, but Uryen expects you to be children and you must act as such. If he is not aware of your strength, he may not see the need to guard you too closely. There will be time for both of you to show your metal if we are betrayed. I have seen the strength in both of you. We will find a way. Show no undue affection or care for me or argue too strongly for my freedom if I'm taken. If you keep your own liberty, you may be able to help me in some way, and for my part, I will not allow you to be held prisoner by your Uncle. If it comes to that, be patient. It may take some time to free you, but it will be done."

Timan, Flann, and Liam gave their horses to the women and helped them mount. The party started off down the road. Ailis looked back at Timan sadly, not wanting to be away from his wonderful magic and his protection. Stephan left the mastiffs in Flann's care.

"When you get to the castle, let them run free in the forest. They don't need to be cared for and they will find me when the time comes."

The dogs did not want to leave their master, but Flann talked to them in his way and they did not chase after Stephan.

The party, now reduced by three, moved off at a trot. Stephan was concerned that they could meet more riders before they reached the gates, and with Cadman wounded it would be difficult to stand another attack. All of them felt the absence of their companions and they felt exposed in this place which was not familiar to any of them. Cristin and Brien had been looking forward to the relief of finally being in from the wild and under the protection of their uncle, but now the doubts were beginning to grow. Cristin especially felt anguish at having put her closest friends in peril. She felt herself no better than any of them, even though she was the daughter of a king. She did not want them to suffer for her any more than they had already.

After two hours of hard riding, the ground became steeper and they could see the walls rising from a hill ahead of them in the distance. As they neared the castle, they saw that the gates were closed and archers stood on the parapet, holding them in their sights. Cristin looked at the walls and the closed gates with a feeling of apprehension. It was plain to see the castle was prepared for an attack. All was not well here, and she knew it. Craven was a large structure but not so grand as the castle at Elmet. There was little natural stone here to build walls and buildings. Instead, the walls were comprised of a heavy wooden palisade covered with a thick layer of clay to protect against fire. The large keep beyond was of wattle and daub construction and surrounded by a timber stockade. There were no snow capped mountains around it and no great towers lifting into the sky. This castle was surrounded by thick forest and not as vulnerable to catapults and siege engines as was Elmet, standing as it did before an open plain. Brien came up alongside Stephan.

"Let me go on ahead alone here, Stephan. My name will be known to these men."

The party reined in their horses, and Brien rode ahead to the gate alone. He addressed the guard.

"I am Brien, son of Certic and nephew to your king. I travel with friends from Elmet and we are pursued. Open these gates for us."

In a moment the gates swung open and Brien motioned for the party to follow him. They rode into the bailey and then through the streets of the city. Even though it was still mid-day, there were not very many people about. The few they passed glanced at them quickly and then diverted their eyes. They seemed fearful. There were armed men walking about and not a child to be seen. Even the people of Elmet, preparing for war as they were, showed more life and joy then did these people. Cristin wondered what had caused them to be so frightened. The ground continued to rise as they moved toward the keep. There was a second gate in the stockade around the keep and they were allowed to enter and dismount. Their joy at finally reaching their destination was tempered by what Stephan had told them. The weight of all they had endured fell upon them and they were weary. The horses were led off to the king's stables and the party entered the keep. They were immediately tended to by the king's servants. Cristin hugged Stephan.

"Thank you for all you have done for us."

"Remember what I told you Cristin. Keep your wits about you."

-18-

They were asked to wait outside of the king's hall. Cadman was taken away to have his wound treated and Lucas went with him. Cristin and Brien expected to be invited in to greet their uncle, but instead the door opened and a woman approached them. She was tall and wore a long blue dress of a glossy fabric not often seen. Her hair was blond, just beginning to turn gray, and her eyes were pale blue. There was a thin smile on her face but the deep creases around her eyes spoke of sadness and perhaps some pain. Cristin recognized her, although she had not seen her in many years. Her name was Lesley and she was the king's consort. She came forward and hugged Cristin and Brien. Her smile broadened, but there was a troubled expression on her face.

"This is the Lady Emeline and her daughter Ailis." Cristin said. "They are my companions."

"You have become a woman since I saw you last, Cristin. I was expecting a child. And you have become a man, Brien. The time passes by too quickly. You are all most welcome. Come with me, you must be weary from your long journey and I'll see that you are cared for. The lady and here daughter are welcome as well. I would like to hear about your adventure."

Cristin spoke.

"This man is Stephan. He has been our guide and protector during our journey. I would ask that he be well cared for."

Lesley turned to Stephan and nodded her head. There was no smile on her face.

"I believe Uryen would have a word with Stephan first. After, he will be seen to. Now come with me. I will have a good meal prepared for you and a warm bath to ease your aches and pains."

As they walked away, Cristin looked back at Stephan with a troubled expression on her face. She could sense that all was not well. Brien revealed nothing of his feelings but Stephan could see the tension in his body. There was trouble here for all of them and they knew it.

Inside the hall, the king paced nervously in front of the hearth. A nobleman sat calmly at the table watching him.

"This was not supposed to happen, Grindan. You told me they would be captured before they ever reached Craven and now they appear in my keep like ghosts sent to haunt me."

"I have no explanation for it. They must have had help from someone or else they knew a secret way I was not aware of."

"And what am I to do now? I will be forced to deny my cousin's request for aid. If he wins this war it will go badly for us."

"You worry too much on that score. Certic can not defeat our army. At best he can hide behind his walls for a time until his people begin to starve. This is a minor inconvenience that is all. The prince and princess will be dealt with in due time. For now, I suggest you treat them as guests, but do not spend time with them. The less they know the better."

The king sat down at the head of his table and he was silent for a while. At last he motioned to the guard at the door.

"Allow the courier to enter."

Stephan was waiting patiently in the hall when the two soldiers came for him. He already knew in his heart, that Uryen had made some bargain with Edwin, but there was nothing for it but to see his mission through to the end. He didn't think Cristin and Brien would be harmed. At least not until the war was settled, but Elmet would now have to stand alone. The soldiers demanded his weapons and Stephan gave them up, knowing there would be no use in resisting. He was led into the king's hall. It was not so grand a place as the castle at Elmet, with bare torches lighting the walls and decorated mainly with mounted animal heads and horns. Still, the hall was a place of power and all who entered it knew they were in the presence of a king.

When he entered, Uryen was sitting at the end of the table. Next to him was a man of noble rank, whom he did not recognize. Two more soldiers stood guard at the door. Stephan bowed to the king and then waited. The king lifted his hand and motioned for him to come over.

"Sit here, Stephan. I am told you have a message for me from Certic."

He sat and removed a deer hide envelope from an inside pocket. He handed it to the king. The king opened it and removed a piece of parchment. As Uryen read Certic's message, Stephan studied the nobleman. He had an arrogant expression on his face and by his attitude; he was not one of the king's subjects. At length, the king spoke.

"You are known to me Stephan. I was quite surprised that you agreed to carry this message, considering your relationship with my cousin. None the less, I suppose you know he asks for my hclp."

"Yes, I know what he asks of you. I also know he believes it is in your best interest to come to his aid."

"Why would he believe such a thing? I have no quarrel with Edwin. It was not I who slaughtered his army and killed his son."

"Edwin came with his army to attack Elmet. He was defeated and he lost his son in the battle. Such are the fortunes of war."

"It was no battle." The nobleman said, angrily. "It was a slaughter and an act of cowardice and treachery."

"It was an unprovoked invasion of Certic's land. How the army was defeated does not change that. You should keep that in mind Uryen. Edwin is not the kind of king who will stop at conquering Elmet. Your kingdom can not stand against him alone. It is only by joining forces that you may prevail."

The nobleman looked at Stephan and sneered.

"What do you know of Edwin?"

"Before I answer that question, I would know who asks it."

"I am Grindan and I am sworn to Edwin, who is my king."

Stephan turned to Uryen.

"So we have come too late. You have already made your bargain. Does it include the slaughter of your niece and nephew?"

"I have made no bargain. Edwin has offered his friendship to me and my people. There are no hostilities between us. I have Edwin's word the children will not be harmed. What I have agreed, is to willingly hand over a criminal who is responsible for the deaths of hundreds of Edwin's men. Eventually, Edwin will wish to deal with you in person. Until then you will be a guest in my dungeon. You should have though long on your decision to come here."

"And you will live to regret betraying your Celtic blood and falling in league with these Saxons. What you have purchased is some time, and not much of it. You should use it well to prepare the grave you will rest in before this matter is settled."

Uryen nodded to his guards. They came over and took Stephan roughly by his arms and pulled him to his feet.

"Our discussion is ended. Take this prisoner to the dungeon."

***

The three travelers arrived at the main gate at dusk. The guards were reluctant to allow them entry but Flann told them his old father was ill and needed to rest. Liam had to bend over completely to fit through the small door cut into the gate. When he stood, the guards peered up at him with an awestruck look on their faces. He had his massive sword slung over his back so as to look less threatening and the old man with his staff and the boy they saw did not appear to be any danger to them.

"Can you direct us to an inn, good sirs?" Flann asked, smiling brightly.

"There is only one. The Wolf and Moon. Straight along this road on the left."

They walked up the hill as the guard had indicated. Timan chuckled.

"So I am your old father now. I may have to send you to bed without your supper."

"No offence, Timan. I said the first thing I thought of."

"None taken, anyway I took it as a complement. Except for the 'old' part."

The city was large and the wall encircled the entire top of a high hill. There were many one and two story houses and shops of wattle and daub along dirt roads that all wound upward to the large public square before the keep. The stables and forges were out by the walls as were the military barracks. There were several small wooded areas some of which contained public wells. Even though it was still early in the evening, the city was quiet and not many were walking about. In a short while, they came upon a building with the sign of a wolf howling at the moon. They entered and found the place nearly empty. It was dimly lit by the light of the fire in the hearth and by candles on the tables. A few men were gathered around the hearth, smoking their pipes and there were some men at the bar. They all turned and stared at the giant, but knew better than to stare too long. Timan walked up to the proprietor.

"We are in need of a good meal and a place to sleep tonight."

"Well you've come to the right place, gentlemen. Make yourselves comfortable over at the table and I'll bring something for you. We have some delicious lamb and herbs in the pot tonight. Would you care for some ale?"

"As soon as you can bring it. My throat has too much of your road in it." Liam said.

"I'll have one also." Flann said.

"I don't suppose you have any tea?" Timan asked.

"Don't get much call for tea, but we just might. Let me ask my wife. I'll be back as fast as I can."

"Where do you think they are?" Liam asked Timan when they were alone.

"Well, Brien and the women are no doubt in the keep. Stephan is probably there also, either as a guest or a prisoner. I don't have a guess about Cadman and Lucas."

"How should we go about finding out?" Flann asked.

"We need to be careful here. If Stephan is in custody, we don't want to be showing too much interest in him."

The proprietor came back to the table with two tankards of ale. They were equal in size but the one he placed in front of Liam looked tiny and the one in front of Flann looked impossibly large.

"We do have some tea in the kitchen; my wife will brew it up for you."

"Do you have any other recent guests?" Timan asked. "We were hoping to meet some friends."

"No, you are the first guests I've had in quite some time, sorry to say. Ever since the troubles people don't seem to come to visit much."

"What troubles are they?"

"You haven't heard about the new overseer then? Being strangers and all I guess. Run's everything outside of the keep."

The man leaned over and whispered.

"He's a brutal bastard, and no mistake about it. But don't mention I said anything about him or I'll find myself flogged in the public square. Mind how you conduct yourselves when you're out and about. They don't need much of a reason to grab you by the scruff of your neck."

"It is as we feared." Timan said after the proprietor had left. "Uryen no longer controls this place. At least not entirely. We will find Stephan in his dungeon, perhaps Cadman and Lucas also."

"Do you think Cristin has been harmed?"

"No, I don't think so, Flann. If this is Edwin's work I expect he will move deliberately. Cristin and Brien are not his immediate concern. He will hold them until the larger matters are settled."

"If he harms her, I will visit him in the night and he will know who takes his life."

The proprietor returned with three large bowls of stew and a cup of tea for Timan.

"Here you are gentlemen. Is there anything else I can get for you?"

"Some bread." Liam said. "The biggest loaf you have, and great slabs of butter."

They were quiet as they ate their meal. Flann was able to listen in to some of the conversations going on around them but beyond the hearing of Timan and Liam."

"These men are frightened." He said at last. They talk of spies and of their friends who have been unjustly arrested. One man says many officers of the army have been arrested as well. Some men were hanged for speaking out. I'm afraid Cristin and Brien have not found a place of refuge here. I think we have taken them to a place of grave danger."

Timan nodded. His face showed deep concern but he remained silent. They were eating their meal when the door opened and Cadman and Lucas came in. They saw Liam but they kept their heads down and did not walk up to the table. They went instead over to the bar and ordered some ale. Cadman's arm was in a sling. Flann started to greet them but Timan put his hand on his shoulder and shook his head. Timan waited a while and then he got up and walked over to the bar.

"Could I have a bit more tea?"

"Certainly, I'll have my wife brew you another cup."

The proprietor walked back into the kitchen.

"What news, Cadman?"

"It is as you feared. Stephan has been taken. Brien and the women are being well treated, as far as I can tell but I don't think they are free to leave. We only managed to get out of the keep because Cristin told the guard she did not know us. She told them we had only met on the road. She is wise beyond her years. There is a stockade fence around the keep and we were stopped and questioned at the gate before they allowed us to leave. We were stopped again in the city before we got to this place.

"How is your wound?"

"They have sewn it together. My left arm is not much use to me at the moment, but it will improve in time. I have no feeling in my fingers, but it is not my sword hand."

The proprietor came back out with a fresh cup of tea. Timan spoke to Cadman.

"Come and join us at our table, strangers. We also know no one in this place."

When they had all settled at the table, Timan spoke quietly.

"The first thing we must do is to talk to Stephan and find out what Uryen has told him."

"That will not be easily done." Liam said. "It is nearly as hard to break into a dungeon as it is to break out."

"I'm willing to try." Flann said.

Timan looked at him and nodded.

"Let us find out the lay of the land before we decide our next course of action. We don't even know where the dungeon is. That I will find out tomorrow. We should not be seen together. Tomorrow we will mingle with the people and learn what we can. Let's plan to meet back here tomorrow evening for dinner. By then I will have a better idea how to proceed. Be on your guard and try not to bring too much attention to yourselves. If you are stopped, have a story ready to explain your visit to this place. Be careful who you talk to. There are no doubt spies and informants among the people. You will need to use your own judgment but be wary of anyone who seems to take any great interest in you.

Make no mention of Cristin or Brien and especially, do not mention Stephan or tell anyone that you are from Elmet. We need to find out where they are all being kept and as much as we can about the strength of the guard."

-19-

The guards took Stephan outside and then walked him over to a different building. It looked to be a barracks where the palace guard would be headquartered. They entered and descended a stone stairway into a cellar. It was a large space lined on both sides with arched stone alcoves covered in the front and sides with iron bars. Stephan was surprised at how many men he found imprisoned there. They were mainly young men with the desperate look that confinement brings, but they did not look like criminals. They stared at Stephan but said nothing. He was taken to an empty cell at the back of the cellar and pushed through the door. He heard it slam shut behind him. There was a low wooden shelf along the wall which served as a bed. He sat down and removed his boots. In a while, a prisoner in the adjoining cell called over to him.

"I do not recognize you stranger. Are you a soldier?"

"I was once a soldier, but no more."

"In what garrison did you serve?"

"I am not from this place."

"From where then?"

Stephan looked at the man. He was tall and muscular and his blond hair was cut short like the other men in the jail. He was in his middle years and Stephan guessed he was a man of high standing. He was wary of divulging too much to someone he didn't know, but he needed to find out what was happening in the castle, and whether the king had struck his bargain with Edwin freely, or if he had been coerced.

"I would ask who you are, before I tell you more."

"My name is Petar, and my rank is captain. Or I should I say that was my rank."

Stephan reached through the bars and shook is hand.

"My name is Stephan and I come from Elmet. I carried a message from king Certic."

"And for this they arrested you?"

"It would appear your king has fallen in with Edwin. He will soon lay siege to Elmet and therefore I am now his enemy."

"Aye, there are many who are now held to be Uryen's enemies, including nearly every man in this dungeon."

Stephan started to speak but the sound of someone approaching interrupted him. In a moment Grindan was standing in front of his cell. Several guards were with him.

"So the legendary Stephan of Elmet is just a man after all. It will please Edwin greatly, when I tell him I put you in a cage where you belong."

Stephan said nothing.

"You know there is no hope for you, so I will not pretend to offer you your life. There is however, the matter of Certic's children. There is a possibility they can still be saved. I am interested in Elmet's defenses, and in the strength of its army. There are certain details I would like to learn about the construction of the walls. Also we have heard of a secret way into the castle. If you agree to provide me with the information I seek, I will spare the children. You know Elmet is going to fall. Why not cooperate with me and save Certic's people from a great deal of suffering. You are no friend of Certic. That is well known. We have no grudge against the people of Elmet. Once we have taken Certic, they will be free to carry on with their lives under our rule."

"I know your kind, Grindan. You are a man without honor. You will do what you want with Certic's children whether I give you information or not. There is only one thing I will tell you and it is this. You, and every man inside these walls who serves Edwin will be dead before the new moon rises if you do not leave this city. So I will offer you this bargain. Take your men and ride back to Edwin. Tell him that the Celtic people are united and that he cannot stand against us. Tell him this time he will die along with his army."

Grindan laughed. "You amuse me Stephan. I did not take you for a man with a sense of humor. I admit I did not expect you to tell me what I wish to know, but there are other ways to get information and I have had enough of your arrogance."

He called his guards over.

"Remove this man's tunic and bind him to the post. The other prisoners will need to see the price for failure to cooperate with me."

The guards opened Stephan's cell and pulled him out into the center of the floor where a stout wooden post with iron rings protruded from the floor. They stripped him to his waist and pushed him against the post and then bound his hands through the iron ring so that he could not move. The other prisoners stood at the bars watching.

"Hand me my whip."

Grindan took his whip and laid it out behind him on the floor. A look of malice and cruelty was on his face. He pulled his arm back and whipped the leather cord forward. He was standing too close and the whip wrapped itself behind the post and only gave Stephan a glancing blow on his side. He flinched but did not cry out. Grindan stepped back a bit and prepared to swing again. Before he could strike a second blow, a man came down the stairs at a run and went up to Grindan. He whispered something in his ear. Grindan looked disappointed. He walked up to Stephan.

"It appears I have more important matters to attend to at the moment, so I will give you some time to consider my offer. Then we will see if you will die like a man or beg for an end to your suffering. Or perhaps a hot iron held to the princess's face will loosen your tongue. We shall see. Put this man back in his cell."

With that, Grindan turned and walked away. Stephan was taken back over to his cell and pushed through the door. They threw his clothing on the floor and then locked the door behind him. Stephan sat for a moment and then put his tunic back on. He knew there would not be much time to plan an escape and his mind was racing. In a moment Petar called to Stephan again. He motioned for him to come closer and he spoke in a hushed tone so that he would not be overheard.

"When you told me your were Stephan, I did not know you were the Stephan of legend. Your name is held in high regard among our men. It is an honor to meet you."

Stephan nodded to him.

"And I you. Are all these men soldiers, Petar?"

"Most of us, yes."

"Why are you imprisoned?"

We dared speak out against the allegiance Uryen has forged with Edwin. For that we have been condemned to death."

"How many are you?"

"There are near a hundred of us here, but there are many more in the ranks who feel as we do but did not speak their minds. We all feel we have been betrayed by our king. We don't trust the Saxon's to keep their word. They desire our lands for themselves and our king is blind to it."

"How many of Edwin's soldiers control this place?"

"Not many now. They came and infiltrated our ranks and identified those of us who would be trouble to them, and then they took us in the dead of night. We were ordered by our king not to resist. Shortly after we were imprisoned, many of Edwin's soldiers departed as well as a party of our horseman who are now loyal to Edwin. They have not returned."

"If those are the horsemen we encountered, you will find their bodies out on the moor. Will these men here follow you, Petar? Would they be willing to rise up against the king if they are set free?"

"Yes, we have no allegiance to Uryen now."

"Who is next in line to be your king?"

"Uryen has no heir. There are some here from wealthy houses who may try to claim the throne, but some of them have made this devil's bargain along with Uryen. I know that Certic has a son and as a blood relative, he may have some claim to the throne. Whoever seeks the crown will have to earn it. It will not be handed to him because of his bloodline. He would have to show himself worthy of it and be willing to defend the people."

"The son is named Brien and he and his sister Cristin are here; held in the keep. I have friends on the outside who will be planning an escape for me. Do you have a way to contact those on the outside who would stand with you?"

"Yes, we can get a message to them. One of the guards here is with us."

"Then make them ready. I don't know when we will be freed, but it will be soon. Prepare your men here as well, so they will move quickly when the time comes. Could there be spies among you?"

"There are a few I suspect may be in league with the king, still."

"Make sure you keep your plans away from them. Whatever that takes."

"Have no fear, Stephan. They will be dealt with."

In the evening, when the dungeon had fallen into darkness, Stephan was lying on the wooden bench, but sleep would not come to him. There was little more he could do until Timan and Liam contacted him. He hoped they would be in time. He heard someone calling to him softly form the adjoining cell and he turned, unable to see who it was in the dim light. He arose and walked over to the bars. A man stood before him. Stephan could not make out his face. The man spoke in a quiet voice.

"I saw the symbol tattooed on your shoulder, stranger. How did you come by it?"

"I've had it since I was a child. I have no memory of how it came to be there. Who are you and why do you ask?"

"I am like you. I am not of this place. I came here a few weeks ago with a message from the chieftain of my clan at Argyll north of the wall. We desire a treaty with Uryen for trade and mutual defense from the raiders that have come to besiege our lands. Instead, I find myself held hostage in the place."

"I don't think Uryen ordered you held. This kingdom has fallen under the control of the Saxon, Edwin."

"Aye, but that means little now. If I do not return soon with Uryen's reply they will come for me and there could be a war."

"I don't think you will be held here much longer. Don't lose heart."

"The mark you wear on your shoulder tells me you are of a people known to me. Their land lies to the north of us. That mark is worn by their chieftain. I saw it once when he was tossing the caber against us at our games. Is that where you're from?"

"I don't know the place of my birth. I was found on a field of battle by a stranger, long ago. What tribe are they?"

"They call themselves the Caledonians but many call them the Picts. For a time they were our enemies, but we are at peace now, at least for a while. The mark you wear tells me you are a chieftain or the son of a chieftain.

"What is your name?"

"I am Robert from the Clan Chanann."

"What do you know of these Caledonians, Robert?"

"They are large men, many with red hair. They are fierce and fearless in battle. I know them to be a proud and noble race. The Romans named them the Picti. It means the painted people. The Britons call them Picts. They united the clans north of the wall and fought often against the Romans. The Romans sent an entire legion north to fight them and it vanished into the forest, never to be seen again. They finally despaired of defeating them. They retreated

247

behind the long wall and gave up on conquering the lands to the north of it."

"And they are friendly with your tribe?"

"For the most part yes. When the Romans tried to take our lands, the Caledonians united us. Now we still join with them when the tribes of Germania sail into our rivers. We only wish peace and to till our land, but these are harsh times and have been for many generations."

"Yes, and they do not look to become less so, at least for a time. Thank you for this news, Robert. I hope we have a chance to talk again. Seek me out when we are released from this place."

***

Cristin, Brien, Emma, and Ailis were taken to the living quarters on the top floor of the keep. They were treated courteously. Once they had bathed and had a meal, they asked to go down to talk to their uncle. They were told he was busy with affairs of the kingdom and would see them later. When they tried to leave their quarters they found the way barred by armed guards. Lesley told them it was for their safety, but they knew they were now prisoners. Brien's sword had been taken from him while he bathed and they all felt bewildered. He visited the women in their chambers.

"I'm afraid Stephan was right. We are indeed prisoners in this castle." Cristin said.

"They have taken my sword. I feel helpless."

"What do you think happened to the rest of our friends?" Emma asked.

"I believe Cadman and Lucas have been set free. I fear Stephan has been arrested."

"What can we do? We cannot let this happen." Brien said.

"For now, we must do as Stephan asked and remain quiet. Remember that Timan, Liam, and Flann are still free. I'm sure they'll come up with a plan. Let's find out all we can about this place and look for a means of escape. Perhaps we will be permitted to go to the lower floors after a while, so long as we don't show our alarm."

"Have you thought about what this means for us, Cristin? Unless our father can prevail against Edwin, we are cast adrift on the earth."

"Perhaps, Brien. But we are not alone. We have made good friends and I have faith there will be a way. I fear many will be cast adrift before this matter is settled. We should have no better fate than the people of Elmet."

"Perhaps not, but without someone to lead them, the people will suffer. We need to do what we can to gain our freedom."

"Be patient, Brien. Our friends will find a way."

***

On the following evening, the men met at the inn as planned. They had spent the day walking about separately and talking to anyone who was willing. They found that the people were in fear, and few would share their thoughts with strangers. Timan addressed the men.

"This place has been taken over by Edwin's men as we suspected. He has been heavy handed and many have been arrested, including as you heard last night, more than a few officers of high rank from Uryen's army."

"I found out that Brien and Cristin are being held on the top floor of the keep."

"How did you get that information, Liam?"

"There is a scullery maid in the king's kitchen who apparently finds me irresistible. I found her in the market. In any case, there are two staircases leading to their chambers. The main staircase is wide but it is heavily guarded and the servants are not permitted to use it. A second, smaller staircase in the back of the keep rises up from the kitchen. It is less well guarded and the servants are allowed a good deal of freedom in its use, to attend to their duties."

"Well done, Liam. I have found that the dungeon is not actually in the keep but is under the guard's barracks at the side of the main building. At any given time there are upwards of fifty soldiers billeted there."

"I have found the armory." Lucas said. "It's inside the stockade, and I was surprised to find it was not heavily guarded. There are weapons of all kinds kept there and also tools for building fortifications"

Timan smiled at him. "You got inside then? How did you manage that?"

"By showing a boy's interest in the weapons. The yeoman warder likes to brag a little."

"Did you see any rope there?" Flann asked.

"Yes, great coils of it."

Cadman spoke next

"The entrances to the keep are guarded around the clock. Two guards stand at each door."

"I will need a length of rope long enough to reach the top of the keep, as thin as we can find, and some weapons." Flann said.

"What do you have in mind?"

"My first though is for Cristin and our friends held captive. If a skirmish erupts as I think we are planning here, I would feel better if they had arms to defend themselves. I would send some bows and a sword up to them to hide until we're ready to strike."

"And how do you plan to get the rope up to the top of the keep?" Liam asked.

"I will carry it up myself and give it to them tonight?"

"How will you get past the guard?"

"I am a shadow when I wish to be."

Timan nodded his head.

"I will visit Stephan tonight also, and then we can make a plan to free them all. They no doubt close the stockade gate at night, so we will have to find another way in."

"I already found a way." Flann said. "Although you may get your knees a bit dirty. I don't think Liam will fit at all but the rest of us could get in without too much trouble."

-20-

They remained at the inn until late in the evening, sitting by the fire and talking quietly. When the last of the townsmen left, they retired to their rooms. They waited a while longer to make sure the proprietor had retired for the evening, then Flann, Timan, and Lucas climbed out their windows and crept around to the side of the inn. Dressed in his elfin cloak, Flann was nearly invisible. They made their way toward the keep. The city was quiet and the streets deserted. Flann led them around to the back of the stockade where the ground was rocky and the timbers were not sunken into the earth. There, next to a large rock was a gap at the foot of the stockade. Flann passed through easily, but for Timan and Lucas it was a tight squeeze. They moved forward in the shadows and stopped by a row of wagons near the side of the armory. There was a guard stationed at the door, but no other soldiers in sight. Flann removed his sling and picked up some stones from the ground.

"Make ready." He said.

Timan rapped his staff against a wagon. The guard turned and looked their way, but he didn't seem to be alarmed. Timan rapped again and the guard looked over for a second time and shouted.

"Who goes there! Come out where I can see you!"

He started to walk toward them, his hand resting on the hilt of his sword. Flann twirled his sling over his head and let loose a stone, hitting the guard square in the forehead. He buckled to his knees and then fell forward on his face. They rushed over to him. Lucas and Timan dragged him back to the door and propped him up against the front of the building. Timan removed a drinking gourd full of ale from his cloak. He poured some into the guard's mouth and spilled a bit down the front of his tunic. He placed the gourd next to him on the ground. Flann examined the lock. It was heavy and forged of thick iron.

"It may take some time to open this." Flann said.

While Timan and Flann examined the lock, Lucas went through the guard's pockets.

"I think I've found the key." He said.

Timan tried it, and the lock sprung open.

"Well done, Lucas. Now put the key back in the guard's pocket where you found it."

Timan stood watch while Flann and Lucas entered the armory. It took them longer than they wanted because they couldn't light a lamp. Timan was about to go in after them when they emerged. Flann had a coil of rope over his shoulder and Lucas had three short bows, quivers and a good sword. Timan picked up the lock and secured the door. As they were hurrying away, the heard the sound of men approaching. They stepped into the shadows and watched. Two soldiers appeared and found the guard still slumped on the ground. One of the soldiers stooped to rouse him, thinking he had fallen asleep. He shook his head in disgust.

"This man is drunk on duty. He will sober up in the prison well enough. Stand guard here Borin, while I fetch the officer."

The three, crept away in the darkness and didn't stop until they came to the place where they had entered the stockade. Lucas squeezed back through the breach and hurried back to the inn. His mission was complete for the evening. He just needed to get back to the inn without being noticed. Several times he had to duck for cover as guards passed too closely, but he made it back without incident. He climbed back through the window to stay with Cadman and Liam in case the alarm was raised and someone came looking for them. Timan and Flann made their way toward the keep, staying behind trees and making use of the shadows. They crossed behind the barracks and found their way to the back of the building. The only windows were high up the wall on the top two floors. Flann dropped the weapons on the ground but kept the rope coiled around his shoulder. They doubled back to where they could see the guards standing at the door to the scullery.

"Are you sure you can do this, Flann? It is a dangerous thing."

"I'll do it. I can't leave Cristin with any way to defend herself."

"Very well then. I'll go around toward the front of the building and create a disturbance. You will only have a moment to get inside, so as soon as you hear it, enter as quickly as you can."

Timan disappeared into the shadows. Flann crept up toward the scullery door until he was only feet from where the guards were standing. They could have reached out and touched him, but in the dim light, and wearing his elfin cloak, it was nearly impossible to see him. He stood with his back to the wall and waited. In a few moments he saw a flash of light and a wagon filled with straw burst into flames. The guards ran toward the fire and Flann leapt up the stairs and entered the scullery. There were two cooks in the kitchen, preparing food for the next day's meals. He could see the stairway but the only way to reach it was to cross the kitchen. He crouched in the shadows for a moment, trying to think what to do. In a moment a rat appeared, walking along at the bottom of the wall. It stopped and sniffed the air. Flann sat still and waited for it to come closer and then he pounced on it and caught it with his hands. He held it for a moment and stroked its head with his finger to calm it. The two cooks were engrossed in their work. Flann took a peek around the corner and then he threw the rat up onto one of the counter tops. One of the cooks saw it and she screamed, the other grabbed a cleaver and went after it. While they had their backs turned, Flann slid behind them, close enough to untie their aprons. He dashed over to the stairway and hid in the shadow. One of the cooks turned as if she had felt something but Flann had again vanished into the darkness. He moved silently but with great speed. There were no guards at the second or third floor landings but when he approached the fourth floor he could see the arm and leg of a soldier leaning against the wall in the dim light.

At first, he couldn't think of what to do. He could see down a long, dimly lit hallway with a number of doors that were all closed. At the end of the hall there was a fire basket, lighting the top of the main staircase. A bronze shield been hung on the wall behind it to reflect the light. An idea came to him. He removed his sling and placed a stone in it. He twirled it above his head and then let the stone fly. It slammed into the bronze shield with a sound like a gong being rung. The guard started down the hall to investigate, and Flann fell in behind him walking step for step in his shadow, not six inches away. There was a thick, support timber against the wall about half way down the hall and when they reached it, Flann ducked behind into its shadow. Seconds later the door at the end of the hall opened and he saw Ailis stick her head out to see what was going on.

"Did you make this commotion, miss? You were told to stay in your room."

"I made no commotion. I think it must be a goblin come to haunt you for your ill manners."

She stuck her tongue out at him and then hurriedly closed the door. The guard examined the shield for a moment and then stooped down and picked up the stone. He looked at Ailis's door and shook his head. Finally, he walked back toward his station and when he had passed the column, Flann came out from behind it and hurried down to Ailis's door and entered the chamber. Ailis and Cristin were sitting on a bed talking and Ailis almost cried out when she saw Flann but Cristin steadied her. Flann went over to them and they threw their arms around him.

"You took a terrible risk coming to us Flann, but I am so happy to see you. What of the others?"

"We are all safe, save for Stephan who has been thrown into the dungeon. Don't worry though; we're working on a plan to release him. Are you being mistreated here?"

"No they're treating us well enough but we're confined to this place. They won't let us talk to our uncle even. Did you bring that rope for us to climb down to our freedom?"

"No, Cristin, it's too high. I don't know what will unfold next but there will be some trouble coming and soon. You need to be ready. I've brought some weapons and they're waiting for you down below on the ground. I need to secure this rope to a ceiling beam and climb down it. When I get to the ground I'll tie the weapons to the rope and you can pull them up. Is there a place where you can safely hide them?"

"We'll find a place."

"Is Brien here also? I have a sword for him."

"Yes, he is in the room at the other end of the hall, nearest the guard."

"I hope you'll not need these weapons, Cristin, but I think you'll feel better knowing you have them. Do you still have the amulet that was given you?"

"Yes. I always wear it. Why?"

"Make sure you wear it tomorrow night, in case you need to leave this place quickly. It will protect you if I am not able."

Cristin looked at him for a moment with a puzzled expression on her face.

"What can we do to help you, Flann?"

"Just stay safe and be ready. That's all I ask. When you have hauled up the weapons, untie the rope and drop it down to me. We will not act before tomorrow night but be ready and be dressed to travel if you can manage it. If you hear fighting below, stay here until one of us comes for you. If anyone else tries to take you or harm you, show them you are not to be trifled with."

They hugged him again and then he broke away and leapt onto the top of a dresser to reach the cross beam. He secured the rope and then opened the window. With a last grin at the two women he lowered himself out the window and climbed down the rope to the ground. Cristin stood in front of the open window, the chilly night air blowing her hair in front of her face. It seemed like a mile to the ground below and she once again marveled at Flann's great courage. When the weapons had been pulled up and the rope dropped to the ground, Flann went to find Timan, who was waiting for him behind the barracks.

"Did you find them? Are they well?"

"Yes they're safe and I have told them as much as I know. They'll be ready when we act."

"It's time for me to visit Stephan now, Flann. Come with me over to the barracks."

They made their way silently across gap between the two buildings and soon they stood in the shadows near the barracks door.

"How do you plan on getting inside, Timan?"

"I will walk straight through the door but first you will have to open it for me. Do you have some stones for that sling of yours?"

"I have plenty."

"Good, now I don't need you to ring one off of anyone's head. Just go a ways off into the shadows and fling a few at the door until someone opens it. Wait until after I make myself ready and don't let them catch you."

Flann smiled.

"They couldn't catch me if I ran on one leg."

Flann watched as Timan walked over and stood next to the barracks door. He stood very still and placed his forehead against his staff. The air seemed to waver around him, and then he was gone. Vanished into thin air. Flann was a little startled but not entirely surprised. He placed a stone in his sling and let it fly. In a moment the door burst open and a guard leapt out with his sword drawn. He looked around for a few moments but finding nothing, went back inside and closed the door behind him. Timan walked past him into the building and then past the guard standing at the top of the stairway. He descended into the dungeon and walked silently past the cells full of sleeping soldiers. He found Stephan in the last cell and he stood in the shadows. He called to him and then, uttering another incantation, became visible again. Stephan walked over to the door.

"I'm happy to see you, my friend. How did you get past the guard?"

"I stood outside the light. It takes a great deal of energy, and I will need to rest a little while before I do so again."

"I was getting ready to break through these walls myself. How is everyone, are they safe?"

"We are all quite well. Flann is waiting for me outside. Liam, Cadman, and Lucas are at the inn. Cristin and Brien and the women are being held in the keep but they haven't been harmed."

"How is Cadman's wound?"

"It will take time to heal, and he will not be able to use his bow for a while, but he still has his sword hand. We are making preparations. We mean to get you out of here tomorrow night."

"If we escape this place we can only run to save our lives and we will have failed. We cannot take Brien and Cristin back to Elmet now and I know of no other safe place for them."

"I don't see what our other choices are, Stephan."

"These men imprisoned here with me are soldiers. They have been held for speaking out against Uryen and his pact with the Saxons. I am told the great majority of the army is against the king. I've spoken to their leader here and they mean to take the castle and remove Uryen from power."

"That is something not easily done, I think."

"Not easy, perhaps, but none the less we will do it. I prayed you would find me in time. I think it will not be too difficult to get the keys to these cells and set us free. We will storm the armory and get the weapons we need."

"I can get the keys, but it will not be easy to get out of here without arms. The guard is billeted above us and they could hold you at the stairway with ease."

"These men have made contact with others in the ranks who will stand with them. There is a captain of the guard named Trian. He is billeted in the main barracks near the outer wall. His loyalty is with the men being held here and their leader who is named Petar. Preparations are already under way. They will position themselves throughout the day tomorrow, and in the evening they will overcome those still loyal to the king and march on the keep. This barracks above us holds all of the king's most loyal soldiers. They will no doubt move to intercept Trian's men, leaving only a few here to guard us. Make ready when they depart. It should be a simple thing to overcome the remaining guards. Once we arm ourselves we will have the strength to overcome whatever force stands in front of the keep. We must take the castle quickly to prevent any harm coming to Brien and Cristin."

"You'll be glad to hear they now have arms to defend themselves. Flann brought them weapons tonight before I came here."

"Flann did this? The more I know of him, the more I am amazed. And to think he was no more than a servant before this journey began."

"He was never just a servant, Stephan. He was sent here to protect Cristin."

"Sent? Who sent him?"

"That is a discussion for another time. If we succeed in this thing, what then? Have you though it through?"

"Once we have control of this place we will see what must be done. The people of Craven will have to chart their own fate."

-21-

Cristin paced the floor of her bed chamber late into the evening. Emma and Ailis were both asleep on her bed, even though they were dressed for riding as Flann had told them to do. Earlier in the day she had hidden the sword under her skirt and brought it to Brien. The bows were under her bed, already strung. Despite her friends and her brother, she felt a great emptiness inside of her. It seemed to her that there was no place left for her in the world. She couldn't go home and now she was a prisoner in her uncle's house where she though she would find safety. She thought about all of the men who had died, some at her own hand, trying to prevent her from reaching this place where she never wanted to be. There would be more killing on this night and a chance, even, that someone she loved could dic. The world suddenly seemed a cruel and heartless place and she was troubled by the things Timan told her. She had barely reached her nineteenth year and now, to be told she would be the mother of kings and the hope of her people, seemed laughable. More than anything else she just wanted to run away from it all, but there was nowhere to go. Whatever would occur in the next few weeks was out of her control and she had no choice but to suffer it. She sat in a chair looking out the window at the stars and had nearly fallen asleep herself, when the alarm sounded. It had begun. She shook Emma and Ailis awake and they armed themselves and made ready.

When the watch on the parapet called out the midnight hour, Trian and his loyal men drew their weapons and overcame the barrack's sentries. They were well prepared and they knew who was loyal to Uryen and the Saxon king. There was a brief, vicious skirmish but soon Uryen's men were overwhelmed and those who were not killed, surrendered. A few escaped and ran to the keep to raise the alarm. Liam waited in the shadows at the stockade gate. He allowed the fleeing soldiers to run through but when the command to close the gate came, he charged forward and engaged the sentries, preventing them from reaching it. Uryen's palace guard were now pouring out of their barracks and some ran down the embankment to defend the gate. Liam was facing a half-dozen men and holding his ground but he knew there wasn't much time. The palace guard had nearly reached him when Trian rushed through with his men. There was a brief clash but the guards were quickly overcome and those still standing retreated back up the hill to the keep, forming ranks in front of the main entrance.

Timan and Flann along with Cadman and Lucas were already in place when the alarm went up. They waited in the shadows next to the barracks until it had emptied, and then they charged in and quickly overcame the few guards who remained. Timan took the keys and ran down the stone stairway with Flann, while Cadman and Lucas stood watch. Soon the prisoners were all freed, except for a handful who were thought to be Uryen's spies. These were left locked in one of the cells. The prisoners moved out of the barracks quickly. They ran in a crouch and tried to make as little noise as they could as they hurried toward the armory. Before long, they were seen by the palace guard who then ran to intercept them. The prisoners were unarmed, and for a moment it looked as though they would be cut down before they could get to the weapons. Timan stepped out in front of the charging guardsmen and swung his staff over his head as he had out on the Pennine. As before, there was a blinding flash of light and the soldiers stumbled to the ground, falling over one another and unnerved by what had befallen them. By the time they recovered their senses, it was too late to prevent the prisoners from reaching the armory, and they retreated back up the hill. The guard at the armory door fled when he saw what was happening. Stephan and Petar reached it and kicked it in. They charged inside and began handing out weapons to the prisoners. In less than a half hour after the alarm had first sounded, Petar and Stephan had joined Trian at the bottom of the hill facing the keep. Petar shouted out a command and they began moving uphill toward the king's house. To a man, they knew if they did not prevail on this night, they would all be hung for treason. Soon a fierce battle was raging all over the hill in front of the keep. On both sides there were skilled fighters who had seen more than a few skirmishes and were trained to fight together and to hold their ground. Uryen's men fought well but they were greatly outnumbered and they were gradually forced back until there was no more room to retreat. In a short time they were overwhelmed but not before a large group of them retreated into the keep and barred the door from the inside. Petar called for a battering ram to be brought forward.

While the prisoners were arming themselves. Cadman, Lucas, and Flann attacked the kitchen entrance. Lucas brought down one of the guards with his bow and Cadman engaged the other with his sword until he retreated to the front of the keep. Flann charged into the kitchen, followed by Cadman and Lucas. They made for the servant's stairway. As they ascended the narrow staircase they began to encounter Uryen's soldiers coming down from the upper floors. Flann and Cadman led the charge while Lucas hung back providing cover with his bow. Slowly they fought their way to the top of the stairs. Flann fought like a demon, desperate to reach Cristin before any harm could come to her, but it was difficult fighting on the narrow staircase and as the enemy guards fell, they blocked the way forward and made it difficult to make progress. Cadman still had his arm in a sling and it took time and a great effort to keep the stairway clear as they ascended.

Flann's fears were not unfounded. When Grindan saw that the battle would be lost, he knew he had only one chance to save himself. He took some men and charged up the main staircase. He would hold Brien and Cristin hostage and trade them for his life. When he reached Cristin's door he found it locked. He ordered his men to kick it down. Emma and Ailis were frightened but they had been through enough danger now to deal with their fear and they stood ready. Cristin watched the door shake as the soldiers slammed their bodies against it. She felt the fear also, but more than anything she felt an overwhelming sadness. Until that moment she still held out some hope that her uncle would change his mind, and offer his hand in friendship to the people of Elmet. As she watched the door burst open she knew that was no longer possible.

What the soldiers found when the door flew open, were three women standing in front of them, facing them with arrows notched on their bowstrings. The soldiers hesitated and Grindan stepped forward to see why. When he saw the women, he laughed, ruefully.

"Come now ladies, don't be foolish. Put down those toys and come quietly and I will not harm you. You don't have the strength even to draw them."

With that, the women drew back on their bowstrings.

Cristin's sorrow had quickly been replaced by a feeling of deep anger and resentment. She stiffened and glared at Grindan.

"These are no toys, but I will make an offer to you." Cristin said. "Throw down your arms now and leave this place and we will spare your lives."

Grindan shook his head as a look of anger flashed across his face. He shouted to his soldiers.

"What are you waiting for, take them!"

The women let fly their arrows and three soldiers fell in front of them. The remaining soldier lunged forward before any of them could notch a new arrow. He moved toward Cristin. There was hatred in his eyes and he lifted his sword and swung it at her head. Ailis screamed. Emma tried to step in the way of the blow but she was too late. The sword swung down, but just as there seemed no hope of avoiding a fatal blow, the sword suddenly lifted up and cut through the air above Cristin's head. The soldier paused, a look of surprise on his face, but before he could swing again, Emma thrust a dagger into his side and he stumbled onto the bed, mortally wounded. Grindan became enraged, but as he drew his sword, he heard the sound of running feet. He turned to find Brien charging toward him with his sword raised. The guard lay dead in the hallway behind him. Emma fell to the floor weeping, still holding the bloody dagger in her hand. The fight was moving away from them now but they knew it wasn't over. Ailis tried to comfort her mother but in a moment Emma forced herself to her feet.

"Cristin is in needs of us, Ailis. We cannot fail her now."

They picked up their bows and ran out into the hallway. Grindan was a skilled swordsman and he was wearing a helmet and breastplate. Brien had no armor. The skirmish ranged across the hallway and started down the main staircase. Flann and Cadman finally reached the hallway followed by Lucas and they ran to support Brien. More soldiers were coming up the stairs but Lucas had reached the top and he began picking them off with his arrows. Cristin joined him and soon a fierce fight was raging up and down main staircase. Flann and Cadman stood with Brien and they pressed Uryen's soldiers backward down the stairs. In a while, the keep began to echo with the sound of a battering ram slamming into the main door. The screams of men and the clash of arms echoed off the walls and everywhere there was utter chaos.

Brien drove Grindan backward down the stairs floor by floor and in a while they were fighting in the main hall. Brien was no longer a boy practicing with a wooden stick. The skirmishes against the wild men and against Edwin's soldiers had given him the confidence to match his skill. As he bore down on his opponent, the fight slowed down for him as Stephan said it would. He saw Grindan's moves before they were executed and he fell into the rhythm of the fight, thinking ahead to how he would answer each thrust. Uryen and Lesley were standing by the hearth, barely comprehending the scene unfolding in front of them. Emma and Ailis followed Cristin down the stairway and in a while they were all finding targets for their arrows. The king looked over with amazement at Cristin as she let her arrows fly, and at Brien fighting like a knight against a skilled and battle tested swordsman and he suddenly understood what a mistake he had made. Too late he comprehended the courage and resolve of his kinsmen, and as he looked on he knew that his kingdom had already slipped from his hands.

The dead and the wounded littered the stairway or lay on the floor of the hall where they had fallen. Brien pressed forward and soon Grindan's strength began to falter. After a final fierce exchange, Brien found his opening and he thrust his sword under Grindan's arm and into his chest, killing him instantly. More of Uryen's loyal men rushed into the hall and among them were some archers. They knelt and took aim at the women and Lucas. Ailis took an arrow in her shoulder and she stumbled backward for a moment and cried out. Emma rushed to her side but Ailis refused her aid. The arrow had only sliced the skin open and imbedded itself in her cloak. Ailis reached up and pulled the arrow out with an angry shout and then she took it and notched it onto her own bowstring. She drew back on her bow and let the arrow fly where it found its mark in the chest of the archer who had sent it. Emma looked at her daughter with amazement on her face. It was as if she had been transformed from a gentle young woman to a fierce warrior right before her eyes. Before long, the sound of the door splintering and flying open echoed through the keep. Stephan, Liam, and Petar charged into the main hall with their swords raised, but the enemy wanted no more of this fight. The remaining soldiers dropped their weapons and surrendered. The battle of Craven was over.

At last, Uryen regained his composure and he stepped forward.

"What is the meaning of this outrage! I am your king! I demand you drop your arms, and leave my house immediately."

Petar walked over to the king and with a swipe of his hand he knocked him to the floor. The king starred back at him in shock.

"You are no one's king now."

He raised his sword and was about to strike when Timan rushed through the door.

"Hold. Do not kill the king. He must be dealt with according to the law or you will have gained nothing here."

-22-

When dawn broke on the following day, the people of Craven went about burying the dead and repairing the damage done during the battle. They were relieved to be out from under the tyranny of Grindan and they were glad that the king who had turned against them had been deposed. Still they were uneasy, being without a king at a time when the rumor of war was in the air. They knew their kingdom was now in great peril. Uryen had been removed to the dungeon and was being guarded around the clock. Lesley was spared the king's fate, but she was confined to a room at the top of the keep and she no longer had the freedom to move about unless escorted by a guard. Since Uryen had no heir, a council was quickly formed to decide the matter. It was agreed they would meet on the following morning in the great hall of the keep, to decide what must be done. There were two issues to be settled. The first was to decide who would be their new king. Beyond that, a decision needed to be made as to how to confront the Saxon threat and whether to send their army to fight at Elmet. It would be some time before Edwin would know what befell Grindan and his remaining soldiers, but when he finally learned of it, Craven would be in grave danger.

As the nearest blood relatives of Uryen, both Cristin and Brien were in attendance, as were Timan and Stephan. Petar and Trian represented the army. A Brehon by the name of Faolan was present as were the heads of several wealthy families. The Brehon was a judge with knowledge of the Celtic law known as the Cain Aigillne. The landowners, as was the custom of the times, did not display any signs of their status, and were dressed simply in common clothes. Most, but not all, were relieved that Uryen's pact with Edwin had been broken and the kind deposed. All of them were in fear of what might now befall the kingdom. Cristin looked at each of the men gathered at the table and was aware that they would now determine her fate and that of her father and his kingdom. A feeling of apprehension gripped her, along with an overwhelming sense of disbelief. She wanted no part in this thing that was happening to her, but events were sweeping her along and she was powerless to resist. She looked across at Stephan and he held her glance. There was something in his eyes that reassured her. Whatever happened, she knew she could depend on his help.

Faolan opened the discussion.

"I would like you all to know Timan. He is a druid of the forest and a man of great wisdom. We are fortunate, indeed, to have his guidance and allegiance."

There was a murmur among the landowners. Many of them had heard fantastic tales about Timan, and they looked at him with awe on their faces.

Faolan continued.

"This young woman is Cristin, Certic's daughter and the princess of Elmet. The young man next to her is her brother prince Brien. As blood relations of Uryen, they both have a claim to the throne of this kingdom. This man is Stephan. He is a representative sent by king Certic to seek our aid. As you no doubt have heard by now, The Saxon king, Edwin, is about to launch an attack on Elmet. If Elmet falls, there will be nothing to stop Edwin from attacking us here. So, there are two matters to be decided here today. The first regards the naming of a new king. The second is whether we will send our army in support of Elmet. In the first matter, I would ask Timan to speak."

Timan stood. He looked at each of the men at the table that he did not know and the room went completely silent. When he finally began speaking, he had everyone's full attention.

"The succession to the throne, as Faolan will tell you, is not well defined in Brehon law in a case where the king has no heir. Does anyone at this table disagree that Uryen has forfeited his right to rule this kingdom?"

Petar spoke. "Uryen has betrayed us all and would have given our lands over to our enemy had we not intervened. For this treason he should be put to death."

"The fate of Uryen will be decided in due time." Faolan said. "The task before us now is to decide who will be king."

Timan nodded his head. "The teachings of the druids recorded in The Rods of the Fili would reward the crown to the nearest blood relative to Uryen which would be either Brien or Cristin, depending on who is the eldest.

"I have no desire to be a queen." Cristin said. "If it comes to that, the honor and duty of leadership should pass to my brother Brien."

Petar spoke next

"Forgive me for saying so, Brien, but we do not know you except from what we have been told by Stephan. You have shown your bravery and your skill as a swordsman but you are young, and there are other qualities we would look for in a king."

One of the landowners named Drustan stood.

"And what of Elmet. Would you not be next in line for that kingship when your father, in due time, passes away?"

"I am not sure the choosing of the king is the most important thing to be decided here." Brien said. "It is a near certainty that, should Elmet fall, Edwin will march on Craven. If that happens, there may well be no throne to argue over. Elmet can hold out for many months, but it cannot stand forever without help. Soon, Edwin will learn what has happened here so we only have a short time to organize an attack if that is your choice. It seems to me the most pressing issue here is whether or not Craven will commit to coming to the aid of my father's kingdom. My father believes that Edwin can be defeated if we join forces. All of our fates lie in what is decided here today."

"But if we come to the aid of Elmet, we leave our own city undefended." Trian said.

Stephan spoke next.

"I have thought about this dilemma, and I believe both things can be accomplished. We do not need your entire army to relieve the siege at Elmet. If we can take a stout company of cavalry and bring them around to the rear of Edwin's forces, we can divide his army and defeat it. The Saxons do not have horsemen. The remainder of your army could stay behind to defend these walls. That should provide you with more than enough men to fend off any raiding party you may face. You would not have to fear Edwin since he will be occupied on the plains of Elmet and there are no other large forces of men south of the wall."

"What of the Picts to the north of the wall?" Drustan asked. "They are at peace with no one."

Stephan spoke.

"There is a man I met while I was being held in your dungeon. He is Robert, from the clan Channan, north of the wall. He was sent here as an emissary and desires to make peace with your kingdom. When these discussions are ended, I suggest you invite him here to speak. Your good will in this matter will go a long way to securing your northern borders."

Another of the landowners, named Morcant, leapt to his feet in anger.

"I see no reason to negotiate with these northern tribes, nor for us to come to the aid of Certic. We are strong here on our own land. Strong enough to defend ourselves. Why should we care what happens to the Picts or to Certic. Why should we raise arms against the Saxons and risk facing their wrath if Certic falls, when has he ever shown us his goodwill or kinship. Our army is strong enough if we do not divide it in half. We have no allegiance to Certic, nor do we wish to be ruled by his children. Someone needs to tell me how that would be any different than being ruled by Edwin or any other foreign king."

"Your recent experience with Grindan should tell you what kind of ruler Edwin would be." Timan said. "We saw for ourselves the fear on the faces of your people. Whatever your decision here, remember that we are all Celts and we are all brothers. Do not be so ready to put yourselves under the yoke of Saxon rule. I have traveled in the lands to the south and I have seen with my own eyes how the Saxon's treat their captives."

The meeting broke down into arguing for a time, until Timan stood again.

"I think we are all aware of the choices facing us and time is short. It is up to the people of Craven to decide what to do. You are the leaders of the people so the choice is yours. I think it will take more deliberation than we have time for now, to determine who will rule this kingdom. It is not a decision that should be made in haste, no matter the urgency of the task that faces us. I propose a vote among you to decide if you will march to the aid of Elmet or not. If your answer is no, than we will depart, and the discussion can turn to the matter of who will accede to the throne. If your answer is yes, then I would propose a temporary ruling council be formed to administer the affairs of the city until the battle for Elmet is decided. If we are victorious, you can meet again and decide who will be your king, without the threat of a war on your minds. Does anyone have a different idea?"

The room was silent.

"Very well then, let us have a vote. All those in favor of mounting an attack on Edwin's forces at Elmet, and of choosing a temporary ruling council, raise your hands."

All but a few of the landowners raised their hands. Brien looked around the room and then he stood.

"On behalf of my father and the people of Elmet we thank you for your help in this hour of our need. Now that we stand together, we will not be defeated."

"That matter being settled." Faolan said. "Let us now decide who will sit on the ruling council until a new king is named."

Morcant stood again.

"I will not participate in this farce. Do what you wish, but don't blame me if war comes to this kingdom and the people suffer because of your foolishness."

With that he turned and stormed out of the room. Two others joined him, but the majority remained at the table, talking quietly among themselves. In a while, Brien stood again.

"For my part, I would ride with your knights to Elmet to break the siege."

"I have no part in this decision, nor does Stephan." Timan said. "The make up of the council should be decided by the rest of you."

"I will order Trian to remain here and take charge of the army in my absence." Petar said. "I would like him to sit on the council to represent the army."

"This would be my proposal then." Faolan said. "Let the landowners take a vote and elect one man to represent them all. Trian will represent the army. I would also propose that Cristin be included to represent the royal blood line."

A look of dismay crossed over Cristin's face, but she said nothing.

"Three is a good number." Petar said. "Any matter can be settled then by a majority vote."

"I agree." Timan said. "And although Faolan will not have a vote, he should sit with the council to advise them according to the Brehon Law."

Faolan nodded. "I would be happy to provide my advice. Let us have another show of hands. How many agree to a council made up of Trian, Cristin and a representative of the landowners."

"Everyone remaining raised their hands."

"Very well." Faolan said. "That is how it shall be. Please elect your representative as soon as possible. There will be pressing matters to attend to."

With that, the landowners stood and left the hall. They agreed to meet later at the tavern to choose a leader. Stephan addressed Petar.

"Our attack on Edwin will have to be closely coordinated. How long will it take to make ready your knights?"

"Perhaps two or three days in preparation."

"And how long to ride to Elmet?"

"We will have to ride to the east for several leagues before turning south, or we may be discovered. I don't know if any of Edwin's men remain on the moor. It should take no more than five days from our departure to reach the banks of the river."

"Very well." Stephan said. "If I may have the use of a few of your mounts, I will take the direct route to Elmet and let Certic know you are coming to his aid. When you are ready to attack at the rear, we will ride out of Elmet and attack him from the front. We will wait for five days from the time you ride from these gates. On the sixth day, and on every day hence, we will be prepared to ride out at dawn, as soon as you are ready."

"How will you know when we are in position?" Petar asked

"Leave that to me." Timan replied. "I will give you something that will announce your presence without any question."

Petar turned to Trian.

"After we ride out, you will need to be vigilant. The guard should be doubled and outriders will need to patrol the borders, especially to the east. If we are victorious, I will send you a rider with the news. If we do not return, you will have to decide whether to stand against Edwin or to surrender. I don't believe that choice will ever come to you. I don't believe Edwin can defeat our combined forces. He thinks Craven is already in his camp and he will not be prepared for our attack if we move swiftly. Be wary. There are still those in the city who are loyal to Uryen. Allow no man to ride out to inform him."

-23-

After the meeting was over, Stephan walked out through the main gate to find his mastiffs. Timan walked with him.

"I'm afraid Cristin will not be altogether safe in this place when we leave, Stephan. I'm sure there are some here who would wish to restore Uryen to the throne and there could be some of Edwin's spies remaining in the city."

"Yes, I've been worried about it. I know Flann will remain by her side and he has proven himself to be a skillful and courageous fighter."

"That is so, but with all that, he may not be enough. There are also Emma and Ailis to think about. Their fates are bound with Cristin and I value their lives nearly as much as I do her own."

Stephan was silent for a moment. Suddenly, they heard the sound of movement in the underbrush nearby, and in a moment the two mastiffs came bounding in from the forest and jumped up on Stephan, nearly knocking him to the ground. He wrestled with them a bit and then reached into his pocket and gave them some scraps of dried meat he had brought for them.

"My dogs have taken a great liking to Cristin. I think I'll leave them in her care while I'm gone. They would protect her with their lives. Also, I know that Lucas is keen to show his metal in battle, but he has never fought on horseback and his skills with a sword are not as good as he will need. This will be a mounted attack and it could go badly for him. Cadman does not have the full use of his arm yet and this will be no fight for an injured man. They may not like to be left behind, but I think their best use will be to stay here to protect the women."

"I agree. I think also that Emma and Ailis will not be unhappy if they remain here."

"I'll speak with Petar and ask him to provide men he trusts without question, to stand guard in the keep."

"When will you ride to Craven?"

"When the army departs. Liam will ride with me. We'll reach the castle at least two days ahead of Petar and his men. What will you do Timan?"

"I have some urgent matters of my own to attend to. If you're going back the way we came, I'll ride with you as far as my forest. For now, I will talk to Uryen. I am keen to know how far he has fallen. Perhaps he acted out of fear and still had the interest of his people in mind, but I think there is another tale to be told here."

That evening, Cristin had the second of her lucid dreams. She was in the glass tower again. She heard someone calling to her as before, but it was not Timan and she was unsure of the voice. A long spiral staircase reached down through the tower and she walked down it. It led to a door and when she had passed through, she saw a boat pulled up onto the shore. She looked across the waters and a man was looking back at her. She could not see his face. She got into the boat and it began to move of its own accord toward the man on the other shore. She awoke before she came close enough to recognize him. She lay in bed for a few moments, thinking about her dream and wondering what it meant. A feeling of restlessness came over her and she suddenly felt the urge to speak to Timan. There was a candlestick on the bureau and she lit it with an ember from the night fire. She carried it out into the hallway. No one was about and the keep was quiet. She walked down the long, dimly lit stairway where she had fought only days before, feeling the stillness of the place. Her candle cast a soft, circle of light against the wall as she descended and in her long, white dressing gown, she looked like an apparition come to haunt the castle. When she reached the main hall she found Timan, sitting in a chair before the hearth, puffing on a long clay pipe. She walked over to him.

"Do you never sleep, Timan?"

"Oh yes. But often I sleep during the day while I'm walking about and doing other things."

Cristin smiled at him.

"Sometimes I can't tell when you are jesting and when you're serious."

"I am always serious. Even when I'm jesting. But sit with me for a while, Cristin. Tell me how you're feeling. These last few days have been harrowing."

"I am troubled by many things. I have taken men's lives. It is a thing I never imagined I was even capable of. When I close my eyes, I can see their faces still. I hate the thought of it."

"We are engaged in a struggle of good against evil, Cristin. Often evil can only be defeated in this way. To my way of thinking, it matters little whether a man who is trying to take your life is killed by your own hand or by someone who is protecting you. It is justified in either case. Still, for your sake I am sorry your life has taken this turn. I hope that happier times will come to you soon. But what has wakened you at this late hour? Did you have a bad dream?"

"No, but I had another of the lucid dreams you talked to me about."

"What was it like?"

"It was very much like the one I told you about, except that this time it was not you standing on the shore. It was a different man. I could not see his face."

Timan nodded. "That is the man you will marry."

"But who is he?"

"You will have to wait for your dreams to tell you. I'm afraid I have little knowledge of the affairs of the heart."

Cristin nodded and was silent for a moment. When she spoke there was a look of concern on her face.

"I haven't had the chance to talk to you since the battle. Something very strange happened to me."

"Tell me."

"Well, you know Flann came to us in the night and brought weapons so we could defend ourselves. He asked me if I was still wearing my amulet. I thought it a strange thing to ask. I was surprised he even knew of it. He told me to make sure I had it on if there was fighting. He said it would protect me. That night when Grindan attempted to take us, there was a skirmish in my bed chamber. One of his soldiers swung his sword at my head and I was sure I was about to die. For some reason, the sword lifted in the air at the last moment and passed above me. I saw surprise on that man's face, as if he had not intended it."

Timan nodded his head.

"May I see the amulet, Cristin?"

She removed it from around her neck and handed it to Timan. He examined it closely, puffing on his pipe as he turned the amulet over in his hands. It was a gem of some kind, deep red in color but shaped like a rod. It was encased in fine gold threads, as if suspended in a spider web.

"This was given to you when you were a little girl, do you remember?"

"Yes, how could I forget it? My mother gave it to me on the night she was killed. She took it from around her neck and told me to wear it always. I never saw her again. I remember a boy came and took me away to hide."

"That boy was Flann."

"Flann? But how could that be? Flann is not much older that I am, if at all."

"Flann is much older that you think, Cristin. He has been watching over you since you were born."

"Watching over me? Why?"

"It was what his father asked him to do. The elves who remained behind on this earth were given tasks to complete. Unlike men, they do not harbor personal ambition nor do they desire wealth or power. They see themselves as a part of a whole and they strive always to serve and protect each other and act for the greater good and for the preservation of their kind. Men cannot function in this way because they are cut off from each other and each seeks his own happiness. Often at the expense of other men. For the elves, all happiness is shared. If an elf feels joy, those around him feel it just as strongly. The same is true when they feel pain. They don't understand the idea of acting for personal gain. It is meaningless to them. At all times they feel the absence of their people. Always they desire to rejoin with the others. Those who remained behind on this earth long for communion with their people always. I was with Flann's father when he died. It was a sad time for me because he was my great friend. But it was a thing of great joy for him, because he knew he had completed his task well, and he was going home to join with the others. The only thing that eases the sorrow of their separation is to share what love they have with someone they have been asked to care for. They are remarkable creatures, as I am sure you have begun to see with Flann. That second echo stone you found in your room the night an attempt was made on your life was one that I gave to Flann long ago. The same day I gave one to you. It was the only stone he could find for his sling when the assassin attacked you."

"How do you know all of this?"

"Flann told me about the attempt on your life. He knew it was about to occur in the way elves know things. It is something beyond me even. He sat in the shadows in your room that night while you slept, waiting to defend you. Flann is a creature of great courage, and his love for you is unwavering. As for the amulet, I have known of this jewel for many years. It is called by the few who are aware of it, the Gardd Rhuddem. The ruby key. What you have here is the rarest of gifts, Cristin. It is the only one of its kind in the world."

"But who made it?"

"No one knows. There is a legend among the elves that in the great battle of good against evil, the god Lugh intervened on behalf of the elves and was wounded. His blood was collected in a small glass vial since it was believed to be sacred. In time the blood hardened into stone and was fashioned into this amulet. The elves believe it will serve some great purpose at the end of time. The druids, however, say it is not of this world at all. They say it is a kind of key, that allows passage between worlds and it was left here by the others when they walked the earth."

"Of what others do you speak?"

"As I told you before, Cristin. Not everyone who is on this earth is of this earth."

"But how do you know of these things?"

"I have lived on this earth a very long time, Cristin. I have seen many things which you cannot understand. In any case, the legend says the amulet offers some protection to whoever wears it, but only as long as the bearer is acting in a way to insure its safe passage through time. The amulet is supposed to play a part in the preservation of the human race, at the end of history. Just how, or what that means, is unknown to me or to any living being, as far as I know. As I told you before, your bloodline carries the hope of mankind in this world. It is no accident that you carry this key. It was passed along through the generations from mother to daughter and now to you."

"But how did it come to my family?"

"It was in the possession of the elves long before men walked this earth. It was passed along to mankind because the elves have almost completely left this world. They thought it would be their destiny to defeat the forces of evil in the final battle at the end of time. But no one knows when this battle will come. For now, it is the fate of mankind to fight this battle, and it is given to you and your descendents to carry the amulet forward so that it will be there when it is needed."

"But why me?"

"I have no answer to that question. I know that Flann's father was the last of the elves to hold it, and that he gave it to Breyanna, knowing she would someday have a daughter and that daughter would continue the Celtic bloodline. There is a special connection between the elves and the Celtic peoples."

"But why did my mother give this amulet to me on the night she was killed? Would it not have protected her?"

"She had to make a choice on that night Cristin. Your life or hers. She chose to protect you as almost any mother would. She knew the time had come, just as you will know when the time comes for you, many years in the future. She had the courage to give up her life for you."

"There must have been some mistake, Timan. I am not much more than a girl. Why has this thing befallen me?"

"I can only say that there is an uncommon strength and goodness in you. It is your destiny. As I told you before, you will be the mother of kings."

"That is not an easy responsibility to bear."

"It is not easy and it is not hard. All you need do is be who you are and the rest will follow. It is not something you need to puzzle about, in fact, the less you think about it, the better it will be for you. Our destiny is in the choices we make. You will make the right ones. Of that I am sure. Wear the amulet always Cristin. At some point in time, you will pass it along to your daughter, and she to hers. I have no knowledge of the progression of this gift through time and it may not always be carried by your descendents. But that's were it will be at the end. In the hands of the last of your blood line."

"And what will happen then?"

"I have not seen it in my dreams, Cristin. At least not yet."

"But what will happen now, Timan? Will this war be won?"

"I don't know. I believe that it will but I cannot see through to the end of it. But in the end, I don't believe your future lies here, Cristin, whatever the outcome of this war."

"Where then?"

"That I cannot say. You must be careful while we're gone. Flann, Cadman, and Lucas will remain behind to help you, as will Emeline and Ailis of course. Trust in them but do not give all of your trust to others you do not know. There will be some in this place who desire the throne and they may see you as an enemy, even if they do not show it. Beware especially of anyone who makes a great effort to gain your confidence. That is how treachery begins. I have spoken to your uncle and he pretends to be contrite but I believe he acted in his own benefit and not for his people. He threw in with Edwin because he was promised to keep the crown after swearing allegiance to him. Don't allow him to play upon your sympathies and by no means allow him to walk free. If all goes well, we will be back here in a short time to help you sort out your future and the future of this kingdom."

-24-

At dawn of the third day after the battle of Craven, Petar and his army assembled in front of the keep with their mounts. Brien rode next to Petar at the head of the column. There were nearly four hundred knights and several dozen men to lead the pack animals that carried their weapons and armor. As they prepared to ride forth, Timan and Stephan came out of the keep. Timan had been busy in a vacant workhouse for more than a day. He was seen moving about the city carrying bags and sacks of unknown things, but he would not stop to talk to anyone nor would he let anyone see what he was up to. Now he was carrying a round bundle the size of a hogshead. He handed it to Brien.

"Don't let this get wet, whatever you do. When you are ready to make your attack, place it on the ground, farther away than you can shoot an arrow. This mark must face toward the enemy. Make sure the knights are not mounted. They will need to control their horses. Set fire to this string and then run back quickly. In half a minute after you light it, you will see a great flash of light and a sound like thunder. It will shake the earth under your feet and there will also be a great amount of smoke. Edwin's men will not be prepared for it and it will no doubt unnerve them, at least for a moment. Let your knights know what to expect, Petar. It will be a shock to them as well, if they are not prepared. The explosion will be heard as far as the gates of Elmet and it will be Certic's signal to ride out of the city and attack."

Stephan took Brien aside.

"Have you practiced fighting from horseback, Brien?"

"Not very much."

"Stay with Petar and keep in a tight formation. In that way you will only have to protect one flank. If your horse is brought down, look to a comrade to pull you up behind him. At some point you will need to abandon your mounts and the fight will be on foot. We will meet you in the middle."

Cristin came out from the keep and hugged her brother.

"Farewell Brien and give my love to our father when you see him. I pray I will see you both again soon."

"Have no fear Cristin. We will not be defeated."

At Petar's command, the knights mounted. They rode forth through the stockade gate in a column of fours, and down through the bailey. The people gathered to watch them depart. They waved and shouted their support. Trian and the remainder of the army stood in formation on either side of the road and saluted as the knights passed in front of them and out through the main gate. There was a great feeling of pride among the knights. It helped them forget for a moment, the dangers they would be facing. When they had departed, Trian ordered the gates of the city closed and he set the watch on the parapet. The army would remain on alert now, until the battle for Elmet was settled.

After the knights had departed, Stephan took Cristin aside. They walked together on the grounds in front of the keep and the mastiffs followed them.

"I know Timan has spoken to you about the danger you may face while we're gone."

"Don't worry about me, Stephan. I am not easily fooled."

"Trian is a man of honor and there will be nothing to fear from him, but there still could be soldiers in his ranks who secretly support Uryen. Be careful around the palace guard and try not to move about alone."

"I think you worry too much for me, and not enough for yourself, Stephan. Surely this will be a terrible battle, and many will die. I fear for my father and brother and I fear for you."

"No one can tell the fortunes of war, not even Timan. I believe we will prevail at Elmet and each of us according to our fate."

Cristin put her arms around him and held him tightly. She looked up at him and there were tears in her eyes.

"Come back to me Stephan. I could not bear to be separated from you again."

**

Not more than an hour after the army departed, Stephan, Timan and Liam mounted their horses and rode out through the main gate. Their journey back to Elmet would go much more quickly on horseback and they did not expect to meet any of the enemy. Nonetheless, they were wary when they rode out across the moor and they spurred their mounts, riding like the wind with their long cloaks flying out behind them under a cloudless blue sky. They rested a few hours at the ravine, and again for a while at the Rosendale Fells, but they didn't tarry long. They reached Timan's house well past midnight and there they fed and watered the horses and took their rest. In the morning, Stephan and Liam joined Timan at his table and they took breakfast together.

"How do you feel about this fight, Stephan?" Timan asked.

"As with all battles, much will depend on fate. Certic thinks Edwin's army may be three times the size of his own. We have many mounted men, but they will not decide this battle. We will have the element of surprise. The horses will cause panic in the enemy for a time and we will kill many, but in not too long a time the fighting will be on foot and we will still be outnumbered. It will be a close thing."

"Are you sure you still wish to throw in with Certic after all that's happened. You've fulfilled your promise to him and won him the help he needs. He could not ask for more."

"I will not fight for Certic, but I'll fight for his people. They have become my people as well. I can't turn my back on them in their hour of need."

"And what of you Liam? You are not of this place."

"Perhaps, but a good fight is not so easy to come by these days. I don't want to take my ease until I'm sure my name will be properly praised in song and legend. I can't let Stephan have all the glory."

"What will you do it the battle is lost, Timan?" Stephan asked.

"I don't believe it will be lost. But if it is, I'll try to get back to Craven before Edwin has time to regroup and make his attack. I'll take Cristin and the remainder of the party away where they'll be out of harm's way. If the Saxon's prevail, this forest will no longer be safe, even for me."

"When will we see you again?"

"That depends on many things that I cannot foresee. I expect you will see me again before this battle is settled. I will render what help I'm able. For now, I have an important task I must attend to. Then we shall see."

Stephan and Liam rode back the way they had come. They encountered no one on the way and even the wild men's forest had gone still. It was as if the world was holding its breath, waiting for the new page in history to be turned. They stayed overnight at the hunters lodging but they took a different route back to Elmet, not wanting to trust to the road. Late in the day they stood on a high hill where they could see out over the valley before the castle. An awesome sight greeted their eyes. Edwin had assembled several large mangonels and they were flinging great stones at Elmet's walls. They watched as the huge stones arced through the air and exploded against the hard rock face of the outer wall. The walls were scarred at their base from many blows, but they were not breached. Many large stones lay imbedded in the mud before the walls, where they had fallen short of their target.

Stephan was surprised to see the mangonels so early into the siege.

"I have not seen machines of this size before, Liam. It appears they will be able to send stones over the walls when they get close enough. I don't think they built them here. They must have been brought in pieces on Edwin's boats."

"Aye. Edwin has had many years to prepare for this fight. He does not mean to lose it."

As they watched they could see what Edwin intended. The mangonels were being pulled forward slowly by teams of oxen. The progress was slow because the mud was deep and the machines unwieldy, but it looked as though they would be close enough in a day or a little more to begin hurling the stones over the wall and into the city. They were beyond the range of Certic's archers and there was no way to stop them without riding out and taking them by force. Wagons were being pulled up to the front. They too were making slow progress through the mud. The oxen strained at their yokes and men, covered in mud and with their feet slipping out from under them, pushed against the spokes of the wheels. The rocks they carried were so large, only two or three filled an entire wagon. It took a large force of men to handle them and load them into the machines. Behind them, Edwin's army made their camp. Their numbers were so great that it was barely possible to see the end of them.

There was nothing for the army to do now except wait. They knew that sooner or later, Certic would need to ride forth or allow the machines to completely flatten his city. When he did, they would overwhelm him with their superior numbers. Stephan and Liam watched for a while, noting how Edwin's forces were arrayed and discussing how they might be attacked.

"Look over at the south side of the valley, Liam. Do you see where the ground begins to rise?"

"Yes, right before it begins to sprout rocks."

"The ground will be firmer there. When we ride forth from the gate, we should swing around to the south. We will be able to hit Edwin's forces on their quarter and avoid the large front he will array against us."

"Aye, but the first rank that charges through the gate should go head on to prevent Edwin from seeing our intention. It will slow them from reforming against our attack."

"I think you may get your wish here Liam. This is going to be a fight long remembered."

They watched until the sun began to set over the mountain and then they made their way around to the back of the walls. Before they climbed down to the cave entrance, they lct the horses run free.

-25-

As the armies prepared themselves for battle on the plains of Elmet, an uneasy calm settled over the people of Craven. The joy of regaining their freedom was tempered by the dread of a war that none of them wanted, even if they understood it could not be avoided. The taste of Saxon rule had erased any idea that they could escape hardship by suing for peace or by hiding behind their walls. And now they knew for certain, if Elmet fell, it would go badly for them all. So they tried to push it out of their minds and go on with their lives.

Out by the public well near the south wall, a dark figure lingered in the shadows. Night had fallen and he was nearly impossible to see. A group of people passed close by and he shrunk back farther into the darkness. In a while, a man approached. He was Morcant, one of the landowners of Craven who had professed loyalty to the king to the very last. The same man who had stormed out of the meeting in the great hall to protest the formation of a ruling council. It was not that he had any great love for Uryen, but he was ambitious, with his own aspirations to the throne. He was also shrewd, and he understood well what the Saxon's wanted. Why spend blood and fortune on a battle, when a kingdom could be taken from within. Edwin knew that Elmet would have to be taken by force, but Uryen was weak and he expected Craven to fall into his hands like a ripe plum. Morcant had been quick to ingratiate himself to the Saxon overseer, hoping to curry favor for the time when Uryen would be brushed aside. The Saxons would want a man they could do business with, and Morcant was just such a man. But now the cursed, meddling wizard and his cronies had ruined everything. Certic's children held a legitimate claim to the throne that would be difficult to refute. Somehow they had to be eliminated. The prince had gone off to war and with any luck he would not return. Even if he did survive and Edwin was defeated, it was more likely that he would take his father's seat at Elmet. The princess was the problem. There was a strange light around her that even he could see. He knew, if nothing were done to prevent it, the people would fall under her spell and she would be named queen. She had to be stopped.

When he reached the well, the man stepped forward out of the shadows and approached him.

Even in the dim light, Morcant could see that his skin had an olive color to it and his nose was long and sharp. He had small, dark eyes that darted about nervously and he wore a hood over his head that kept his face in shadow. He had seen Moorish men like these once on a visit to Londinium and he did not trust them. Morcant was nervous and his hand rested on the dagger in his belt. He did not know why he had been chosen for this meeting. His ambitions were well known, but there were other ambitious men and he was not the only one opposed to the idea of a council. It bothered him that someone had singled him out and his temper was short.

"You have asked to meet with me stranger, and now I'm here. What is your reason for coming to this place? What do you want from me?"

The dark man looked at Morcant and smiled.

"This conversation will go much better for you if your hand comes off your belt without a dagger in it."

Morcant let his hand fall to his side, but he did not relax. The man nodded.

"You waste no time with small talk Morcant, which is to my liking. You will get none of it from me. I have my own reasons for being here, but that is not the question, rather you should ask me what service I can render to you."

"What makes you think I am in need of your services?"

"Your king is overthrown and a pretender makes claim to your throne. Is that to your liking?"

"You know it isn't, or we would not be talking. What do you imagine could be done about it?"

"I am a man of many skills. I may be able to take care of your problem for you. The young princess is well guarded but not so well that I cannot get to her. If she were to suddenly disappear, there would be nothing to stop you from making your own claim to the throne. Is that not what you wish?"

"I will not say if it is what I wish, or if I would be willing to do anything to make such a thing happen."

"I will not play games with you, Morcant. Either you want my help or not. This matter will be decided now or not at all."

"And what would you want in payment for your services?"

"If you ask am I looking for payment in gold, the answer is no."

"What then? Such an offer cannot be without conditions."

"Let us just say, if I help you take care of your problem and clear the way to the throne for you, I might in the future ask for a small favor from time to time?"

"What kind of favor?"

"Nothing to cause you much trouble. Perhaps you may rule in favor of the sale of a parcel of land to certain parties, or award a contract for the trade of certain goods. You may be asked to rule in a dispute over the ownership of certain resources. Nothing that would raise undue suspicion."

"You assume I cannot take care of my problem on my own."

"I assume nothing, but think of this. If you were to act on your own and were discovered, it would be the end of you. This is not so large a city that secrets can be hidden for long. The people will talk. Should you seek out someone to do your bidding, it would become known to some and soon to all. It is no small matter to kill the daughter of a king and I don't think you have the stomach for it. On the other hand, you need not make any formal pact with me. Nothing will change hands. Nothing will link us. All I need is your word that, should you become king, you will help us as I have asked."

"Who are you? Who do you represent?"

"That you will know when the need arises. I will tell you only that we have no interest in ruling a kingdom. We are merchants. We do what we do for profit and nothing more. Now we have already spent too much time discussing this matter. If you desire my services simply say so and you will not see me again until you sit on the throne."

"All right. I agree."

"Very well, it is done. Remember this and remember it well. It is no more trouble for me to kill a king than the daughter of a king. If you cross me, it will be at your peril."

***

Cristin sat in the king's hall talking with Lesley, the king's consort. She was convinced Lesley had no part in giving up the kingdom to the Saxon overseer and she felt sorry for her. It seemed to her Lesley was a kind soul with the good of the people of Craven foremost in her heart. Lesley had taken a particular interest in the children of the kingdom. In most places children were put to work as soon as they had the strength to do so, and few of them learned to read or write or to count higher than the fingers on their hands. She had been active in organizing informal schools for the children, which met during the winter months when there was little work to be done in the fields and forests. She also looked after the health of the families and appointed women with healing skills to travel throughout the city, teaching the women about sanitation and infant care. Cristin was interested in these things as well and she desired very much to start such programs at Elmet when she returned. Even though she had been cautioned not to give Uryen his freedom, she saw no harm in allowing Lesley to visit some of the families she had been helping. Emma and Ailis were also very much interested in Lesley's work and they were bored sitting aground the castle with little to do. Cristin had already become overwhelmed with the administration of the city and her days were now spent hearing grievances and attending to matters that required urgent action. It was not how she wanted to spend her time, but she did her best to look after the concerns of the people. She would have preferred to help Lesley with her work but there was already too much to attend to.

On a warm afternoon, several days after the army had departed for Elmet, Emma and Ailis, accompanied by Lesley and one of her nurses, walked down through the stockade and through the streets of the city to visit some homes. The nurse was named Mavis and she was a jolly soul, full of laughter and skilled at healing. The city was quiet. The army was on high alert but there had been no trouble inside the walls since the overthrow of the king and the people were happy to return to their work. Now that the overseer had been defeated and his soldiers removed from the city, at least some joy had returned to their daily lives. Many had relatives who had gone off to war so the mood was still a bit somber. The women visited several homes, listening to the nurse giving instructions and allowing the children to show them their letters and numbers, written with chalkstones on flat pieces of shale they had found in the forest. Ailis loved playing with the children and they were enchanted by this beautiful young woman who talked to them as if she were also a child. Leslie instructed the women about sanitation and the safe preparation of food. She knew that great care was taken in these matters in the king's own kitchen, and that there was much less sickness in the keep than there was in the city. They had visited many families and it was getting to be late in the day when a man approached them and spoke to Lesley. She nodded and then took the nurse aside. After a few minutes, the nurse hurried off and Lesley returned to Emma and Ailis.

"We have a woman in labor and she is having difficulty. Mavis has gone off to help. We have just one more family to see, if you don't mind."

Emma and Ailis followed Lesley and in a while, they took a turn down a narrow alley that was strewn with litter and did not look like a place where families lived. Emma in particular felt some alarm, but Lesley was chatting happily with Ailis and did not seem at all concerned. They stopped in front of a building that looked more like a stable than a house. Lesley knocked on the door but no one answered. She lifted the latch and pushed the door open. It was dark inside but Lesley went in anyway and Emma and Ailis followed her reluctantly. Emma started to ask Lesley where the family was when she and Ailis were grabbed from behind and quickly subdued. Their hands were tied and their mouths gagged. Lesley spoke to a man who was standing in the shadows.

"Keep them quiet but they must not be hurt, do you understand? If any harm comes to them you will pay with your lives."

With that she walked over to Emma.

"What I do here is for my husband. He will be killed if I do not win his freedom. I'm sorry to treat you in this manner but I could think of no other way. This should all be over quickly and you will be set free. Please don't resist. I do not wish to see any harm come to you."

Stephan and Liam emerged from the mine after dark had fallen and they were immediately challenged by the guard. They were nearly attacked, except that one of the soldiers recognized Liam and after their officer was called over, they were permitted to pass. The city was much more crowded now that the farmers and herdsmen had brought their families in behind the walls. The livestock pens were full and even though night had fallen, men were hurrying about and there was much movement of wagons and horses. Preparations had been made to fortify some of the buildings and some near the wall had been abandoned completely. Archers were in position on the parapet in case an attempt was made to breach the gates under cover of night. The army waited, prepared to march out through the gates at the king's command. Stephan and Liam made their way up to the gate in the inner wall and were stopped as they had been before. Martin was close by and they did not have to wait long before they were admitted to the keep. Once inside, Martin took Stephan aside.

"What news do you bring?"

"When we arrived at Craven we found that Uryen had turned against his people. He made a bargain with Edwin to stay out of this war. I was arrested and held captive for a time."

"This is bad news indeed. Uryen has betrayed his own people? I can't believe it. Our hopes are dashed. It appears we will now have to stand alone."

"Take heart Martin, you will get the help you need. Uryen's army has risen up against him and the king has been deposed. A vote was taken. Even now, Craven's knights are riding to your aid. If all goes as planned, they will reach the river in no more than three days time. They will send us a signal when they're ready to attack. It will come at dawn."

"How many men?"

"Near four hundred mounted knights. They could not send more without leaving Craven vulnerable to an attack."

"They will be most welcome. That number is fewer than I had wished for but I hope it will be enough to divide Edwin's army."

"Where is the king? Stephan asked. "He will want to hear that his children are safe."

"The king is gravely ill, I'm afraid. No one knows what has befallen him. His physician suspects someone has made an attempt to poison him. He lies in his chambers and is unable to stand."

"Can I speak to him?"

"I'll see if I can arrange it. He is very weak. I fear he may not live to see the outcome of this war. I don't think it would be wise to tell him what has befallen his cousin if it can be avoided. There are more than enough troubles to deprive him of his rest, and rest is what he needs."

Later in the evening Stephan was allowed to see the king. He was lying in his bed chamber and when Stephan saw him it was a shock. His skin was ashen and his hair almost white. It looked as though he had aged years in less then a few weeks. When Stephan went over to him he raised his hand weakly. His voice was thin, and his words frequently interrupted by a great effort to breathe.

"Stephan. I dared not hope I would see you again. How are my children?"

"They are safe. You should be proud of them. I have come to know them both well on our journey and I count them among my friends."

"I am pleased to hear it. And Uryen. How did it go with him?"

"Craven will send an army to help you. They are riding overland and will be behind the enemy lines in two or three days. Brien rides with them."

"So, my son will now discover the bitter taste of war. I would have spared him such knowledge so soon in his life, but in these times I suppose it was too much to hope for."

"We have already fought some skirmishes together. He is a skilled fighter and has courage. He will acquit himself well on the field of battle."

"And what of my daughter?"

"She is safe at Craven, awaiting news of the battle."

"I never should have removed you from my side, Stephan. Who could have told that now in my greatest hour of need, it would be you who would stand to save my kingdom. I'm sorry for the years that have been lost to us. I hope you will remain here when this war is ended to give us your wisdom and strength. They will not tell me so, Stephan, but I know I'm dying. I had hoped to ride out with my army once more to finally defeat this Saxon devil who has plagued all of my years. When I die, my crown will pass to Brien. He will need a man like you to help him."

"For now, I can think no farther than the battle that faces us. Don't lose hope. The fates will have much to say about the future of this kingdom and of the Celtic people in Britannia."

"How many men does Uryen send us?"

"Nearly four hundred horse."

"Not many to face the host encamped before my walls. How do you feel about this fight?"

"The Saxon's will not have faced a mounted force as large as we will throw at them. If we indeed take them by surprise we will make the odds more even than they are now. Beyond that, the fates will decide. You have good men who are fighting for their homes. I believe we will prevail."

The king started to speak, but lapsed into a fit of coughing and the physician went to his side.

"He is in need of rest now, sir. I would ask you to see him again when his strength is better."

The king reached up and took Stephan by his hand.

"Do not tell my children of my condition. They'll find out soon enough. Tell them I love them and my thoughts are with them now and always."

Later in the evening, Stephan and Liam joined Martin on the parapet above the gate. The fires of the enemy camp filled the plain like fireflies on a summer's eve. Stephan pointed out to the north.

"We watched some of the assault from a hill above the valley as we approached the castle. It appears the walls are holding well."

"They will hold, but in a short time the stones will come over the top and begin to land in the city. Then he will begin throwing fire at us and it will take many men just to keep the city from burning to the ground. Whether Uryen's knights are ready or not, we will need to prevent that from happening. As it is, we are fortunate that the mud has slowed their approach. Yesterday, one of the mangonels toppled over and it took them most of the day to put it back to use. I think we have another day, not more."

Stephan looked up into the night sky. The moon was barely visible behind a thick cloud layer. He turned to Liam.

"What say you my friend? Would you like a little adventure before you find your bed tonight?"

"I find myself in ill humor, Stephan. I think I need to swing my sword a little."

"How closely do they watch these walls at night, Martin?"

"On the first few nights after they arrived they probed our defenses with small parties of men. We found them without too much difficulty. We have not seen them again, although I can't be sure there are not men hiding in the forest nearby. What do you have in mind?"

"I will need to put some men over the wall here on the north side. At least three good marksmen and three or four more. I need men who can climb. Also some bowman above the gate."

"I can give you the men, but the archers will not be of much use on the wall in this darkness."

"When we need them, Martin, they will not lack for light. Be prepared to open the gate for us when we return. We will be pursued."

Stephan and Liam made their way back out through the mine. In the darkness, even the descent down the ladder was treacherous. Stephan lit a torch and turned to make sure Liam was behind him.

"Are you ready?"

"Of course I'm ready, but when this fight is over I don't think I'll let you take me into any more holes in the ground. I like this place less every time you make me crawl through it."

"Please keep your grumbling to a minimum tonight, Liam. It's hard enough to hide you as it is."

When they were outside they made their way along the back of the castle wall. It was pitch black and they had to feel their way. When they reached the corner, Stephan stopped and listened. He turned to Liam and spoke to him in a soft voice.

"There are men close by, I can feel them. I'll move forward. Stay back in the shadows and prepare to come to my aid. I don't know how many there are."

Stephan moved forward, trusting to his instincts. He had not gone far when three men crept out of the darkness and fell in behind him. He felt their presence and let them come closer.

Before they could move to strike, Stephan pivoted with his sword drawn and cut down the closest man. The other two moved to attack but they never saw Liam come up behind them. He killed them both with one stroke of his sword. They hurried forward toward the front wall and then Stephan gave the call of an owl. Ropes were thrown over the wall and soon a number of men came climbing down. When they had reached the ground some buckets filled with pitch were lowered to them and then the ropes withdrawn. They moved out in front of the walls keeping low. It was difficult moving through the thick mud and it took nearly a half hour to reach the mangonels. There was a guard posted at each of them, as well as a number of pickets walking the edges of the camp. Stephan positioned his archers and gave them their targets. Liam remained with them in case there were more spies lurking in the darkness.

Stephan took the remainder of the men with their buckets toward the mangonels. He crept forward with his dagger drawn and took out the guard at the first machine. The men moved in silently and poured the black pitch over the torsion ropes and timbers. When they had finished they moved to the next machine. It took most of an hour for all six of the mangonels to be prepared, then they crept back to where the archers waited. The men notched arrows that had cloth soaked in pitch wrapped around their points. Stephan lit them with a flint. In seconds the flaming arrows arced through the air and found their marks. The mangonels burst into flame. Stephan drew his bow and knelt on the ground with his archers. Soon the scene was lit brightly by the fires. Men came running to douse the flames but Stephan and his archers cut them down before they could reach the machines. In a short time they were burning like torches and beyond saving. A large company of Edwin's soldiers came charging toward them from the camp. Stephan watched for a moment and then he spoke to Liam.

"I think we have done enough here for tonight. This time we will return by the main gate."

"You are spoiling all my fun."

"You'll have more of that than you'll want on the morrow."

They turned and ran back toward the gate. In seconds, they could hear arrows singing through the air and landing in the mud around them. One of the archers yelled out as an arrow hit him in the leg. Liam picked the man up and threw him over his shoulder. The pursuers had a more direct angle to the gate and they were gaining. The mangonels were fully engulfed and they lit the night with an angry red glow. Martin waited for the enemy to come into range and then gave his command. His archers stood behind the parapet and arrows rained down from the top of the wall. Many found their mark. The pursuit faltered and then stopped and retreated. The gates were open and Stephan led his party back into the castle. A great cheer leapt up from the soldiers manning the wall.

-27-

On the morning of the fifth day after Petar and Brien rode out from Craven, a light mist clung to the valley floor in front of Elmet. The sky was leaden and there was a chill in the air. The burnt out wreckage of the mangonels lay smoldering in the mud. Timbers had been brought forth from the forest and Edwin's engineers were busy building machines to replace them. While they labored, the rest of the army sat around their cooking fires, grumbling as soldiers will do when there's too much time and nothing much to do with it. They were a large force of men and it took a great effort to keep them fed. The livestock that were left behind by the farmers were being slaughtered to feed the army but it was easy to see they wouldn't last for long. Hunting parties roamed the neighboring forest looking for game, but it had long since been hunted out and they were having to go farther afield to find the herds. As they did so, they inevitably ran into bands of wild men who did not take kindly to trespassers in their forest. Edwin was counting on resupply by ship, but the Spring storms had been fierce and the supply lines stretched thin. He had planned for a long siege, but keeping a large army busy and supplied was a daunting task. He was running out of patience and desperate to find a way to force a battle.

Suddenly, from the east there came a brilliant flash of light and a sound like thunder that shook the earth below them. An acrid smell permeated the air. The soldiers stood and looked with great alarm toward the rising sun. An enormous black cloud in the shape of a mushroom, rose up into the sky and hovered for a moment. As they watched, not comprehending what had happened, the cloud formed itself into the shape of a huge black raven that lifted its wings and swooped toward them with its talons raised. Some of the men ran in terror. Many more fell to their knees, trembling in fear. The raven dove down to the earth and then suddenly dissipated into a thick black smoke that burned their throats and their eyes. Soon a new rumble of thunder arose low and in the distance. The ground began to shake again. The soldiers stood frozen in fear, not knowing what to expect. Suddenly, up through the smoke came the sight of Petar's cavalry coming at them at a full gallop.

Four hundred war horses coming at them across the entire width of the battlefield. They were slow to react and then many ran in terror. Finally, the army took to their weapons but they had waited too long. They did not expect an attack from the rear. The knights charged into the camp like a giant wave breaking on a beach. They cut men down as the ran and trampled them under the horses hooves. In the middle of the camp, Edwin came out of his tent and saw what was happening. He thought somehow Certic had managed to bring his army around to his rear and he became enraged. In his fury, he began shouting orders to his officers. The army turned and rushed to the rear to meet the on-charging knights. In a while, Petar's line was broken and he ordered a retreat. The cavalry wheeled and rode back to the east where it reformed its ranks and prepared to charge again. As Edwin watched he heard the sound of a horn ringing in the air behind him and he turned; a look of alarm on his face. He watched as the gates of Elmet were flung open. Martin and his knights rode forth proudly and formed a line in front of the walls. Edwin looked across the field at them and could not comprehend what was happening. He shouted orders again, and some of his men turned to face the new threat. His soldiers were confused and suddenly unnerved. They had expected an easy victory, even if it would be a long siege. Many of them believed that, in the end, Certic would surrender and they would not have to fight at all. They had never faced such a number of mounted men before and the sight of the horses bearing down on them was terrifying. The mud which had been Certic's ally, however, now became his army's enemy. It was difficult for the horses to gallop through it and the knights did not want to spend their strength too soon. Instead they came forward slowly, holding their formation and saving their horses for the charge when they were close to the enemy line.

As Martin's line moved forward, Stephan and Liam rode out leading the second rank of Certic's knights. They wheeled to the south behind Martin's line and rode hard until they came to where the earth was firm under the horse's hooves and then they wheeled again to the east. Edwin's line stood to face Martin's charge but they did not see the new threat until it was too late. Martin finally shouted his command, and his knights charged forward. With the enemy forces focused on the charge, Stephan's riders suddenly appeared and tore into the flank of Edwin's army. Their line buckled. The men who were rebuilding the mangonels ran and abandoned them in the field. Behind the mounted knights, Certic's foot soldiers rushed forward. The archers knelt and began reining arrows down into the center of Edwin's ranks. Some ran to the partially completed machines with buckets of pitch, and set them aflame again. Soon the battle raged all over the valley, with pockets of men engaged in fierce hand to hand combat. The mounted knights had killed many of the enemy but in time the field was too chaotic for them to be effective. The knights abandoned their mounts and fought on foot.

The fight raged for hours. There were no longer any defined lines on the battlefield. Instead, clusters of men fought pitched battles with neither side gaining a clear advantage. Dead and dying men littered the field of battle and blood ran across the ground. In the end, most of the men were too exhausted to fight effectively and they flailed about, hoping only for an end to it.

Stephan found Martin and he took him aside.

"We would do well to regroup now Martin. Our forces are too scattered to be effective. There is no advantage here."

"What of Craven's men. We cannot abandon them on the field?"

"I'll find them. Give me a little time and then sound the retreat. We can reform and see how Edwin reacts. If I'm right, he wants no more of this fight today. You can shelter your army behind the walls tonight and we can ride out again in the morning."

Stephan and Liam, with a dozen of Martin's soldiers formed into a wedge and moved off toward the east at a run. With Liam leading the charge, few of the enemy were willing to stand in their way. It was difficult to tell friend from foe and Stephan began to doubt that he would find them. At last, he caught sight of Brien fighting with a handful of men against a much larger force of soldiers at the far end of the battlefield. Stephan and Liam charged forward and engaged the enemy. These men were not dressed as the other Saxon's they had faced on the field and they had a different look about them. On both sides were exhausted men and there was not much fight left in any of them. Stephan pressed the attack against one who appeared to be a captain. As he pushed forward he noticed the symbol on the man's shield and it gave him pause. With a violent thrust of his own shield he toppled the soldier onto his back and held his sword at the man's throat. The remainder of the enemy force dropped their swords and surrendered. Liam moved toward them but Stephan shouted out.

"Hold now, Liam. I wish to question these men."

Brien fell to his knee, breathing heavily and unable to speak. Stephan turned to the man lying on the ground before him.

"You are no Saxon. Why do you take up arms against us in this place?"

"We fight because we have no choice. We were taken at sea by this Saxon army as they moved to attack you."

"And the Saxon's left you here at the back of the army, unguarded?"

"No, we were held here by the Saxon's rear guard. More than twice our number. They were keeping us in reserve. Most of the soldiers who guarded us were killed in your cavalry charge. Some we killed ourselves when the opportunity arose. We were preparing to escape when your men found us."

"What tribe are you?"

"We are the Caledonians, from the land called Fortriu far to the north. We sailed a week ago with our merchants to afford them protection on a voyage of trade. We were bound for Londinium when we were taken at sea."

"What is your name?"

"I am Talorc. Son of Bridei."

"How many are you?"

"We were near four score when the fight began. Fewer now."

"Do the Saxon's hold hostages to keep you here?"

"No. It was a simple choice they gave us. Fight or die."

"What if I make you a better bargain. Join with us and fight by our side to regain your freedom. It is a better offer than the Saxons will give you if they prevail in this fight."

"Why would you make such an offer?"

Stephan held the haft of his sword up to the man's face. The symbol on his sword was identical to the one painted on the man's wooden shield.

Talorc looked shocked.

"I know this sword. How did you come by it?"

"That is a discussion for another time. I am a man of my word. If you join us, those who live will be free to return to their homes. What say you?"

"I will need to speak to my men."

"Do so quickly."

Stephan turned to Brien.

"Are you injured, Brien?"

"Not badly, but I confess I thought I had seen my last morning until you arrived. My thanks for your help."

"Where is Petar?"

"He has fallen, along with many of his knights. We have slain many more of the enemy, but we are not many more than half what we were and our mounts are scattered to the wind."

"That is bad news indeed. The knights of Craven will feel Petar's loss greatly. It's time to fall back and regroup. Martin will soon sound the retreat. Let's gather as many of your wounded as we can before we leave the field."

Talorc returned.

"My men will fight with you. What do you want us to do?"

"There will be no more fighting this day. We will retreat to the east. Help us with our wounded and come with us."

In a while, Martin's horn rang out and the men of Elmet retired from the field. They fell back to the castle wall and reformed their lines. Many of the men were wounded and some had to be helped. The badly wounded were taken to the gate and as the army stood guard, the gates were opened and stretcher bearers rushed out to help them. Martin braced for an attack but Edwin's forces were bloodied and exhausted. Neither side had the strength to launch another assault. At the other end of the field, Brien led the knights back toward the river. They found a place where the terrain afforded some protection and they slumped to the ground exhausted. They had lost many men and they grieved for their captain, Petar.

"What will we do now, Stephan?" Brien asked. "We have not routed the enemy as I'd hoped."

Stephan looked around at the exhausted soldiers. They were in a dangerous position. If Edwin decided to retreat they stood between his army and the river and there were too few to make an effective defense.

"I think we should make our way back to Elmet and join your father's army. There is no advantage to remaining here and we are badly exposed. Many of your mounts have run off and it would be too dangerous to try to retrieve them now."

"How is my father? I thought I would see him on the field today."

"Your father is sick, Brien and too weak to hold a sword. The fates willing, you will see him tonight."

"But how will we get to the castle, with Edwin in our way."

"I know a way through the forest. You will have to wrap the horse's hooves in cloth to silence them. Have your men prepare many fires and post sentries out in front of us. We'll make it look like we are encamped for the night, but we'll move off quietly when the moon sets and make our way back through the forest."

Stephan helped with the preparation of the horses and then he sought out Talorc who was gathered with his men.

"It is for me to decide what is to be done with you now Talorc. We will find our way back to the castle later this night. I do not know if the king will be happy to have men who fought against us behind his walls."

"Then let me make you a different offer, Stephan. There are few enough of us left here to make much of a difference in this fight, but Edwin has left fewer still to guard his boats and ours. We are keen to get our vessels and trade goods back. Turn us loose and we will take back what is ours, and put Edwin's boats to the torch in the bargain. Without his food stores, I wager he will not be able to hold this siege for very long."

Stephan looked in the eyes of the man who sat before him and he wondered if they might even be of the same clan. In any case he found he trusted Talorc and though his idea to be a good one.

"All right Talorc. I give you and your men my leave. I would ask only that you not put all of Edwin's boats to the torch. Take as much of his supplies as you can carry and set fire to the rest, but leave enough boats to allow him to escape. I would rather see him run for his boats than be forced to fight to the last man because he has no retreat."

"That is what we will do then. Farewell on the field tomorrow."

"And you in your journey to your homes."

"You said you would tell me of the sword you carry."

"I will tell you what I know. I was found holding this sword in my hand on a battlefield like this one somewhere north of the great wall. I was just a small boy. I have never known where I came from or who were my kinsmen."

Talorc seemed awe struck.

"That would be the battle our people fought against Graban of the Scotii who had been raiding our settlements to the north. Our king Brude was lost on that day. If I am not mistaken, that is his sword you carry. You are kin to my people, Stephan. When this business is done, I hope you will come to meet with us. There is much for us to learn from each other. It is said in our legends that the sword you carry is the one that will unite our people. When we have fought as one, we have never been defeated. Now, we are besieged from every land and are too often defeated when we do not hold the tribes together."

"Where will I find you?"

"Find the ruins of the second Roman wall that crosses the land between the Firth of Clyde and the Firth of Forth. It is called the Antonine wall. Travel northward. The journey is many days by foot. Ask anyone you see about the great loch called Ness where the serpent dwells and the place called Inverness on its shores. That is where you will find us. Beyond us lies no nation. Nothing but waves and rocks. If you are questioned, tell anyone you meet you travel under the protection of Talorc of the Caledonians. Take much care for these have always been dangerous lands."

***

In his camp, Edwin paced to and fro, berating his captains and blaming them for the surprise attack. A man entered the tent and kneeled before the king.

"What is it? Why have you interrupted me!"

"The mounted knights who attacked us from our rear were king Uryen's men from Craven, sire."

"Nonsense. Grindan has control of Craven's army."

"We found a few still alive, sire. They have told us as much."

Edwin flew into a rage, refusing to believe his plans had failed.

"Take me to these men. I will question them myself."

Night fell and the soldiers of Edwin's army nursed their wounds and lay on the cold ground, too exhausted to sleep. To a man, they took the appearance of the giant raven as a sign they would be all be killed and many of them wanted no more of this fight. They did not all share their king's obsession with revenge. Many were farmers and craftsmen who have been pressed into service and although they were loyal to their king, they wished to be back home on their own land. They were now surrounded by the enemy and they knew there would be no escape should the battle turn against them. More than anything, they feared facing the charging war horses again. Edwin could be heard raving in his tent, late into the night. He resolved to hold back nothing and to take the city on the following day, no matter the cost.

***

Brien made sure the campfires were built large and placed at intervals across the entire width of the field. The knights of Craven had taken many casualties, but in spite of their great loss, the men were encouraged by the battle and their spirits lifted by the sight of Edwin's men running in panic in front of their mounts. They took some food and slept a little. Brien and Stephan waited until the darkness had completely fallen, and then they led the knights off into the forest. It was a difficult trek over broken ground with little light to guide them. They had to move in single file and quietly to avoid being discovered. They moved through a narrow strip of forest between the plain and the southern mountain and they knew there would be nowhere to run if they were found out. The grim procession wound off through the forest like the ghost of a lost army. The wounded were put up on the horses and the soldiers wrapped their weapons in cloth to keep them silent. It took them until well past midnight to reach the south wall of the castle.

"Be ready to move at my signal." Stephan said. "A fire will be lit on top of the wall. Move as quickly as you can. We will provide cover for you from the parapet."

Liam waited in the forest with Brien and his knights while Stephan made his way back through the cave and into the city. Some of the wounded were too exhausted even to speak and a few fell dead off their horses. The knights stood by their mounts, calming them and keeping them silent. The chill and damp of the forest seeped under their clothes and all they wanted was some food and a fire to warm themselves by. The day had gone well, but they had taken great losses and they knew to a man that the next battle would be far worse. It seemed like too much time had passed and the men began to wonder if Stephan had been discovered. Finally, a torch was lit at the corner of the parapet and Brien roused his men. They moved out into the open and made for the main gate. An alarm rang out from the enemy camp and men rushed forth to repel what they thought was an attack. When they saw what was happening they charged forward to intercept Brien's men but they were met with a hail of arrows from the walls. The gates were thrown open and Brien and Liam rushed through with what remained of Craven's knights. In spite of their losses, it took a great deal of time to get Craven's men safely behind the walls, but Edwin's army did not have the strength or the will to oppose them.

Brien ran up into the keep to see his father while Stephan came down off the wall and joined Liam. They went off to find Martin. Houses had been turned into hospitals and everywhere the women were trying to bandage wounds and offer what care they could. The air was full of the moans of injured and dying men. They found Martin at the stables where he had gone to count his horses. A cold rain had begun to fall.

"Your army fought well today, Martin." Stephan said. "Edwin has lost many men."

"Aye, but so have we and Craven's army has also been decimated. At least they will not be able to throw more stones over our walls."

"What will you do now?" Liam asked.

"When I look at my army, my instincts tell me they need some time to rest and recover before the battle is joined again. Yet I know that time would also help Edwin prepare for us. If we wait, the advantage we have given ourselves today will be lost. I think we have little choice but to press the issue in the morning."

"How many horse can you bring to bear?"

"Not many more than a hundred. Not enough for a full assault across his line."

"We have brought another hundred or so with us and many knights who have lost their mounts."

"We will provide mounts for as many as we can, but it is still not enough. I'll form them into smaller cadres to drive gaps in the line. I think we are still outnumbered, but our odds are a good bit better than they were at the beginning of this day."

"It's true Edwin's army is still more than our own, but even the few horse we have will give us an advantage. We will break his line."

"Aye." Liam said. "Also, soon enough he will learn that the way behind him is open now and if we hit him hard enough in the morning, perhaps he will retreat rather than lose the rest of his army."

As they made their way back to the keep, they heard a shout from the lookouts in the tower. In a few moments, a runner approached them.

"There are fires out on the river, Sir. It appears the enemy's boats are burning."

"So, it appears this will be a fight to the death after all." Martin said.

"Perhaps not. We have left him enough boats for an escape if he chooses it."

-28-

When Lesley and the women did not return to the keep in the evening, alarm spread through the city. Cristin sat up with Flann long into the night, hoping to hear that their friends had been found unharmed. Mavis had returned and when questioned, she gave an alarming account of what had occurred. There had been no woman in labor and she was bewildered by the events that had befallen Lesley and her companions. She did not know the man who had come to Lesley, but she told Cristin that Lesley seemed to know him. Search parties spent hours combing the city looking for the women, but they seemed to have vanished into thin air and they resolved to renew the search at first light. Cadman and Lucas had joined in with the search but Flann feared it could be a diversion to draw the protection away from Cristin, so he remained behind in the keep.

After hearing the account Mavis had made of the events before the women vanished, Cristin was overcome with a sickening feeling that Lesley had betrayed her and was behind whatever plot was unfolding. She chastised herself bitterly for ignoring the warning Timan had given her.

"This is my fault, and mine alone." Cristin said. "I was warned not to trust Lesley and now it appears she has betrayed us."

"Lesley could have been taken as well." Flann said. "We cannot be sure she's not a victim also. Don't blame yourself. No one could have foreseen this treachery."

"Perhaps not, but my heart is telling me she is behind this."

Cadman and Lucas returned. They were exhausted from the search and growing more fearful by the hour. Lucas set to pacing the room, unable to sit and barely able to speak. Finally he slammed his fist on the table and cried out.

"If they are harmed I will kill whoever is responsible, including the king himself."

Cadman put his hand on his son's shoulder.

"It's possible Uryen knows nothing about this. He has been kept isolated."

"But what could be the reason for this. Who would gain from kidnapping Emma and Ailis?"

"If Lesley is behind this." Flann said. "Then this is an attempt to gain freedom for Uryen."

"But why take Emma and Ailis." Cristin asked. "They have no part in any of this."

"Perhaps because it would have been too difficult to come after you." Flann said. "If I'm right, they will threaten to kill Emma and Ailis unless Uryen is released."

"Then I will have him released." Cristin said. "As long as he leaves the city I care not what happens to him."

Flann looked at her with a sad expression on his face.

"To do so would rob the people of their justice. I think we need to know who is behind this, or they may seek to harm you as well. We cannot let the king go. We need to find out who is responsible. There are evil forces about in this city. I can feel it."

"But what can we do? I feel so powerless."

"I don't know." Cadman said. "But I think in the morning Lucas and I will take Stephan's dogs out into the city. If we give them the scent from Ailis and Emma's clothing, they may be able to track her."

"I will remain here with Cristin." Flann said. "We can't be sure an attempt will not be made against her."

It was already past midnight when Cristin returned to her bed chamber. With Uryen's imprisonment, she had been moved into the king's rooms so that she would not have to climb the long stairway every day to see to her new duties. Since her departure from Elmet, in spite of the danger she faced, she had felt that somehow everything would come to a good end. Now, she felt unsure of herself and very much alone. She longed to have Stephan to talk to and the wisdom of Timan to guide her. She sat on her bed, unable to even undress for the evening. She could not decide what to do. Finally, too exhausted to think about it any more, she fell back on her bed. When she reached for her pillow she discovered a note, written on heavy parchment. She took it over to the fire to read:

CRISTIN. I KNOW YOU WILL NOT FORGIVE ME FOR WHAT I HAVE DONE AND THAT GRIEVES ME MORE THAN YOU WILL EVER KNOW. I HAVE COME TO LOVE AND RESPECT YOU IN THESE DAYS SINCE URYEN HAS BEEN IMPRISONED. WHAT I HAVE DONE HERE, IS FOR HIS SAKE. IN SPITE OF WHAT IS BEING SAID OF HIM, HE IS A GOOD MAN. THE PEOPLE ARE ANGRY NOW AND I FEAR FOR HIS LIFE. HE DID WHAT HE THOUGHT BEST FOR THE PEOPLE OF THIS KINGDOM, EVEN IF HE WAS DECEIVED. I HAVE TAKEN EMMA AND AILIS. I COULD THINK OF NO OTHER WAY TO WIN URYEN'S FREEDOM. STILL, I KNOW THE PEOPLE WILL NOT RELEASE HIM FOR THE SAKE OF TWO STRANGERS TO THIS KINGDOM.

I DO BELIEVE THEY WILL RELEASE HIM FOR YOUR SAKE. SO I OFFER YOU THE CHANCE TO SAVE YOUR FRIENDS BY TAKING THEIR PLACE, BUT YOU MUST ACT QUICKLY. THE MEN WHO ARE HOLDING THEM ARE RISKING THEIR LIVES AND THEY WILL NOT WAIT LONG BEFORE THEY ACT. EMMA AND AILIS ARE SAFE FOR NOW, AND WILL NOT BE HARMED IF YOU DO AS I ASK. YOU WILL BE SET FREE ONCE URYEN IS RELEASED.

THERE IS A CLOSET IN THE KINGS BED CHAMBER. ON THE LEFT SIDE YOU WILL FIND THE KINGS HUNTING CLOAK, HANGING ON A HOOK. IF YOU REMOVE THE CLOAK AND PUSH THE HOOK UPWARD, A PANEL WILL OPEN, AND YOU WILL FIND A STAIRCASE. THIS PASSAGE WAS BUILT TO ALLOW THE KING TO ESCAPE IF THE KEEP WERE TAKEN. IF ONLY HE HAD USED IT WHEN HE HAD THE CHANCE. YOU WILL FIND A TORCH JUST INSIDE AND A FLINT TO LIGHT IT. FOLLOW THE STAIRWAY DOWN AND YOU WILL COME TO A TUNNEL. FOLLOW IT TO THE END WHERE YOU WILL FIND A HEAVY DOOR, BARRED FROM THE INSIDE. ONCE THROUGH THIS DOOR YOU WILL FIND YOURSELF IN THE CELLAR OF A STORAGE BUILDING JUST ON THE OTHER SIDE OF THE STOCKADE. TAKE THE STAIRS AND EXIT THROUGH THE REAR DOOR. MAKE SURE YOU ARE NOT SEEN AND YOU MUST COME ALONE.

FROM THERE, MAKE YOUR WAY TO THE WELL NEAR THE SOUTH WALL. WE WILL BE WAITING FOR YOU. IF YOU TELL ANYONE, YOU RISK THE LIVES OF YOUR FRIENDS.

MY DEEPEST REGRETS.

LESLEY.

Cristin read the letter several times, and then she crumpled it in her hands and threw it angrily into the fire. It seemed to her she had become the cause of all the difficulties her friends had been subjected to. The hardship of the journey and the wound's suffered on her behalf and now the taking of her friends. She knew she would be in peril for her life if she did as Lesley demanded, but there did not seem to be any other way. She was no longer willing to live, if it meant the continued suffering of those she loved. She quickly changed into her riding clothes and put on her elfin cloak. She stood for a moment looking around the room, trying to find her courage and then she went into the king's chamber and found the secret door. The torch did not want to light and she could smell a foul odor coming from the cellar. Finally she managed to start a flame. The stone stairway was covered in dust and spider webs hung from the walls. The passageway was dank and she could hear the sound of rats scurrying about. She found the entrance to the tunnel and entered. The floor was wet under her feet and there was a bad smell in the air. The tunnel seemed endless and she prayed the torch would not burn out before she reached the end. The further along she went, the more an icy hand gripped her heart. It seemed to her she was moving down the long dark passage that led to her death, and she could not stop the tears from coming to her eyes. She kept imagining she heard footsteps behind her and several times she turned around, holding the torch high, but she saw no one. The only sound was the steady drip of water seeping through the rocks and the soft splashing of her boots on the wet stone. Finally, she came to a thick oaken door with a heavy iron latch. It took all of her strength to lift it, but finally it fell open and she pushed the door forward. She entered another cellar, which appeared to be empty. She held the torch high over her head and looked about the room. The stairway was on the opposite wall. When she reached the first floor, she found herself in a large open space with windows and a door on one wall and a single door at the back. She walked over to the back door and doused the torch in a bucket of water. Finally, she opened the door and stepped out into the chill and gloom of the night.

Cristin had not spent much time in the city and it took her a while to orient herself. She looked up at the heavens, grateful that it was a clear night, and in a moment she found the North Star. She faced north and then turned around and walked off in the opposite direction toward the city wall looming in the distance. In a while, she came to a small park and she could just make out the well at its center. When she reached it she stopped and looked around, hoping she was at the right place. There didn't seem to be anyone about and the city was still. As she glanced about herself, she felt as if she could see shapes moving in the shadows but no one appeared. Nearly an hour passed and with each minute the dread grew in her heart. Perhaps she had come to the wrong place or perhaps they had meant her to come on the following night. She didn't know what to do. Suddenly she was grabbed from behind. She was gagged with a piece of cloth and a sack was pulled down over her head. Her hands were tied behind her back and she was taken away into the night.

Men walked on either side of her, holding her arms. She stumbled several times but the firm grip of her captors kept her from falling. In a while thy stopped her and she heard the sound of a large door being opened. She was pushed forward into what seemed like a large space. The door was closed behind her and she was led further into the room. It was a dirt floor under her feet and the place had the smell of a stable. Finally she was stopped, and forced to sit on the floor. Someone lifted the sack off of her head and she found herself sitting next to Emma and Ailis on the floor of a warehouse. The walls were stacked with crates and barrels and a number of wagons were lined up ready to be loaded. She looked at Emma and Ailis. They did not seem to be harmed but their eyes were red from crying and their dresses soiled and torn in places. A woman walked over to them from out of the shadows. It was Leslie and there was a strange looking man with her. Cristin had never seen anyone like him in the kingdom and she did not like the look of him. His eyes were cold and cruel looking and his skin looked almost the color of an elm leaf.

"I'm sorry to have done this to you and your friends, Cristin, but I had no other choice. When Uryen is released, you will be released also."

The man standing next to her laughed in a shrill voice. He motioned to a group of men who were standing by one of the wagons. Two of them came over and gripped Leslie by her arms.

"What is the meaning of this! I demand you let me go!"

The man reached out and slapped Leslie across her face so hard that she staggered and her knees buckled.

"If you think we did this to release that fool of a king, you are sadly mistaken. All we wanted here was to get our hands on the princess and clear the way for others to take the throne of Craven. You are as big a fool as your husband if you thought we wanted otherwise, and now you will all share his fate. He looked at the men holding Leslie. Bind her and put her with the others."

"Why not kill them now and get it over with?" One of the men said.

"No, the sun will rise in a few hours and they will turn the city upside down to find the princess. We need to be out of this place before the dawn. Bring those large barrels over here. Make sure their bonds are secure before you place them inside."

-29-

In the morning, Edwin's army awoke to a cold, stinging rain. When the sun rose, it cast only a dim gray light that gave no heat and made no shadows. It was as if a perpetual twilight had fallen upon the land. As they prepared themselves, they felt the fear of the upcoming battle in their hearts. They knew they were where they should not be and they looked at each with dread. The omens from the previous day did not bode well. They had carried off the wounded after the battle ended, but night fell before they could care for the dead. As they stood, shivering around the campfires, the corpses of their comrades and their enemies, seemed to stare back at them through hollow eyes. The stench of death and the buzzing of the flies filled the air. A warning, perhaps, of what was yet to come. When the call came to form their lines, many felt that their legs had turned to stone.

Behind the castle walls, Elmet's soldiers had warmth and shelter at least, and a good meal if they could stomach it. They made themselves ready in the dim light and thought of their wives and their children. Martin shouted orders to his captains and the army was organized into ranks. The mounted knights were formed into columns. They would lead the army through the gate and then divide into four cadres in front of their foot soldiers. Stephan and Liam chose to fight on foot while Brien led one of the four groups of knights. Martin left a full complement of archers on his wall. They knelt behind the parapet so that they could not be seen by the enemy. Martin rode out in front of his army and called to his men.

"Take heart all you men of Elmet. You fight for your families and your homes and for your king. Yesterday you showed the enemy your metal and his army has been reduced greatly in numbers and his morale is low. Today you will make him regret that he ever placed his feet on our soil. This fight will end today and Edwin will be vanquished on this field. Look to your comrade's in arms and fight for each other. We will not fail."

At that, the gates were flung open and Martin took the knights out through the wall. They broke right and left and then held their mounts while the army marched out behind them. They formed their lines across the entire front wall of the castle, ten men deep. When they had all filed out, they waited. The gates slammed closed with a hollow boom that sounded like the closing of a crypt. Then, from atop the tower, two pipers began to play and the wail of their bagpipes filled the air. The men of Elmet stood proudly as the haunting, plaintive song echoed off the low gray clouds, lifting their spirits and steeling their resolve. A chill ran through the ranks of the enemy as they stood with the cold rain running down their faces and into their clothes. Many a man's hand took to shaking and all of them wished to be home with their kin. When the song had ended, Elmet's soldiers raised their swords into the air with a shout. Martin blew his horn, and the knights formed into their cadre's and raced out in front of the enemy line. One more command and the battle was joined.

The cadres of cavalry galloped along Edwin's front wheeling in and out, feigning a charge so that the enemy could not anticipate where his line would be hit. Martin's soldiers marched steadily on, keeping in their ranks. Again, Martin sounded his horn and his army ran forward. The cadres of cavalry wheeled and slammed into Edwin's line, driving deep wedges in the ranks, throwing men backward and forcing them together until there was no room to swing their swords. At last, the two lines met with a great shout and clash of arms. Edwin's line sagged but it did not break. After the initial shock it again became a matter of individual battles and the fighting skill of each man. The soldiers of Elmet showed more discipline and individual skill, but the Saxon army had fought many battles and their experience gave them confidence. The battle raged on with neither side gaining an advantage. When his army had become too scattered, Martin sounded his horn and his men retreated to reform again in front of the wall. The enemy, thinking it was a rout charged after them, throwing caution to the wind. Martin signaled with his horn again and the archers stood on the parapet and fired down on Edwin's charging soldiers, leaving a mound of fallen men across the entire front. Martin charged again and this time drove his line almost to Edwin's tent. Most of Elmet's men now fought on foot, since the battlefield was too chaotic to make good use of the cavalry. The two armies were now roughly equal in number and all of the men were exhausted. It appeared that both of the armies would have to fight to the last man. Edwin could not accept defeat and Elmet's men would not surrender their city. Stephan and Liam had found Brien again and they fought together, watching each other's backs.

"I never though you would hear me say this, Stephan, but I grow tired of swinging this sword. These Saxons do not know when they're beaten."

"Aye, and I fear we will have to kill all of them before we can end this fight."

In a while it appeared that the Saxon's had gained the upper hand. Elmet's army was losing ground and being pushed back toward the walls. Edwin had kept a company of fresh soldiers in reserve and just when Martin's forces were nearly spent, Edwin released them into the fight. Martin's line buckled and they were driven back toward their city. Some stumbled in the mud and were slain where they lay. Stephan knew that the war would be won or lost in the next hour and that the men of Elmet were beginning to lose heart. He ran to Martin's side in an attempt to rally the army just one more time. The strain was beginning to show on Martin's face.

"The army has little left to continue this fight, Stephan."

"Yes, but I fear if we withdraw from the field now we will not have the strength to ride forth again. Edwin will rebuild his mangonels and resume his assault on the city. Many will die inside the walls."

"I will not withdraw from the field. We will fight to the last man and let the fates decide what happens here."

"Then you should sound your horn once more and prepare your defense. The Saxons smell blood, and they are making ready their final attack."

The men of Elmet stood battered and bloodied before the walls of their city. They had given their all in the face of an enemy that at the beginning of the fight had them vastly outnumbered. Although they stood firmly, with courage and resolve on their faces, they feared in their hearts they were defeated. Many a man turned and looked at the great stone wall of the city and thought of his wife and his children and what horrors would be visited upon them if they failed. There would be no surrender. No retreat. To a man, they were prepared to give the last measure of their strength and resolve for the sake of their families and their kingdom. They looked across the field at the Saxon's who were forming their lines and preparing to attack. The sky was nearly as dark as night and a chill wind blew up from the water. Many prayed to their gods and petitioned for the safety of their families. Many more let their anger build to a fever pitch, until they were ready to throw themselves into the fight, giving no quarter and expecting none in return. At last the moment came, and the two armies faced each other in a struggle to the death. The Saxon line came on.

Suddenly, there came the sound of a different horn and a great flash of light from the forest on the north side of the valley. The Saxon advance ceased for a moment and all of the soldiers turned and looked toward the trees. In a moment, Timan and Danius emerged from the forest at a run followed by a host of wild men, running naked across the field with their axes raised in the air. Their bodies painted blue and their eyes crazed with bloodlust. Stephan shouted to Martin above the din.

"Pull your army back, Martin. They will kill anyone in their path."

Martin sounded the retreat and his army returned to the wall. They reformed their line but there was no one left to fight. The Saxons had never faced such a host of the wild men and many were already exhausted from the long battle. They were terrified by the sight of it and their confidence crumbled as did their courage. They turned to meet the new threat and tried to hold their ground but in a short time they were overwhelmed and began to flee toward the river. The wild men caught them as they ran and showed them no mercy. The men of Elmet watched in awe, as the wild men shredded the Saxon army. To a man they rejoiced that it was not they who had to stand the bloody onslaught. Many fell to the ground exhausted and the gates were opened so that the wounded could be taken inside the walls. The field was so littered with the dead that a man could walk nearly to the river on the bodies of the fallen without touching the earth. In the distance, Stephan could see the last skirmish of the war. A group of men stood by Edwin's tent, surrounding their king in a fight to the death. In not too long a time, the issue was settled. Steven and Martin mounted horses and galloped out onto the battlefield. The wild men were too busy taking trophies to bother with them. They found Timan and Danius in front of Edwin's tent. Danius was admiring, Edwin's sword with its gold pummel inlayed with almandine garnets. The king was lying face down in the mud and the bodies of his personal guard were piled around him, many with their heads removed.

Stephan nodded to Timan and then leapt off his horse and greeted Danius.

"So you have decided to swing your axe again Danius. I thank you for your help."

Danius nodded. "This dead man has violated my forest one too many times. He fell on this sword before I had the pleasure of removing his head. I will decorate my hut with it to remind me of the foolishness of kings. Certic will be unhappy that he did not have the chance to look in this fool's eyes while the axe is lowered on his neck. How is your king? I did not see him on the field. Is he alive still?"

"He is but he is very ill. This is Martin, who represents his king."

"Certic and the people of Elmet give you their thanks." Martin said. " Please ride with us to the city. I'm sure the king will want to thank you in person."

"I am no rider of horses. I have not been inside your walls since I came to sign the treaty that binds us and I swore I would never enter those gates again. But your king and I are old adversaries and I think it would be good that we greet each other one more time before we no longer walk this earth. Ride back and let Certic know I'm coming. I will bring him this trophy to admire when I have completed my business here."

***

The people of Elmet awoke on the morning following the battle feeling they had been reborn. The fear was gone, but it was replaced by grief and uncertainty, and by the dread of the task that lay ahead of them. There were few in the kingdom who had not been touched by the loss of a husband or a father or a friend. There was relief, but little joy at the great victory. Men traversed the battlefield, retrieving the bodies of their fallen comrades for a proper burial. The bodies of Edwin's soldiers were piled into a mound and burned. The grizzly bonfire lasted well into the night, but the people of Elmet were too exhausted to notice. Brien sent two of Craven's riders back to tell the people of the great victory they had won. The wild men had returned to their forest, laden with what plunder they could carry and many had new heads to decorate their belts. The soldiers of Elmet were grateful for their help, but unhappy to see them now so well armed with Saxon steel. Many watched them depart fearing they might have to face those weapons again. For now, they only wished to return to their families and a normal life.

Certic lay in his bed chamber, talking quietly to Brien and Stephan. His skin was ashen and his voice weak.

"I'm glad to have lived long enough at least to see Edwin finally defeated here and our lands secure. I only wish I had been able to ride forth to lead my army in victory."

"You were in the soldier's hearts as they fought, father. You would have been proud of them."

"I am proud of you, my son. To see you become a man and to know your strength and courage is a gift every father longs for. I know now I will leave my kingdom in good hands. Stephan, there are no words to thank you for what you have done for me and for my kingdom. Without you, we would not have prevailed here. I know it is true. Name your reward and you shall have it."

"I seek no reward, Certic. I wish only to live in peace and to hunt the forests as I always have."

"Will you not find a home here in the city?"

"Perhaps in time. For now, another journey calls me."

"I think I have come to understand you after all these years, and of course, you are free to do as you please. In spite of all you have done though, there is one more thing I would ask of you."

"Ask it."

"I know my days are numbered and I desire to see my daughter again before I pass from this life. The road to Craven is still a dangerous place. Will you bring her back to me Stephan? I fear there is little time."

"Yes, I'll do that. I plan to depart in the morning with Craven's knights."

"Once again I thank you. How do you think Craven will fare now that this business is ended."

"As Brien has told you, Uryen has been deposed and they are without a king. At least their kingdom is safe once more. As safe as it can be in times such as these. The Saxon's will not lose their desire for these lands. They are defeated for the moment, but I wager they will return when they have regained their strength. The wild Norsemen also covet this land. Both

Elmet and Craven will need to stay on guard and keep their armies strong."

"Yes. I was saddened to hear of the choice Uryen made. I suppose he thought it best to avoid a fight. I wish I had been able to talk to him directly so he would have known better than to trust in Edwin's bargain. Who will Craven choose to be their new king? Uryen has no heir."

"That remains to be seen. Some say that Cristin should become the queen of Craven, since she is a blood relation to Uryen, but I know she doesn't desire it."

"That is not a burden I would see my daughter carry. She is a gentle soul and not made to rule a kingdom."

"There is more strength in your daughter than you may imagine, Certic. But I also hope she doesn't take this path. In any case, she and the people of Craven will decide the matter. For now, I'll bring her back to you as quickly as I can."

***

At dawn on the following day, the knights of Craven formed into ranks in front of the walls of Elmet. Most of the horses had been recovered, but there were not enough men to ride them. Of the nearly four hundred knights who had ridden forth from Craven, a few more than two hundred remained. Many had been killed and others would be carried home in wagons, unable to mount a horse. The army of Elmet stood on the parapet to honor their comrades in arms. The pipers played again and many a man had tears in his eyes and love in his heart for his brothers in arms. When the song had ended, a command was shouted and the men on the walls shouted out and lifted their swords in salute. The knight's below raised their own swords in reply and then a command was given and they turned and rode slowly down through the field of battle, their banners flying proudly above them. Stephan, Liam, and Timan rode off with them but soon went out ahead. Stephan feared that Certic would die before Cristin could see him again and he knew how badly she would be hurt by it. With the wild men drunk with mead and victory and the Saxon's vanquished, they did not fear attack on the road and they raced off to Craven, throwing caution to the wind.

-30-

With the first light of dawn, the doors of the warehouse were opened and the wagon, laden with casks of ale and several large barrels, moved slowly out onto the road. Three men sat up on the bench and two more followed on horseback. They were stopped at the city gate and asked for a bill of lading. The guard looked over the manifest and then took a quick look at the load. The barrels had been turned inward so that no one would see the open bung holes. He looked at each of the men, and his eyes fell on the strange looking rider who followed the wagon.

"You are making an early start this morning. The sun has barely risen." The guard said.

"We have a long journey ahead of us. These goods are for the docks at Lindisware for shipment to Gaul."

"You are a lot of men for one wagon."

The strange man answered.

"We have nothing to do with these goods, except that we all have the same destination.

These are troubled times. It's better to travel together."

The guard nodded and called for the gate to be opened. As everyone looked toward the gate, a small figure barely visible in the dim light moved quickly out of the shadows and scurried under the wagon, climbing into the small gap above the rear axel. In a moment the driver cracked his whip and whistled. The team of horses hauled against their yoke, and the wagon moved slowly through the gate, and off down the road.

At the keep, the cooks and servants began to move about, preparing for the new day. Cadman and Lucas had been up late into the night and they were still sleeping even though the sun had already risen above the trees. They were awakened by the two mastiffs who were making a commotion in the hallway in front of Cristin's bed chamber. The men went to quiet the dogs, but the animals crouched and growled and refused to be led away. Finally, Cadman knocked on the door. There was no answer. He knocked again and then called out.

"Cristin, is everything all right?"

No answer came and he lifted the latch and pushed the door open. Cristin's bed had not been slept in and she was nowhere to be found. The dogs were extremely agitated, sniffing about the room, and whining. In a moment they stood in front of the door to the king's chambers and scratched against it. Lucas opened the door and the dogs ran in and sniffed about the room for a moment and then went into the king's closet. Lucas followed. Cristin had not drawn the hidden door shut and the dogs leapt through the doorway and down the stone staircase. Lucas, still dressed in his sleeping clothes followed them a short distance but without a torch he could go no further. He could hear the dogs barking and they sounded as if they were some distance away.

He returned and found Cadman.

"Cristin has left by a secret door. The dogs are on her scent."

"There are evil deeds afoot here, Lucas. I can't find Flann either. We must make ready and search for them."

The two men dressed quickly and took their weapons. A servant came with two torches and the men went quickly down the stairs, holding the torches out in front of them. They could hear the dogs barking in the distance. They followed the sound and found the entrance to the tunnel. In a few minutes they arrived at the heavy door and pushed it open. The dogs ran into the cellar and followed the scent to the stairway and up into the room above. Lucas and Cadman followed. The dogs went immediately to the rear door and began barking and scratching at it.

Lucas let them out and the two men had to run to keep the dogs in sight. In a few moments they caught up with the dogs at the public well. Several women, holding buckets in their hands, were cowering off to the side while the huge animals sniffed about the ground for a moment and then bolted off again. Lucas and Cadman were out of breath when they finally caught up to the dogs again, at the door of a warehouse. They drew their swords and flung the door open. There were two men inside loading crates onto a wagon and when they saw Lucas and Cadman with their swords drawn, they ran and cowered in a corner. Cadman ran after them. The dogs sniffed around the floor but then sat on their haunches and whined. They had lost the scent.

"What do you want with us?" The men screamed. "We have committed no crime."

"Where is she." Cadman yelled, raising his sword above his head."

"Please sir, we don't know what you're talking about. We are here doing our work, nothing more."

"A woman came here this morning. What has become of her?"

"We know nothing about a woman. There was no one else here when we arrived this morning."

"Has anyone come here since you arrived?"

"No only us. Please put your weapons away. We have done nothing."

Cadman lowered his sword and looked at Lucas, not knowing what to do.

Lucas thought for a moment and then looked around the warehouse.

"Were any wagons moved from this place this morning?"

"Yes, there was one. It was gone when we arrived. A strange thing it was too. We were to load that wagon today but the cargo has not yet arrived to do the work. Also we are short some casks of ale. We were going to report the theft as soon as were done with this load."

"There is our answer." Cadman said. We must find Trian and get horses for ourselves. I fear the women have been taken out of the city by wagon and they may be several hours ahead of us."

"And what of Flann?" Lucas asked.

"I can't be sure, but if I know him, he is already in pursuit."

***

The wagon had been on the road for two hours when the strange man moved to the front to talk to the driver.

"Turn off onto the next trail that's wide enough for the wagon. The longer we stay on this road, the greater the danger we will be discovered."

They passed several deer trails but it took nearly another hour to find something useable. It was an old, partially overgrown logging trail. The driver turned his horses and they moved off into the forest. The road was rough and the women were being sorely jostled in the cramped barrels, and nearly suffocating with their mouths gagged. The two men on horseback dismounted after the wagon turned and they used fallen branches to remove the wheel tracks leading off the road. When the work was done, they remounted and caught up with the wagon. In a while they arrived at a clearing and the wagon halted. The men unloaded the barrels and removed the lids. The women were frantic with relief at being set free, yet overwhelmed with the fear of what would happen next. The strange man gave orders and the women's gags were removed. Lesley flashed with anger.

"You will not get away with this. Do you think by taking a few women hostage, you'll get what you want? You will be discovered and my people will deal with you."

The strange man laughed.

"They are no longer your people. Do you not understand that? You are nothing now. You have no kingdom and soon you will have no husband. The people of Craven hate you and if they do not execute you along with Uryen, you will be cast out into the wild with nowhere to live and none to give you shelter. You have even betrayed these women here with you, who at least had sympathy for you. We already have what we want. We came for the princess and now we have her. Nothing will change that."

"Why are you doing this?"

"As I have already told you, what we want is simply to clear the way to the throne for one who will be, let us say, cooperative. Your husband was a fool. First trusting the Saxons to keep their bargain and then allowing himself to be overthrown by a handful of zealots. Now he will pay for his stupidity with his life. The princess and her brother are full of foolish notions about charity and the rights of the people. They don't understand how the world is run and how wealth is created. Do you think the Romans cared a moment for the rights of men? The Emperors gave what was required to keep the people under control. Nothing more. We have heard this dull tale before. Worthless ideas like equality and the rights of man. Men have no rights. Only the strong survive in this world. It will always be so. The weak will be used like beasts of burden and discarded when they can no longer produce. They are sheep, and like sheep they will be shorn. Men like us will run this world. Men with the ambition to take what we want, no matter who tries to stand in our way. Men will have their kings and they will be granted enough freedom to keep them in check, but it is all an illusion. The real power in the world will always be in the hands of those who take it, and the people be damned."

"Who are you? On whose behalf do you commit this treachery?" Cristin asked.

"You may call me Abbas. I tell you my name so you can carry it with you to your grave. As for who I represent, that is not for you to know."

He turned to his men.

"Hold the princess; tie the others to the trees so they can see what becomes of lofty ideas."

Emma, Ailis, and Lesley were pulled roughly over to the side. Lesley struggled and broke free. She ran into the forest, but Abbas nodded to his men. One of them notched an arrow and shot her in the back before she could get away. She fell to the ground and did not move again. Emma and Ailis cried out, but the men quickly gagged them again and tied them to a tree. Cristin was left standing alone in the clearing. She looked over at Emma and Ailis who were sobbing uncontrollably. She wanted to console them but there were no words to take away their fear and despair. Her eyes looked over the meadow where she stood and knew that it would likely be the last place she would ever see on this earth. There was no fear in her. Of all the emotions that were coursing through her, the one she felt the strongest was regret. Regret that she would never see her father and brother again, nor Stephan, nor any of the friends she had come to love during her journey. Regret that she would never have a family or know the love of a husband. And finally, regret that she would not be able to fulfill the destiny that Timan said would be hers. Suddenly, a feeling of acceptance came over her and she felt like a great weight had been lifted from her shoulders. She smiled then, and accepted her fate. Abbas walked over to her and forced her to her knees. He drew his sword and looked at her with a kind of cruel amusement. Cristin ignored him. She was holding onto her amulet and looking up into the sky. A lone falcon circled high overhead as if to be the world's witness to her last mortal breath. At last, she smiled at Abbas and he became infuriated. He was a man who lived for the thrill of seeing men shrink in fear before him and beg for their lives. He raised his sword in the air, but then he hesitated as a shout rang out behind him and he turned. There, behind them in the clearing stood a small man in an elfin cloak, not much bigger than a boy. He held a sword in his hand and he moved toward them slowly. Abbas looked at the small man and laughed.

"It appears we have brought a rat with us. Put down that sword, little man, or I will spank you with it."

Flann looked at Abbas and smiled.

"Look well on this sword, evil one, for it is the weapon that will take your life. You have harmed my princess, and now you will die for it."

"No, Flann. Please don't do this!" Cristin screamed.

Flann looked at her and smiled.

"This is the thing I was put on this earth to do, Cristin. I do not wish any more from this life. It has been my great joy to know you and to love you as I have. Enough for many lifetimes. We will meet again, long from now at the end of your days. Do not grieve for me. I go to join my people."

With that, he charged forward with such speed that he appeared no more than a glint of light, flashing through the forest. The men formed in front of their leader to shield him. They swung their swords, but found only air. Flann was already by them and as Abbas swung his sword, Flann ducked under the blow and thrust his sword up under his ribs. Abbas staggered and fell backward with a fatal wound, but with his last dying breath escaping his lips, he reached out and seized Flann by the ankle, causing him to fall. The men leapt upon him before he could free himself and they thrust their swords into his body. Cristin screamed in horror. Flann lay on the ground before her. He was writhing in pain and bleeding from many wounds, but he looked over at her and managed to raise his arm, beckoning her to come. She ran over to him and cradled his head in her arms. He looked into her eyes one last time and smiled.

"I have loved you all my life and now it is time for me to go."

He touched her face with his hand and kissed her on the cheek.

"Do not remain in this place, Cristin. There is nothing for you here. Your destiny lies elsewhere. Follow your heart, and farewell."

Then the light left his eyes and his body went still. The men who had stabbed Flann were confused. They felt their arms go numb and a great fear fell upon them. Cristin cried out in despair and the forest rang with her anguish. The men looked at each other with panic on their faces. One of them yelled out.

"Finish the rest of them and let's get out of here before we're discovered."

As they moved to attack, the two mastiffs suddenly came charging out of the forest and leapt upon them, tearing at their flesh. They screamed and tried to defend themselves but soon they lost heart, and they dropped their weapons and ran. In a moment, Cadman and Lucas, with Trian and two of his soldiers charged into the clearing and rode them down. Three were slain and the other badly wounded. Cadman and Lucas dismounted and ran to the women and quickly untied them. They ran to Cristin who had flung herself across the body of the fallen Flann and was crying in disbelief. Emma threw her arms around Cadman and buried her face into his shoulder. Ailis held Lucas and cried. Cristin remained kneeling, gently stroking Flann's hair, lost in her grief and unable to speak.

Out in the clearing, Trian held his sword at the throat of the wounded man. He was begging for his life.

"You have one chance only to save your miserable life, assassin. Tell me who is behind this treachery."

The man was trembling with fear and his voice quavered as he spoke.

"Abbas was our leader. He lies yonder on the ground. Slain by the boy."

"Abbas is a foreigner. What would he have to gain by this?"

"I was paid to do what I was told. I know nothing more."

"If you know nothing more than I have no reason to spare your life."

Trian held his sword in the air. The man threw his arms up to protect himself and he cried out.

"Wait. I know a name. I don't know who he is, but I heard Abbas speak of a man called Morcant. That is all I know. I swear it."

Trian looked at his men.

"So that snake, Morcant is behind this murder. Bind this man. I will deal with him in due time.

-31-

While Cristin still knelt next to the body of Flann, the mastiffs came over to her and pressed against her, feeling her anguish. They remained like that for some time while the others spoke quietly. Suddenly, the dog's leapt to their feet and charged off into the forest toward the road. Alarmed, Trian and his men drew their swords, expecting an attack. Cadman and Lucas moved in front of the women and stood ready. In a few moments they could hear the sound of horses coming toward them through the trees and they prepared themselves. Soon three riders could be seen, moving with great speed. As they came closer, Trian saw that it was Stephan and the wizard and the giant that traveled with them. They charged into the clearing and quickly dismounted, running to the fallen body of Flann. Timan fell to his knees and put his hand on Flann's forehead. He bowed his head and a great darkness crossed his face. The anger rose inside of him and those around him swore that the sun had gone dim and a chill wind swirled around them all. Cristin leapt to her feet and ran to Stephan, throwing her arms around him and releasing the flood of grief and anguish that she had been holding inside of her. The party remained standing in silence for a long time, feeling the loss of their friend and companion and wishing they had been able to save him. Such was the love that each of them had for the fallen elf-man. Finally, Timan spoke. There was great sadness in his voice.

"Today the world has lost a being of the light and we shall all be the poorer for it. We must take him now back to the Sidhe mound so that he may be reunited with his ancestors."

Trian spoke. "Let us bear his body back to Craven so he can be prepared for burial."

"No, we must go now." Timan said. "Flann's spirit dwells in his body still, but in a short while it will let go and be adrift in the darkness, searching for the way home. I would spare Flann this wandering and take him where he can find peace."

Trian pointed at the dead men lying in the field.

"These assassins were sent to make sure the princess never would wear the crown of Craven. A landowner, named Morcant is behind this. We will decide his fate when we return. I'm glad you will at least be able to sit in judgment over those who took you and killed your friend."

Cristin turned to Trian and spoke. There was great sadness in her voice.

"I will not return to Craven, Trian. I do not desire nor am I worthy to rule your kingdom. I fear your city will forever carry memories that I wish to push far from me. You do not need me to decide for you who should wear the crown. Give your people my thanks for helping us in our time of need and let them know that Elmet stands ready to come to their aid should you ever be in need of us."

"As you wish." Trian said. "For my part, I'm sorry for what has befallen you here. I hope in time you think better of our kingdom and come to visit with us. The people of Craven and Elmet are now forever bound together in friendship, even if a great price has been paid to make it so."

"We need to make haste, Cristin. Your father is in ill health and I'm afraid he doesn't have much time. He asks for your return."

"And what of Brien?" She asked.

"He has some wounds but he will recover from them. He waits by your father's side."

"We can ride back across the Pennine." Timan said. "I will stop there to help Flann on his journey."

"We will all stop with you, Timan. I would be there to say my farewell and see Flann safely away. I pray only that my father recovers from this illness so that I can come to know him again before he passes."

Stephan and Liam bore Flann's body over to the wagon. With a final salute, Trian and his men rode off to Craven, leading their captive and carrying the body of Lesley who would be given a proper burial in the city. The women rode behind Stephan, Cadman, and Lucas as they had on the journey to Craven. The sad procession moved off toward the Pennine moors. They rode behind Timan and Liam who drove the wagon in silence. Each rode with the memory of Flann in their hearts.

It was well past midnight when they reached the Sidhe mound. As before, Timan raised his staff and the mound seemed to rise up out of the moor. They secured the horses and then entered through the low doorway. They placed Flann's body on the floor, dressed still in his elfin cloak, and with his sword lying on his chest and his arms crossed over it, as was the burial custom for warriors. The party sat around Flann's body in a circle. They sat in silence, each to his own thoughts and prayers while Timan spoke quietly in a language that they did not understand. They sat in the dark place, lit only by the soft glow from Timan's staff with the weight of their grief heavy on their hearts. They had no consciousness of time passing and none wished to leave Flann alone in this dark place. In a while, an intense humming sound could be heard and a soft glow appeared at the center of the mound. The light became slowly brighter and soon, the tiny luminous being they had wondered at before, emerged from the ground followed by many others. They formed a circle around the party. They made no sound, and it seemed to them all that these spirits also grieved at the passing of Flann from the world. Then, with a sudden closing of their circle, they moved in and surrounded the body of Flann as if they were one ring of light. Flann's body itself began to glow, and suddenly a light rose up out of him which bore the shape of his body and his visage in pure light. The spirit stood and first moved to Timan and stood before him. The great wizard bowed and the spirit placed its hand on his gray head, and Timan wept. The spirit then move to each of the party, touching them in turn. It lingered with Stephan for a time and even he could not cease from weeping. Finally the spirit stood before Cristin. Cristin herself began to glow with a golden light and that light merged with the light of Flann's spirit until they were one. The light swirled in many colors and flared brightly until it filled the dark space, and then the spirit pulled away. It hovered in the air for a moment and then the spirit lights of the Daoine Sidhe surrounded it and carried it with them into the earth.

The party remained sitting for a time, but they no longer felt grief. Each in turn had felt the presence of Flann and heard his voice talking to them. A deep feeling of calm passed through the party and their grief was replaced with a kind of quiet joy that Flann had now gone safely to his home. At last they stood and took one last look at the body of their fallen friend. Then they turned and filed out through the entrance into the night. Timan raised his staff into the air one last time and spoke in the ancient tongue and the Sidhe mound wavered, and returned to the earth, never to be seen again by mortal men.

***

Certic passed away two weeks to the day after Cristin returned home to him. Although he remained frail and weak, the return of his daughter seemed to bring the joy back into his face and they spent many hours talking together and even laughing at the happy memories they shared from her childhood. Cristin was grateful for the time they had together at the end but it did not ease the pain of his passing. To lose two men who were both so dear to her, in such a short time was nearly more than she could bear. Stephan felt for her and he stayed close by, even though he didn't know how to help ease her pain. The people of Elmet also grieved for their king and for the loss of their kinsmen. A deep sadness had fallen over the city.

Cristin threw herself into the task of finding homes and care for the widows and orphans of the war, and that more than any kind words of sympathy, seemed to help her overcome her great loss. There was much to be done and after a few weeks, her thoughts turned to the crowning of Brien as the new king of Elmet. It was hard to know when it would be proper to have such a joyous ceremony. Timan, in his wisdom, suggested the festival at mid-summers' eve. The night before the Summer Solstice which the druids called the Alban Hefin. The people needed to find their joy again and there was no better time than this great, yearly celebration of life. Everyone agreed that it should be a party the likes of which had never been known in the kingdom.

When the first day of June arrived, Cristin learned with great happiness that Cadman had proposed marriage to Emma and Lucas as well to Ailis. Cristin wanted them to have the wedding at the castle on the day of the coronation ceremony, but they chose instead a small gathering with only a few of their closest friends in attendance. After what they had been through, they desired no more than a quiet wedding, away from the turmoil that seemed to surround the royal house always. They met in the forest in a grove of tall oak trees. Stephan and Cristin stood as witnesses and Liam and Brien with a few friends came as guests. A piper led the couples into the grove with a merry tune that seemed to fill the forest with joy. The brides were dressed in satin gowns of green and gold and with flower garlands in their hair. Cadman and Lucas wore leather tunics and high boots and each wore a belt comprised of linked bronze medallions. These were crafted in the king's forge and were gifts from Brien.

It was a simple ceremony. Timan performed the blessing and read them the sacred vowels from the Cain Aigillne. The couples swore their lives to each other and knelt on the forest floor. Cristin came forward and wrapped each of couples joined hands in a garland of mistletoe and furze. Timan placed his hand on each of their heads and pronounced them husband and wife. He wished them long lives and happiness, and then he raised his staff over the newly married couples and spoke some words in his ancient language. They remained still and quiet in that forest glade as a feeling of deep peace and contentment came over all of them. In a while they rose and hugged each other. An unbreakable bond had formed among all of them who had traveled out from Elmet those months ago and who had each in their own way helped to preserve the kingdom. Finally, as they were about to depart for the castle, Brien spoke.

"Over these last months all of you have risked your lives for the kingdom of Elmet. In doing so, each of you has taught me, in your own way, what is required of a king. I know now, that a king cannot rule well without the consent and respect of his people and that more than any man, he needs the wisdom and judgment of those who are close to him. There is no way I can truly repay you all for what you have done for me, and for this kingdom. It is my wish that you will continue to stand by me as we face an uncertain future together. And so it will be with great gratitude, and humility, that on the day of my coronation, I will name Cadman, Lucas, and Liam knights of Elmet. With your titles will come estates befitting your service. In return, I ask only that you continue to serve the people of this kingdom, and to be my friends, and support me with your wisdom and courage and the strength of your arms."

That evening, Stephan walked the parapet overlooking the field of battle. Out in the great valley, now so well nourished with the blood of men, new crops were growing. In the city, wounds were healing, babies were born, and life continued. He thought in his heart, that it must have always been so. That men had always labored and fought and died for the love of their homeland and their wives and children, as if a great unknown force was pushing mankind toward some prize that could only be won at the cost of their endless strife. He was grateful for the great victory that had been won beyond the wall, but his joy was tempered by the knowledge that this peace would not last. These were turbulent times for all the Britons and many coveted this rich, temperate land. The Viking raids had become more frequent since the Romans abandoned the island and the wild tribes across the eastern sea were restless for new lands to conquer. He heard someone approaching and he turned to find Brien standing behind him.

"You stand the watch still, Stephan, even though the war is won."

"Good evening, Brien. I think that everyone has their part to play in this life. Yours is to rule a kingdom. It would seem that mine is to forever stand atop a wall, or a mountain top, and try to see what lies over the horizon. Have you come to take the night air?"

"No, though it is a fine evening. I came to talk to you."

"I'm glad you sought me out. I've been wanting to talk to you also."

"I want to thank you Stephan, not just for what you have done for this kingdom, but for what you have done for me. I wouldn't have been ready to wear the crown had we not traveled and fought together. I needed the lessons you taught me, even when my pride was wounded by them."

"You are a fine man, Brien. You just needed to learn some things that only a great struggle can teach you. You've earned the crown you will wear. You have great courage and I have seen how you care for the people. I hope you never forget how you came to wear the crown of Elmet. I think you will be surprised at the weight of it."

"You know I did not forget you when I offered knighthood to our friends. I would give you whatever lands and titles you wanted if you would agree to stay here with us. I value your wisdom and courage above all others. Still, I know you do not desire to remain in this kingdom."

"This is not my place, Brien. There is some destiny I need to fulfill. I know it's true, even if I don't know what it is."

"When will you leave us?"

"Soon after the festival. I wish to depart with the joy of my friends still fresh in my memory."

"Could I ask one more thing of you, before you go?"

"If it is in my power to give it."

"I wish you would stand with Timan when he places the crown on my head. I would want the two of you to stand for my father who cannot be there with me."

"I will be honored to be there."

On the morning of the coronation, the people gathered in the great open space before the keep. A platform had been erected so that all could see. There was barely room inside the wall to fit all those who wished to be part of the great celebration. It was a fine warm day with towering cumulus clouds rising up high above them into the deep blue sky. By now, the people had all heard the legend of their new king. How he had traveled through the land of the wild men to come to the rescue of the kingdom of Craven. How he had deposed their evil king and won the help of Craven's knights to come and fight the Saxons. How he had ridden into battle at the head of an army of nights and charged into the enemy ranks with no care for his own life. He would be a fine king and there were no voices raised against him. Stephan had heard the tales and he smiled. It was good for the people to see their king as an invincible warrior, singlehandedly vanquishing his enemies, even if the truth was somewhat less. Brien had proven himself more than worthy of the crown.

In a while, a horn sounded, and Brien emerged from the keep with Cristin on his arm. He was dressed as a knight of high rank and his officers walked behind him. Cristin wore a gown of white and gold and no one could remember seeing a princess of such beauty. Cristin moved off to the side, joining Emma and Ailis who were dressed in the gowns they had worn at their weddings. They could not contain the joy they were feeling, and Ailis had tears streaming down her face. On the other side of the platform stood Cadman, Lucas and Liam, all looking uncomfortable in formal uniforms that they could barely stand wearing. Brien stood at the front of the platform and bowed to his people. A great applause rose up and it continued much too long for Timan's liking. He was not comfortable being exposed in front of such a throng and desired to get the thing done as quickly as possible. Stephan stood next to Timan. He looked over at Cristin and she glanced back at him with a look on her face that he had come to know well. It was a look of love and of sadness and he did not know what to do with it.

Finally the cheering stopped and there came the sound of Martin's Great War horn ringing out under the clear summer sky. A hush fell over the crowd. Timan stepped out in front of Brien carrying the crown on a cushion of crimson. Stephan held the wizard's staff and it was the only time in memory that Timan had ever permitted a mortal man to hold it. Brien went down on one knee, and Timan spoke strange sounding words of his ancient tongue. It was the oath of the Tuatha De Danann used to bind the king to his people and they to him forever. When he was done speaking, he took the crown and placed it on Brien's head. Then he took his staff from Stephan and tapped the crown lightly. He lifted the staff above his head and again a great flash of light came forth, evoking the awe of all who witnessed it. They turned to each other and knew that they once again had a king. A great cheer rose up from the people and it didn't end until Brien raised his hands in the air. The new king then addressed his people.

"We have lived through a terrible war that has tested us all and brought great sorrow to many. We have prevailed through our bravery and our love for each other. My first command as your king is that the time of mourning now be ended. We must look to the future and build our city strong once again and make a safe and prosperous place for our children. We would not have prevailed in this war without the help of mighty men whose legend will be bound to us forever. I give my grateful thanks to Stephan and Timan who now stand here with me. Without their help, we would not have prevailed. Also for their service, I will bestow knighthood on three who served as my brothers in arms and my protectors through my long dark journey.

Cadman and Lucas of Elmet and Liam of Keld, now Liam of Elmet, please come forth."

The three men walked to the front and knelt before their new king. Brien drew his sword and tapped each man on his right shoulder and then his left.

"I proclaim that you three brave men and true are now knights of the kingdom of Elmet. May all who witness this proclamation, hold these men in great honor and esteem, and give thanks to them for their service."

The people applauded again and the three men bowed before the people, glad that the ceremony was finally over. Liam looked over at Stephan and whispered loudly.

"I am in need of great quantities of ale, my friend. I hope you can find the keg for me."

Stephan laughed at his stout friend, and was glad for the journey they had shared together. Brien lifted his hands in the air one more time.

"I am told there are wagons filled to the brim with delicious cooked meat and warm, freshly baked bread, and rivers of ale and honey for you to enjoy. Do any of you wish to sample these delights?"

The crowd roared again.

"As you wish. Let the festivities begin."

The party had been going strong for hours and the sun was beginning to set behind the mountains. Stephan and Timan walked together out by the wall.

"How are you feeling, Stephan? It must be a relief to you that this business is well finished."

"It is that. But I don't know what is facing me. This chapter of my life has finally closed and at least that gives me some peace."

"Do you wish to remain here with your friends?"

"Yes, a part of me would like to finally claim this as my home, but as you have told me, there is more for me to do."

"Yes, but there is nothing wrong with taking some time. This journey has been hard on all of us. No one could fault you for taking your rest for a while."

"I know that's true. Many have asked me to stay for a while, but the longer I remain the more difficult it will become to leave. Who knows how long before another army marches toward this wall? Who knows how soon these people will be in need of stout arms? I could not refuse to fight for them, even if I know there is another fate for me. I have thought about it a great deal, but I need to do this thing and I feel I must do it now."

"When will you leave then?"

"Tomorrow, sometime. I have some goodbyes to say."

"I will depart tomorrow as well. The children here have taken to following me around and asking me to turn frogs into cats. Some of the people now refer to me as a magician. A magician! It is a good thing for them that I am not in a foul mood. It reminds me why I choose to live alone. Perhaps you would you like some company on the road?"

"I always welcome your company, Timan. Where will the road take you?"

"I have no destination. I will let my dreams tell me. You will find me in the keep when you wish to leave. For tonight at least, I hope you will relax and enjoy yourself."

Stephan began to walk away, but Timan grabbed his arm.

"And what of Cristin?"

"She is safe here now, Timan. After all she has suffered, there is nothing I want more for her?"

"Nothing?"

"What else, can I give her?"

"You can give her what she desires more than all things in her heart. You can take her with you when you leave Elmet."

"How could I take her back into the wild after all she's been through? How could I put her at risk again?"

"It is not for you to say what risk Cristin must abide or what danger she must face. Her future is also not in this place. If she doesn't leave here with you, she will leave on her own and she will be in greater danger even than she has seen over our long journey together. She loves you Stephan. Surely you have not grown so dense as to miss what is plain for all to see. Can you tell me you don't love her? If you do, I won't believe you."

"Of course I love her. I love her enough to want her to be safe behind these walls."

"And how long will she be safe if she remains here. How long is anyone safe in this world? We cannot hide from life, Stephan. None of us can. We cannot hide in our beds with the covers pulled up around our ears. If we try to shut out the dangers of living, we also shut out the joy in it."

"I don't know Timan. Tell me what I should do."

"That I will not do. It is for you alone to decide. I will be ready to depart when you come to find me."

Stephan rejoined the party and found a seat at a table with Liam who was feeling the affects of all the ale.

"So, Sir Liam. I wonder what you will do with your new lands and titles."

"The first thing I will do is build a stout house, large enough so that I don't have to bend over every time I walk into a room."

"And will you find someone to live there with you?"

"Of course. Now that I am a man of substance, who could resist me?"

"Do you have someone in mind?"

"Well it seems there is a sweet little scullery maid with a fine fat bottom, pining away for me over at Craven. I plan to ride over and steal her away as soon as I get around to it."

"And how do you know she would have a great oaf like you."

"Bah! She fell in love with me the first day we met, whcn I was merely the most strong and handsome man in the world. Now that I am a knight, I will simply ride up to her, and tell hcr to climb up behind me."

Stephan laughed.

"Some day, Liam, you will find your confidence and then you will be impossible to talk to."

"Just wait and see what my seven sons will be like. I expect at least a few kings from the lot."

"You will have seven sons, then. And how many daughters?"

"Oh, three or four. They will all be so beautiful that suitors will melt at their feet. That is, any of them who can stand my scrutiny."

They both paused for a moment, looking out over the happy crowd. Many were dancing and the children were chasing each other laughing such as had not been heard for many hard months. Finally, Liam looked over at him.

"When will you leave, my friend."

"I think tomorrow."

"I'm not sure I can let you go. Mark my words, you will soon be in need of me, and you will not find another giant willing to put up with you."

Stephan looked over at the huge man and placed his hand on his arm.

"You are my true great friend, Liam. I could not have asked for better company in all the years we have traveled together."

"And I you, Stephan. I will have a hard time finding someone who will get me into as much trouble as you have done."

"Don't close that book too soon, Liam. I have a feeling the days of my future will not be entirely peaceful ones. It is my fate I guess. You may yet find me at your door some evening, needing some heads to be collected."

"I hope you will come anyway. Even if just to share a bit of ale."

"You can count on that, my friend."

They were silent again. Stephan began to say something when he saw Cristin coming toward him. Liam took a long pull from his mug.

"I think I need to refill my tankard. I'll see you before you go."

Liam greeted Cristin and then went off to find the keg. Cristin stood before Stephan and smiled.

"Will you walk with me a while, Stephan?"

"Of course I will."

They walked away from the crowd and soon were alone at a quiet corner of the keep. Cristin stopped suddenly and threw her arms around him. She was silent for a while, holding him tightly and Stephan didn't know what to say. He had kept his feelings for Cristin at bay over the long course of their journey together, but he knew he would have to come to grips with them sooner or later. Now the immediate danger was past, but with his own future still uncertain, he had been trying to decide what was best for her. In the end he though it better to put some distance between them so they both could think with a clear head. She had depended on him for her survival and he knew that sometimes made people misjudge the depth of their feelings. He was sure that, in time, she would find her future and he would be just a memory. For his part, he didn't believe he had the right to share her life with her, and so he refused to wish for it.

"When are you leaving, Stephan?"

"Tomorrow, after I have said my farewell to my friends."

Cristin began to cry.

"You cannot leave me, Stephan. Not after all we've been through. There is nothing for me here if you are gone."

"You know my destiny does not lie here Cristin. Flann knew it also. Did his spirit not speak to you when we laid him to rest?"

"Yes, he told me to follow my heart and then I saw the faces of scores of women stretching down through many years. I think he was showing me the faces of my descendents through the ages. It frightened me a little, but I was overcome with my love for him. I can't say that I fully understood what he tried to tell me. Did he speak to you as well?"

"Yes. He spoke of my kinsmen to the north and about a future that will be full of war and strife."

"That was not a happy vision to leave you with."

"No, but he told me something else also. He said that my happiness will be found, not in the comforts of a peaceful life, but in the love and gratitude of my people."

"And what about a wife. Is your fate to be alone always, with no one to care for you or listen to you in the dark hours?"

"He did not speak of it. Who can tell of these things?"

"I know only this Stephan. If you go off and leave me here we will never see each other again. First I lost Flann, and then my father. I cannot bear to lose you too. Take me with you, Stephan. You know I love you and I know you love me also. Can you say it isn't true?"

"Of course it's true Cristin. I have loved you since you were a child. You know that."

"Then take me with you now. I want nothing more than to be by your side."

"You are a young and beautiful woman, Cristin and I have already passed two score years on this earth. You deserve a fine young man of your age, to live with and to have a family together."

"How could you speak to me of age, Stephan? After what I've been through, do you still see me as a naïve young woman? Have I not suffered the forest and the moor and the cold and

401

the attacks of assassins and of wild men of the forest? Have I not killed men with my bow to help preserve all of our lives? Show me a young man who has done such things in so few years and if you can find one, ask if he still feels a young."

"I don't know how much time I have left on this earth, Cristin. You deserve a companion who can see you through your years. Men who live their lives as I do, do not become old men."

"No one has such knowledge. A star could fall from the heavens tomorrow and kill us all. Flann told you there was a destiny for you to fulfill. Even if it is only a few years, I would stand with you while you complete this task. If I am to be the mother of kings, as Timan has told me, then I will need a king beside me. And you are a king, Stephan. Timan said this to me. He said that the only thing remaining was for you to find your kingdom. That is why he is sending you off to the lands to the north."

"Who knows what I will find at the end of this journey, Cristin. Who can say what peril you would face if you came with me."

"Enough of these foolish arguments. I will not listen to any more of them. Either you love me or you do not. If you do not, than say so and I will accept it, even though it would tear my heart from my breast. If you love me than it is for me to decide what I would risk to be with you. I will not beg you, Stephan. I will be ready to travel on the morrow. You need only to knock on my door and I will be at your side for all of the remainder of your years."

***

In the last still hour before dawn, she awoke from a troubling dream and sat up in her bed. The room was lit by the dying embers of the night fire and by the cool, dim light of a waxing moon. She knew she was at a crossroad in her life, and before the sun set again in the west, the direction her life would take would be known to her. She told herself that she was prepared no mater what Stephan decided, but she could not stop her heart from beating wildly in her chest. She had packed her bags the night before and they sat by her door like an unanswered question. She dressed quietly and made herself ready for travel. The sun finally rose and the sky was clear and bright. She sat looking out her window as the hours passed slowly by, refusing to leave her room. Later in the morning a servant brought some breakfast for her, but she barely touched it.

She was having some tea when the latch on her door lifted and the door opened. She almost jumped out of her skin. Emma and Ailis entered the room. They knew why Cristin waited, and they could not leave her sitting by herself, not knowing what her fate would be. They stayed and chatted until late in the morning. Cristin had never seen them so happy and for her part, she was pleased to know that they had chosen such good men to spend their lives with. It seemed that their futures were secure and it was something she had always hoped for. When they finally stood to leave, Cristin stopped them. She went over to her dresser and opened her jewelry box. She removed the two echo stones and held them in her hand a moment, than she turned and gave one of them to Emma and one to Ailis.

"I don't know if I will be here on the morrow or not. But if I am gone, I would ask you to hold these echo stones for me. Timan told me if you give them to someone you love, they will always return to you in time. Wherever my fate takes me then, I know we will meet again."

Midday passed and her spirits began to fail. She could not read, or sew or do any of the things that normally helped her pass the time. She paced her room, and wished she could at least be outside in the sun. A feeling of panic was starting to engulf her and at last she lay down on her bed and wept. In a while she fell into a fitful sleep and she dreamed again of the glass tower and the man standing on the distant shore. Once more she heard the man call to her and she climbed down the tower stair and out to the boat that was waiting for her. She stepped into the boat and it began to move toward the far shore, closer and closer to the man who would be her husband and her lover and her companion for the rest of her life. She strained her eyes to see his face but as before, when she came close enough to finally see him, she awakened. She opened her eyes then, and saw Stephan standing over her smiling. She leapt up and threw her arms around him and refused to let him go.

ABOUT THE AUTHOR

Wallace Brown's first novel, <u>The Shepherd Sleeps</u>, was published by Writers-Exchange in 2008. It is available in paperback or as an e-book at both amazon.com and writers-exchange.com/wallace-brown.html. It is set in New Orleans at the height of the Vietnam War and the counter-culture revolution of the 1960s. It is a tale of espionage and betrayal and the risks a man and a woman will take for the sake of forbidden love. A sense of place and historical setting permeates the narrative, providing the reader with the sensation of walking the back streets of the French Quarter where dark characters lurk in the shadows and everyone wears a mask.

His second novel, <u>Jayapura</u>, is set in the dense jungles and teeming cities of South East Asia. A soldier of fortune, burnt out and grieving the loss of the only woman he ever loved, is cast into a desperate struggle for survival. He has stumbled upon a secret that could change the world. Now, everyone wants him dead, even his own government. Along the way, he crosses paths with a beautiful, British agent who is running from her own demons. They join forces in an effort to avert an unspeakable tragedy, and to try to stay alive.

Wallace lives and writes in suburban Philadelphia, Pennsylvania and is a graduate of Villanova University. To contact, log onto his website at www.wallacefbrown.com. You will find a link there to his e-mail address.